Nocturnum's Muse

dpInk

Donnalnk Publications, L.L.C.

This Book Belongs To:

_____

MONTANA Bleeds

United States of America

Nocturnum's Muse

New season,
new books...

MONTANA Bleeds

JILL ENGLAND   ERIC FALCON

GERHARD PLENERT

A Montana Rising Series Novel

Nocturnum's Muse
Publishers Since 2012
An imprint of Donnalnk Publications, L.L.C.

Copyright © 2020 by Dr. Gerhard Plenert.

Library of Congress Cataloging-in-Publications Data: 2020948406.
Name: Plenert, Gerhard, author.
Title: "Montana Bleeds" / Gerhard Plenert

Description: "Montana Bleeds," the inaugural title in the "Montana Rising" mystery, suspense, and procedural series, immerses readers in a world where ancient Aztec and Roman cement technologies are reinvented. Against the backdrop of a small town, the narrative unfolds, weaving a complex tapestry of murder, intrigue, and con-flicting interests. As economic giants clash with individual determination, drama and suspense intertwine, leaving readers emotionally engaged. The story commences at the Falcon Gravel Pit, where a failed kidnapping escalates into a chilling murder. En-ter Detective Jill England, a tenacious investigator who soon realizes she's embroiled in a web of interconnected homicides, jeopardizing her pursuit of justice.

Identifiers: ISBN – 13 – 978-1-947704-65-7 (alk. paper).

BISAC: FIC022060 - FICTION / Mystery & Detective / Historical; FIC022020 - FICTION / Mystery & Detective / Police Procedural; FIC022040 - FICTION / Mystery & Detective / Women Sleuths; FIC022050 - FICTION / Mystery & Detective / Collections & Anthologies.

328 p. cm.
Printed in the United States of America
First Edition: 12 11 10 9 8 7 6 5 4 3 2 1; 2020. All Rights Reserved.

Book design by: dplnk Ltd. Liability Company.

For more information contact:
Donnalnk Publications, L.L.C.
17611 Aquasco Road, Brandywine, MD 20613
www.donnaink.shop

OTHER BOOKS BY

GERHARD PLENERT

The History of The Small World Series
The Siege of the Small World - Dr. Gerhard Plenert
The Uniting of the Small World - Dr. Gerhard Plenert
Saving the Small World

The New Templars Series
Dawn of the New Templars - Gerhard Plenert
Activating the New Templars - Gerhard Plenert

Other Fiction Titles
The Dragon Pit - Gerhard Plenert

Non-fiction Business Titles
Discover Excellence: An Overview of the Shingo Model and Its Principles - Edited by Gerhard Plenert

Driving Strategy to Execution Using Lean Six Sigma: A Framework for Creating High Performance Organizations - Gerhard Plenert | Tom Cluley

Finite Capacity Scheduling: Optimizing A Constrained Supply Chain - Bill Kirchmier | Gerhard Plenert | Gregory Quinn

International Management and Production - Gerhard Johannes Plenert, Ph.D.

International Operations Management - Gerhard Plenert

Lean Management Principles for Information Technology - Gerhard J. Plenert

Making Innovation Happen - Concept Management Through Integration - Gerhard Plenert | Shozo Hibino

Module 17 Operations Management - Gerhard Plenert

Reinventing Lean: Introducing Lean Management Into The Supply Chain - Gerhard Plenert

Strategic Continuous Process Improvement: Which Quality Tools to Use, and When to Use Them - Gerhard Plenert

Strategic Continuous Process Improvement: Which Quality Tools to Use, and When to Use Them - Gerhard Plenert, Ph.D., CPIM

Strategic Excellence in the Architecture, Engineering, and Construction Industries - Gerhard Plenert | Joshua Plenert

Supply Chain Optimization through Segmentation and Analytics - Gerhard Plenert

The eManager: Value Chain Management in an eCommerce World - Gerhard Plenert

The Plant Operations Handbook: A Tactical Guide to Everyday Management - Gerhard J. Plenert

Toyota's Global Marketing Strategy: Innovation through Breakthrough Thinking and Kaizen - Shozo Hibino | Kolchiro Noguchi | Gerhard Plenert

World Class Manager - Gerhard Plenert, Ph.D.

DEDICATION

GERHARD PLENERT

This Book is dedicated to Renee Sangray Plenert

And my parents George and Ida Plenert

And the 8 Kids and the yet to be Numbered Grandkids

Who Work Hard to Bring Mystery into My Life

TABLE OF CONTENTS

OTHER BOOKS BY xiii
 GERHARD PLENERT XIII

DEDICATION xv
 GERHARD PLENERT XV

TABLE OF CONTENTS xvii

TABLE OF NAMES xxi
 KEY ACTORS XXI

CHAPTER ONE 1
 A MURDER 1

CHAPTER TWO 7
 ANOTHER DAY AT WORK 7

CHAPTER THREE 15
 CASE ANALYSIS 15

CHAPTER FOUR 21
 ANOTHER DEATH 21

CHAPTER FIVE 29
 THE INVESTIGATION 29

CHAPTER SIX.. **37**
  MORE TO INVESTIGATE.. 37

CHAPTER SEVEN... **47**
  THE MYSTERY DEEPENS... 47

Chapter Eight.. **55**
  SOME ASSUMPTIONS.. 55

Chapter Nine... **65**
  IS THE KILLER SERIAL?.. 65

CHAPTER TEN **69**
  THREATS... 69

CHAPTER ELEVEN.. **77**
  THE SERIAL OPTION... 77

CHAPTER TWELVE **85**
  THE CONSPIRACY.. 85

CHAPTER THIRTEEN.. **89**
  CONFUSION 89

CHAPTER FOURTEEN... **95**
  STILL ANOTHER MURDER 95

CHAPTER FIFTEEN **101**
  ASSASSINATION 101

CHAPTER SIXTEEN **107**
  THE TRAP 107

CHAPTER SEVENTEEN.. **115**
  CHANGE IN LEADERSHIP 115

CHAPTER EIGHTEEN **123**
  SAMPLES.. 123

CHAPTER NINETEEN... **129**
  MORE CONFUSION 129

CHAPTER TWENTY.. **137**
  HIDDEN EVIDENCE 137

CHAPTER TWENTY-ONE.. **143**
  ANOTHER DEATH 143

CHAPTER TWENTY-TWO **149**
  MORE HIDDEN EVIDENCE... 149

CHAPTER TWENTY-THREE 155
CAN'T TRUST ANYONE 155

CHAPTER TWENTY-FOUR 163
TRACKING 163

CHAPTER TWENTY-FIVE 171
THE MOLE HUNT 171

CHAPTER TWENTY-SIX 177
CAPTURED 177

CHAPTER TWENTY-SEVEN 183
MORE CHANGES 183

CHAPTER TWENTY-EIGHT 188
FRANKLIN'S HIDEOUT 188

CHAPTER TWENTY-NINE 194
BETRAYAL 194

CHAPTER THIRTY 202
LIZZY 202

CHAPTER THIRTY-ONE 208
MISSOULA 208

CHAPTER THIRTY-TWO 216
ROGER 216

CHAPTER THIRTY-THREE 222
RESCUE 222

CHAPTER THIRTY-FOUR 228
VENICIA 228

CHAPTER THIRTY-FIVE 236
BROWNING, MONTANA 236

CHAPTER THIRTY-SIX 242
EAST GLACIER 242

CHAPTER THIRTY-SEVEN 248
FINDING ROGER 248

CHAPTER THIRTY-EIGHT 254
TRACKING 254

CHAPTER THIRTY-NINE 262
THE CHASE 262

Table of Contents

CHAPTER FORTY 268
  THE CHASE CONTINUES 268

CHAPTER FORTY-ONE 274
  SHOWDOWN 274

CHAPTER FORTY-TWO 280
  SHOOTOUT 280

CHAPTER FORTY-THREE 286
  WRAP-UP 286

ABOUT THE AUTHOR 292
  GERHARD PLENERT 292

VISIT THE AUTHOR 294
  SOCIAL MEDIA 294

GIFTS AND EXPRESSIONS 296
  PLENERT CREATIONS 296

TABLE OF NAMES

Key Actors

The Key Players

Roger Falcon – Owner of Falcon Sand and Gravel Company
Eric Falcon – Son of Roger and Judy Falcon
Judy Falcon – Roger's wife
Lizzy Falcon – Daughter of Roger and Judy Falcon

Falcon Employees

Bud – Falcon Cement Truck Driver
Falcon Office Secretary
Chase Mitton – Roger's Lab Technician
Steve Smith – Patent Attorney

Criminals

Joe Basigliano – Tasked with Kidnapping Roger
Fred Fartner – Tasked with Kidnapping Roger
Alfredo – Fred's Assassins
Ricardo – Fred's Assassins
Doug – Employee of Gerd
Gerd Liroza – Boss of the Mobsters Trying to Stop Roger

Gerrard Liroza – Gerd's Father and the Crime Family Godfather
Karl – Employee of Gerd
Pablo – Informant Working for Gerd
Venicia – Agent for Intercontinental Cement
Maria – Works for Venicia
Jonard – Works for Venicia

Local Helena Police

Duke Wilson – Helena Lead Detective
Jill England – Assistant Detective to Duke
Morton Mararac – Mortician / Coroner
Lemery – Jill's Replacement

Montana State Police

Ranel Marinduque – State Police
Brendt George – State Detective from Australia

FBI

Bridger Blakeslee – Lead Agent
Matthew Christ – New Lead Agent
Franklin – Agent
Mason – Agent who is Franklin's Partner

Forest Service

Namid – Cheyenne Indian whose name Means "Star Dancer"

Deaths

Bud
Joe Basigliano
Fred Fartner
Office Secretary at Falcon Sand & Gravel
FBI Officer in the Car with Duke
Doug
Karl
Gerd Liroza

Mason
Pablo
One Indian
Maria
Jonard
Brendt
Two More Indians
Ranel
Two More Indians
Venicia
Four More Indians

CHAPTER ONE

A MURDER

June 2020, Helena, Montana, Gravel Pit

"There he is," whispered Joe as he hid behind a gravel pile. Joe and Fred had been given an assignment by their boss. They were to kidnap Roger and bring him to the boss. They weren't supposed to hurt him; just tie him up and deliver him. They knew Roger would be working late at his gravel and cement company based in Helena, Montana. He always worked late.

"Where do you see him?" asked Fred, who was a good six inches taller than Joe, but whose eyesight wasn't as strong. Unlike Joe, Fred enjoyed the suspense and hype of sneaking around and doing things he wasn't supposed to do. He enjoyed the adrenaline rush of being a lifetime criminal. But his eyesight was a disadvantage. Especially at night. It was 9 PM and the only light came from a partial moon and stars. Fred was struggling to see anything.

Fred was annoyed by Joe's interruption. His mind was running through his favorite fantasy and it was just starting to get good. Two girls and only one bed. And he was in the middle. What could be better. But now that Joe had disrupted his mind melt, he had to get back to thinking about the job he needed to do.

Joe was different. When his mind wandered it almost always went to food. His thoughts would dwell on the last good meal and he wondered how he could replicate it. He saw himself as a master chef whose food was everyone's desire.

The reason Joe was here with Fred was because his brother, who was on the police force, had told him he could earn a few bucks, and he was running short on cash. Besides, he reasoned that if his police brother told him to do it, he should be safe.

"See that guy coming down from the office toward the loading chute? I can tell by his walk that it is him." Joe was chunky compared to Fred's thin and muscular build. Despite the height difference, Joe weighed slightly more than Fred. Joe was bald on top, with hair around the lower parts of his head. He had a scruf-fy, unshaven look, like someone who was still struggling to get out of bed. His clothes were loose and sloppy.

"You must be right. Who else would work late at a job like this? He either loves gravel or else he's avoiding going home." As he spoke to him, Fred looked over at Joe and then looked quickly away. Joe's nose was running from the cold and the snot could be seen running toward his mouth. That sight was something that quickly triggered Fred's gag reflex.

Fred had a scraggly full head of black hair which badly needed a barber's touch. He had a mustache which hid part of a scar that he had across his left cheek. He was presentable but rough looking.

"I know Roger from way back, and he's obsessed with work," whispered Joe. "He was like that already when he was a kid in school. He was constantly busy doing something. Let's get him and get this over with." Joe was fidgety and uncomfortable with their assignment, but there wasn't much else he knew how to do. He was always a bully, growing up, getting his way by threats and force, and now that he was middle aged, he was still the same. It was no accident that he chose this type of work. It allowed him to feel like he was still in control, even though as he aged, it became more of a mirage than reality.

"So, what's the plan?" grumbled Fred. He didn't like the idea of crawling around in the dirty gravel, but he took these types of jobs because the money was good. He wasn't happy about working with Joe, who was a constant complainer, and his allergies caused him to have a never-ending runny nose, which grossed Fred out. But here he was, again, stuck doing someone else's dirty work, and literally crawling around in the dirt.

"We put a bag over his head, bungie tie his hands and legs, and haul him off to the van. And if he puts up a fight, we whack him on the head to calm him down."

The two snuck as quietly as possible over to the side of the loading chute. The chute was a large piece of equipment about two stories high, used for loading the cement trucks. It was a large four-sided container, raised high on four corner legs. The chute was high enough so that a cement truck could drive under it and have the contents of the chute dumped into the back end of the cement truck, where the truck's loading chute was located.

The two carefully and slowly walked around the side of the loader and successfully positioned themselves behind their vic-tim. Joe jumped into action and threw the bag over Roger's head, but they soon learned that this wasn't going to be an easy snatch and grab. Roger started punching, clawing, and screaming. Fred grabbed a rock and whacked him over the head causing Roger to crumble to the ground.

"Something's wrong here," suggested Joe. "His yelling and screaming didn't sound like Roger."

They pulled the bag off the head of their victim. Blood was streaming from a gash in his head. The victim was about the same height and build as Roger and coming up from behind in the dark he could easily be mistaken for Roger, but it definitely was not Roger. This man was slightly bald, and at least ten years old-er.

"Oh crap! You're right," said Fred. "That's not him. Who is that?"

"Are you kidding me? You stupid idiot. You said it was him. Beats me who it is. I was sure it was Roger by the way he walked, but obviously I was wrong."

"You're the one who screwed up, you jerk. So now what do we do?"

"How about we just leave him here for someone else to find."

Fred protested, "Then they'll know we were trying to kidnap someone, and they'll be on the lookout. They'll probably even have the police out here watching for us. We need a better plan than that."

"Maybe we'll just have to kill him and get rid of the body."

"That would also be a warning sign and get us unnecessary attention."

Joe was desperate to find a solution, "Maybe we leave the body here. Then the police will think that there was an accident. We'll make it look like it wasn't anything intentional."

"I like that plan."

Just then the victim started squirming. Fred was still holding the rock that he had used earlier to hit him in the head and gave him another quick whack.

"Is he dead?" asked Joe.

Fred knelt and checked for a pulse. "I think we finished the job this time. There's no pulse and he's not breathing. So now what do we do?"

"Let's run him up the loading chute belt and dump him into the loader. It will look like an accident. They'll think he bumped his head falling into the chute." The belt he was referring to was a belt that was used to carry gravel from the ground up the two stories and into the top of the cement truck loader. "Finding a body up there should give everyone something to talk about."

"Quit talking and let's get this done," said Fred as he lifted the legs of the body. "Grab the other end and let's load him on the belt."

They made quick work of loading the body. Then Fred hit the belt switch and they both stood and watched as the body slow-ly worked its way up the incline and eventually dumped into the chute.

Fred turned off the switch on the belt and said, "Let's get out of here."

"But what about Roger? We were supposed to bring him back to the boss."

"Obviously, he's not here or he would have come out to see why the conveyor belt was running. We're going to have to come back and get him another time. For now, we're not going to tell the boss about this screw up with the guy we killed. We're just going to report that Roger was a no show and so we weren't able to snag him."

"Got it! Let's go you idiot. This is about the stupidest thing you've ever done. I can't believe I even work with you."

The two made their way to the van that they had stashed behind one of the gravel piles. They quickly jumped in and drove off.

CHAPTER TWO

Another Day at Work

June 2020, Helena, Montana
Gravel Pit

"The load's ready," instructed Roger Falcon. He was telling his 24-year-old son Eric all the components of the cement mix had already been transferred up the belt and into the loading chute and was now ready to be loaded into the cement trucks. Eric had earned the privilege of having his own cement truck allocated to him. It helped to be the son of the owner.

"I'll pull my truck under the loading chute and get going with the delivery." Eric left the office and walked to the area where the cement trucks were parked. Eric was well built, lean and tall, and had built up his strength because of the type of work that a gravel pit required. He was muscular and very few individuals risked making him angry. He was average in looks and had plenty of girls interested in getting to know him, but, like his father, he pre-ferred work. The feeling that came with a job well done, was hard to duplicate in any other way. In fact, most girls were intimidated by him and were too afraid to make the first move, so if any relationships were to develop, Eric would have to be the instigator.

As he walked toward his truck his mind strayed back to Fri-day night. He had received a text message from the girl he was with that night, and she was asking him how he felt about their date. He had taken his high school fling out to dinner and danc-ing, hoping to see if there was some magic that would ignite. He believed that if she, or any other girl, was the right girl, he would be hit by a bolt of lightning. There had to be something different; something that made her stand out. He was convinced that if there wasn't anything magical, then she couldn't be the right one. Dinner went fine, and they reminisced about the old times, when he was on the football team and she was a cheerleader. Those were the days when he could have had the pick of the litter, but he felt the need to be loyal and stick with one girl. But he didn't mention that to her. Instead they talked about the times they would sneak away after a game and hide out under the bleachers, hoping no one would catch them. They even touched on the taboo topic of her pregnancy and miscarriage. They had dodged a bullet there since neither one of them was ready to get married and start a family.

After dinner they went to a country dance hall. They joined the circle of dancers rotating in mass clockwise around the floor, everyone doing the country two step as if that was the only dance step anyone knew how to do. The dancing was fun too and the evening was romantic enough, especially after the dance, but the lightning never hit. It just wasn't there. Eric felt a little sad that she wasn't the one, but he also felt a little relieved that now he knew.

Eric was a religious man, and that made him a social outsider. He felt the spirit of God regularly guiding him and he wondered why his friends would mock his beliefs when he didn't badger them about their lack of belief. When he was in High School, he would openly share stories about how he was guided in his life, and his fellow students and teachers would make fun of even the basic concept of a God. They pretended to be so much smarter, claiming the lack of scientific evidence which would prove the existence of a God. And, of course, he knew that science was not the tool to prove the existence of spiritual things. These self-acclaimed intellectuals would challenge him to prove, using their senses, that God existed. And he would, in return, challenge them to prove, using their senses, that dark matter exists. To this demand, they just scoffed, but produced no evidence. Unfortunately, this left Eric feeling that his classmates were shallow, and sadly, that included many of the girls he associated with during those years in school. It was difficult to have a - relationship with someone who did not know God existed.

He would need to keep looking. This dating game wasn't the fun time everyone claimed. It was frustrating that he couldn't find a companion that understood him. Especially at times like this when he knew he would have to let her off the hook and tell her that he didn't feel the magic. He knew she would most likely cry, and that's what he hated the most. But he didn't want to do it now. He would put it off till later. Right now, he had a job to do, and he jumped into his truck and started the engine.

The gravel and concrete company, owned by Roger, was in a large gravel pit southeast of Helena, Montana. It contained several acres of rock crushing and cement mixing equipment and included dozens of delivery trucks for the gravel, sand, and cement. It also contained a modern, two story office.

Roger Falcon, the owner, was a middle-aged man who was an amazing entrepreneur. He had started his own business while he was still in high school and was always driven by his ambition and passion. He was slightly shorter than his son, Eric, and had dark hair. He had a warm, friendly disposition and a welcoming smile. He was well groomed, and dressed well, even at the gravel pit.

The cement mixing chutes, and equipment were a recent addition, installed just a few years back with the goal of diversifying. Now the concrete business had now taken over and had become the largest portion of his revenue. Concrete was now the primary product of what had previously been a sand and gravel company.

Falcon Sand and Gravel, as the company was called, had eight cement trucks and another dozen trucks were used to deliv-er the raw sand and gravel products. Eric and Roger both drove cement trucks, along with several other drivers who came in on an as-needed basis. Today was an extra busy day. They had ord-ers for a dozen loads of concrete to be delivered on a freeway renovation project. And they had experienced a delay because of a computer glitch which required them to reboot the computer that they used for calculating the exact mix for each load of con-crete based on a set of parameters which included moisture, den-sity, humidity, dry time, etc.

Eric pulled his cement truck out of the lot and drove it under the filler which would pour the correct mixture of sand, gravel, and other materials from the chute into the back end of his truck. Once the truck was in place, he waved to the person responsible for running the dump chute, indicating that he was ready for the truck to be loaded. Eric turned on the mixer in his truck, which caused the conical drum, which was the biggest part of his truck, to slowly spin. This allowed the materials that were dumped into the truck to be mixed together in preparation for delivery.

Suddenly there was a jam. Sand and gravel started spurting out over the top of the truck instead of flowing down into the chute.

Eric yelled out, "Shut down the chute! There's a jam."

The chute was shut down and the flow suddenly stopped. Eric climbed up the metal ladder that was connected to the side of the truck to inspect the truck chute and see why it had jam-med.

"What do you see?" yelled the filler operator from below as he saw Eric arrive at the top of the ladder.

"I see a leg sticking up," responded a shocked Eric. "Some-one's stuck in the chute. Get up here and help me pull him out! Wait. Shut the truck off first so that it quits turning the drum. Then get up here."

"You have to be joking," responded the filler operator as he ran to the truck cab, shut off the truck, and returned to the back of the truck. He quickly climbed up the truck's ladder.

Eric had already started to clear sand and gravel away from around the body. He climbed up on top of the truck's filler chute so the filler operator could join him at the top of the ladder and help him. They both continued to clear materials away from the body, occasionally pulling up on the body to see if they could pull it free. After another ten minutes they were finally successful at getting the body to start to shake loose.

At this point a crowd of people had started to accumulate around the truck. Eric's father yelled up, "What's going on?"

Eric responded, "There's a dead body jammed into the truck's chute. We're trying to pull him out."

"Wait! Shouldn't we wait for the police? They may think we're obstructing evidence if we mess with the body. Do you know who it is?" questioned Roger.

"We have no idea who it is. He's upside down and all we see are his legs. But I think we need to go ahead. What if there's a chance of reviving him? Shouldn't we at least try? I think we need to continue trying to get him out just in case. We're starting to wiggle him out now. We should have him out in a few more minutes."

"Wow. That's scary! How on earth could something like this happen?" expressed a concerned Roger. At this point he was rambling, almost talking to himself. He was obviously in shock, along with everyone else that was in the area watching the active-ities.

Roger pulled out his phone and dialed 9-1-1. The operator answered and said, "What is your emergency?"

Roger responded, "We have a dead man in our cement truck."

Operator, "Are you sure he's dead? Did you check his vital signs?"

Roger, "His head is buried in the sand and gravel. There's no way he's alive. My crew is trying to dig him out now just to make sure."

Operator, "Please check for vital signs to confirm that he's dead."

Roger, "How do I check his vital signs? On his big toe?"

Operator, "I'll send the fire department and an ambulance. Don't touch or move the body until they arrive. Give me your location."

Roger supplied the information and got off the phone mumbling, "Those idiots. They've given me conflicting instructions. Either I check for vital signs, or I don't move the body. I go for checking for vital signs."

Eric called down, "We have him loose enough. He's starting to come up out of the truck's chute.". After another few tugs Eric and the filler operator were able to lay the body out on the top of the truck's drum.

"Who is it?" yelled Roger.

"Holy crap. It's Bud," replied the filler operator. "I just saw him last night when we were both driving out of the parking lot and heading home. I can't believe he's dead. How did he end up in the filler chute?"

"Do you think it was suicide?" questioned Eric.

"It seems like he went through a lot of trouble if he just wanted to kill himself," answered Roger. "Do you see any wounds? Does it look like he might have been in a fight?"

"Nothing obvious," responded Eric as the fire trucks and ambulance started to pull up. "Wait, I do see a gash on his head. I'm not sure if it's accidental from a fall or if he was hit."

"What's going on?" asked the emergency responder.

"A dead man was in the filler chute and ended up getting dumped into the cement truck. We just pulled him out of the truck," replied Rick.

"Get down from there and let us get up there to take a look," commanded the first responder.

Eric and the filler chute operator climbed down, and the responder climbed up on the truck. He checked the vital signs of the body. Then he confirmed the information to the rest of his crew. "He is definitely dead. Hand me a body board. I'll strap him down and then we can off load him from this truck."

The emergency responders took over and it wasn't long before they had Bud off the truck and transferred to an ambulance. Just then the sheriff arrived and started an investigation which included pictures and interviews of everyone on location. It would be hours before they were able to get back to delivering the cement loads for the day.

CHAPTER THREE

Case Analysis

June 2020, Helena, Montana
Police Station

"What do we have on that sand and gravel body?" asked Duke Wilson, the lead detective, directing his question to Jill England, his junior companion. Duke was in his late forties, short, overweight, and balding. He could easily be mistaken as the killer who attempted to kidnap Roger, Joe's twin, except Duke was clean cut and looked ten years younger than his actual age. Unlike Joe, he took care of himself. Duke had a slight stutter, but his intelligence and investi-gative ability made any of his speech defects ignorable.

Duke was the only detective in Helena qualified to handle a murder investigation. He was always assigned to do an initial review of any "unattended" death just in case there was foul play.

"Not a lot," was the response. Jill was in her mid-twenties and had just graduated from the university as a criminal investigator. She was a good-looking American Filipino. Both her parents had immigrated from the Philippines before she was born. She had a killer smile and a cute body. Besides her physical beauty, she had a personality that made everyone comfortable around her. Guys tended to immediately fall in love with her because of her Oriental mystique, which was uncommon in Montana. She was teamed up with Duke because he was an excellent trainer. The plan was for her to learn the ropes of a murder investigator and eventually become a lead detective.

Jill was a little distracted because of an over-the-phone fight she had earlier that day with her parents. She had become estran-ged from her parents who lived in New York. They couldn't understand why anyone would move to a bug and disease infested wilderness, like Montana. They had spent over an hour on the phone that morning lecturing her about her insanity. But she was a little on the rebellious side and the more they lectured her, the more she pushed back and resisted their requests.

She had a happy childhood, and she loved her parents. But the older she got, the more she disagreed with their religious be-liefs. They belonged to a church which was very prominent in the Philippines called Inglesia Ni Cristo. They expected Jill to follow their teachings and would not except the fact that she was a grown woman with her own choices to make. Jill thought of herself as a Christian, but her parents insisted she was a lost soul. This became the major point of contention between Jill and her par-ents. Finally, and a little rudely, she cut their conversation off on the phone and told them she had to get to work.

After the call she felt sad because once again she had allowed them to make her angry. She didn't want to be angry. She wanted to love them and have them love her and be proud of her. But all they seemed to see was the negative. It felt like she was constantly under pressure; like she was never good enough and always had to change something. No matter what she did, there would always be something wrong with it. And she allowed these frustrations to make her feel a slight sense of depression and exasperation. And now it affected her work. It made her feel like she shouldn't care; like it wasn't worth the effort to do a good job. And she hated herself for this feeling.

Jill was glad she had moved so far away from her parents. She loved the beauty of Montana and the freedom of living beyond her parent's reach. She was, however, slightly disappointed in the male selection in Helena. In her view, all the men came out of the same mold. They all looked and thought the same. And she preferred a little more stubbornness and originality in a man. And maybe that was part of the reason she wasn't married yet. In fact, she had never even come close to being married. She never allowed any relationship to move that far along. But she blamed it on the fact that she was a police officer, and she thought that her position intimidated most men. She also liked being free to make her own choices. She decided that life was a trade-off and that she still hadn't decided what trades she was willing to make.

She quickly jumped back to the present when she noticed Duke staring at her, expecting her to explain what she was thinking. "Him being in that chute doesn't make sense," she contin-ued. "If he was climbing around up there, he could easily have slipped and the whack on the head could be an accident. But doing it in the middle of the night doesn't make sense. He was seen leaving the gravel pit earlier, so why did he come back?"

"I will continue to interview everyone at the gravel pit." stated Duke. "I want you to start interviewing his family. Was he showing signs of depression? Was he suicidal? Or another angle could be a secret life of some kind. Was he meeting someone? Did he have an alcohol, drug, gambling, or other addiction? We also need to get a full corner's report. I'm not willing to call this an accident just yet."

"I'll call his wife and see if we can set up a meeting with her and the rest of the family," suggested Jill.

"As always, we want to talk to each member individually. Have them come to the police station if possible so we can put them in separate interview rooms."

"Will do," responded Jill as she headed for the office and sat down at her desk. It would be about three hours before family members started arriving and the interviews were able to begin. Duke had finished the interviews at the gravel pit and joined Jill for the family interviews. They met with Bud's wife and each of his three teenage children. They also met with his two sisters and a brother who lived in the Helena area.

Duke and Jill started their interviews by first meeting with Bud's widow. Bud spoke first, "We apologize for bringing you out here at such an emotional and tragic time. We know this is hard for you. But the longer we wait with this interview the more details will be lost."

"I understand," said the wife. "I assume you're treating this as a murder."

"We haven't made that determination," responded Jill. "Right now, we are considering all possibilities. But the circumstances are suspicious."

Duke interjected, "Until we have the coroner's report, and all the interviews completed, it would be premature to make a statement about the cause of death."

"I understand," said the wife. "You're being careful before you commit, but there's no way this is a suicide."

Duke continued, "There is also the possibility of it being an accident."

"I don't see that as very likely," stated the widow. "Bud always arrived home between six and seven in the evening. Last night, he called me when he was on his way home to say he had forgotten his lunch box and he was returning to the gravel pit to retrieve it. That was the last time I spoke to him. He wasn't going back there to work or to check on the equipment. He was just getting his lunch bucket and coming straight home. An accident which would put him into the loading chute doesn't make sense. And, as for suicide, that doesn't fit either. Our oldest daughter is going to have a baby in about four months, and he was so excited about being a grandad. There wasn't anything in his life that would cause him to be depressed or sad. We are in good shape finan-cially, and everyone in the family is getting along reasonably well. Nothing out of the ordinary. Suicide or an accident just don't fit."

"Has your husband been out late any other evenings?" asked Duke.

"No. This was very unusual for him. We have dinner at 6:30 and he's always home for that. A couple weeks ago the guys at his work went out for a Friday-nighter at the bar, but he told me about that ahead of time so I wouldn't have dinner waiting for him. Other than that life is pretty routine for us."

"So, he normally doesn't go out again after dinner?" asked Jill.

"Rarely."

"What about early mornings?"

"He's up at about 4:30 AM because they often have 6 AM cement deliveries, but that's not unusual either. We're pretty boring when it comes right down to it."

The interview continued for another ten minutes, discussing his work, hobbies, and even the types of shows he watched. He didn't spend a lot of time on the computer, so they didn't dive into a discussion of that.

"We do want one of our computer experts to look at your computer, just in case we find anything suspicious, and the same goes with your cell phones. We don't expect to find anything, but we're expected to be thorough in case any of this ends up in court. For example, we don't want the killer to go free on a tech-nicality, because we weren't thorough. We need your permission to do that. Any problem with that?" requested Duke.

"What are you hoping to find?" asked the wife.

"Honestly, nothing," answered Duke. "We're just being thorough. Based on what you told us we shouldn't find anything. Would you give us permission to have our techies look things over?"

"Of course," she responded. "If there are any clues there then I hope you find them."

With that, the detectives had the widow sign a release form and they finished the interview. At that point Jill and Duke split up and held separate interviews with each of the remaining family members. Once the interviews were completed, they got together again to discuss what they learned.

"Did you come up with anything of interest?" Duke asked Jill.

"Not really," she responded. "I received a lot more details about Bud's life, but nothing that would suggest suicide. And the idea of an accident makes less sense. No one believes that he went back to work to run the loading chute. None of this makes sense."

"I'm in agreement. Everyone I talked to gives a story that's similar to what you're hearing. It looks like we may have a mur-der here. But let's wait for the coroner's report before we make that call. It's just that I'm also not hearing anything that would cause us to conclude that it was a murder."

"Agreed," answered Jill. "The only thing I can think of that might have happened is that he saw something he shouldn't have, or he was in the wrong place at the wrong time."

Jill continued, "I have found something that is interesting. There was a missing person's report filed last night on Bud. Apparently, his wife was reporting that he didn't show up at home as expected. But, as you know, we don't do anything until at least 24 hours, and sometimes 48 hours, after the person goes missing."

Duke responded, "That suggests the spouse didn't have anything to do with Bud going missing, but we can't be sure until we dig a little deeper."

"I listened to the recording and it sounded genuine. I don't think she is involved. She sounded genuinely concerned."

Duke shook his head in agreement as Jill left his office.

After Jill was gone, Duke picked up his phone, punched in a number, and waited for someone to pick up the call.

There was a female voice on the other end of the line that picked up the call, and she said, "Hello Duke. What do you need?"

"I want to know how we're going to play this," responded Duke.

"Just let it play out naturally. Don't interfere yet. We may need to later, so let's not show our cards too early."

"Will do," said Duke. "I'll treat it as a normal investigation."

"Perfect," was her response as she hung up the phone.

CHAPTER FOUR

Another Death

June 2020, Helena, Montana
Holter Lake

Joe and Fred weren't hikers. Climbing over the top of one of the Rocky Mountains to get to a dammed off part of the Missouri River known as Holter Lake wasn't how they had planned to spend their day. They started at a drop-off point along Interstate I-15 slightly northwest of the "Gates of the Mountains" recreation area. From there, they crossed a wheat field arriving at the base of the mountain. Then, it was a climb up one side of the mountain and down the other to arrive at the lake.

"Are you kidding me," complained Joe as they arrived at the base of the mountain. "We're supposed to be killing someone, but this looks more like someone is trying to kill us."

"Quit whining," responded Fred. "I always wanted to climb over the Sleeping Giant, and now's our chance."

"I know the Sleeping Giant nonsense and it always seemed a little spooky to me. When you look north from Helena, the mountains look like a sleeping giant and you see his face and body.

It really is a bit of a stretch of the imagination. But I guess everyone wants to pretend that it's a giant laying there."

"We're climbing his chest. On the other side is Holter Lake, which is where the Falcon cabin is located," explained Fred, ignoring his whining.

"I'm glad it's a he, not a she, or the chest would have been even higher," complained Joe.

Fred continued, "You heard the boss. He didn't want any-thing tying this crime to us. If we went to this cabin by boat, it would be too obvious and there might even be surveillance cam-eras. Consider this as getting our weeks' worth of exercise in one day."

"More like a months' worth of exercise. I'm exhausted just walking across this field. Now we're going to climb a mountain. I'm no Davey friggen Crocket."

"For you that's probably true," added Fred. "Regardless, we have to do this so let's get going and quit the whining."

"I know. I know."

The two slowly started their climb, with Joe stumbling occasionally and always lagging behind.

Eventually, they arrived at the top. The climb took about three hours which made it the middle of the day as they started their descent.

"See the lake?" asked Fred. "Isn't that a pretty sight?"

Joe was huffing and puffing and bent over, resting his hands on his knees as he complained, "What good does pretty do me if I'm dead?"

"It's all downhill now."

"I know better than that. Going down a steep hill is murder on your feet and your back. You're not fooling me. There may be more than one death on this mountain before the day is over."

Fred was frustrated with all the complaining, "It may be me killing you if you don't quit your whining."

"Just try it. We'll see who wins that one," challenged Joe.

The downhill climb was just as strenuous as Joe predicted. It wasn't as exhausting as the uphill climb, but it was every bit as painful on the leg joints and on the lower back.

"Can you see the cabin that we're headed for?" question Joe.

"No. It's hidden in a gulley to the right, but I know it's there because I can see the cabins on either side of it. We're definitely heading to the right place."

"Good! I'd hate for all this to be a waste of time. We already bungled this kidnapping job once. I'd hate to mess it up a second time," responded Joe.

"I'm with you on that one. Let's get this done and get it done right."

"Hopefully, we're not going to grab him and then end up dragging him over the top of this hill, are we?"

"No! We're supposed to grab him and then use his boat to drive to a spot near the end of the road. Apparently, the road that goes by the dam goes a long way along the north side of the lake and there is a drop-off spot at the end of the road where we are to deliver Roger."

"Good. That means we don't have to climb back over this mountain again. That makes me happy."

Fred explained, "Actually, all those details haven't been decided. Roger is supposed to come up to the lake by himself tomorrow - to fish for the day. Hopefully, there won't be any other people that we have to deal with. Either way, us coming up to the back of the cabin, will not be expected. Once we get close enough, we can watch the cabin and figure out if Roger is already there and if he is alone."

"Let's come up with a plan that doesn't require us to have to reclimb that mountain," begged Joe.

It took close to three more hours for them to finally descend the mountain and arrive at the cabin. There were gullies that had to be traversed making it necessary to go down one side and then back up again on the other, and there were areas where rock-slides had occurred. The hikers had to work their way around therm.

"We made it," exclaimed Joe. "Finally! I was about to die from exhaustion. Next time you have a stupid assignment like this, pick someone else. The money isn't worth anything to me if I'm dead."

"We were told that Roger would be coming to the cabin and we were to lie in wait for him," commented Fred. "There's no boat parked at the dock. Let's keep quiet and sneak into the cab-in and wait for him. Let's try not to make any noise just in case someone is already here."

Coming down the hill they approached the cabin from the back side, walking past the outhouse and down onto the upstairs deck. They did their best to be quiet, but unfortunately the deck-ing and the stairs from the upper deck down to the lower deck squeaked as they descended.

Both the upstairs and downstairs doors were locked. "Looks like we're alone," suggested Fred.

"So, what do we do?" asked Joe.

"We break in and relax until someone arrives."

"When will that be?"

"According to the boss, Roger is supposed to be arriving tomorrow," answered Fred. "So, we have to make the best of it and spend the night here and be ready to grab him tomorrow."

Joe was quick to break into the downstairs living room and kitchen area of the house, "They have a TV and a VCR in here. I'm going to find me a movie to watch."

"Go for it," answered Fred. "I'm going to see what food they have and try to find me something to eat."

"Get me something too," answered Joe.

The two went to work on each of their tasks, Joe starting up a movie, and Fred rummaging through the fridge and the cup-boards for something to eat. They ended up eating dry cereal for dinner, but it was better than nothing. It soon became dark and the two, exhausted from their climb, hit the sack early. They knew that tomorrow would include dealing with whoever showed up at the cabin, and possibly more climbing.

Fred, frustrated that they couldn't find anything better to eat, went into one of his temper tantrums. He started pulling off his shoes and threw them up in the air, hitting the ceiling. Joe, who was familiar with Joe's behavior, decided to stay out of the way and said nothing. Eventually he calmed down and the two went to sleep.

When morning came, they were up, alert, and ready. But no one came. It was noon and still there was no one. They sat in the cabin and watched movie after movie, waiting for someone to show up.

It was around three PM when a boat arrived at the dock with two heavily bearded older men who had obviously spent the day fishing. They climbed out of the boat and hauled a large cooler onto the shore.

The first fisherman, looking through the large picture window at the front of the cabin, yelled out to the other, "There's someone in the cabin. What's going on? There's no boat here. There shouldn't be anyone here."

Joe and Fred focused on the movie didn't realize that someone had pulled up in a boat until it was too late. Looking out the window and seeing that they had been spotted, they came out of the cabin and challenged the fishermen, "What the hell are you guys doing here?"

The surprised fishermen responded, "We didn't know anyone was here. Where's your boat?"

"We came off the hill," answered Joe.

"We stop here often," continued one of the fishermen. "We have Roger's permission to clean our catch on shore here before we leave the lake. We do it all the time." Then he asked, "Are you friends of the Falcon's?"

"Yes," responded Fred. "We were expecting to meet them here today."

"If you're friends of the Falcons you should know better than that. There's no way Roger would leave his gravel pit on a weekday."

Joe was put into a rage. "Are you accusing us of lying?" he challenged the fisherman. He didn't like being accused. He jumped off the deck and ran out on the lawn area heading toward the fishermen who quickly put down their cooler and got ready for what looked like a possible fight.

"What are you thinking you idiot?" yelled one of the fishermen as he picked up the fileting knife from off the top of the cooler. "What is your problem?"

Joe didn't say anything. He continued his charge, clenching his fist and obviously planning to strike.

The fight was short lived. Joe threw a punch at the fisherman that had accused them of lying, only to find a fileting knife jammed through the underside of his upper arm. An artery was sliced, and he began to bleed profusely. He fell to the ground screaming, grabbing his arm with his other hand and putting pressure on the stab wound. Fred jumped into action quickly taking off his shirt and using it to tie a tourniquet on the stab wound while the fishermen made a mad dash for their boat, returning their cooler to the boat and driving off. They weren't going to wait around for another attack.

Fred's efforts were in vain. Joe bled out in a matter of minutes and died right there on the front lawn of the cabin. Fred was exasperated. He didn't have any idea what to do. He sat down in the grass resigned to his fate. According to the fishermen, there would be no Roger to kidnap. And now he had lost his companion in crime. What was he going to do with Joe's body? What was he going to tell the boss? Once again everything had gone tragically wrong.

After fifteen minutes Fred decided he was going to make Joe's death look like a suicide. He didn't want anyone to know that there had been other people at the cabin. He didn't want the fishermen to be connected with Joe's death because then they would be able to describe Fred. He didn't want to leave any evidence behind that he or anyone else had even been at the cabin. It needed to appear as if no one else was involved in Joe's death.

Fred struggled as he carried Joe's body upstairs to the upper balcony and laid it out. He used a weak ski rope and tied it around Joe's neck. He also tied another piece on the roof rafter, making it look like a suicide where the rope had busted. He knew that the autopsy would reveal the real cause of death as the stab in his artery, but it would take at least a month before that report came out, and by then any other evidence, like the blood in the lawn, would be washed away by rain. The faked suicide would throw everyone off track, and the officials wouldn't even consider the possibility of murder until it was too late.

Next Fred grabbed a bucket and scooped water out of the lake and dumped it on the blood that was on the lawn. He con-tinued dumping water on the lawn until he felt he had sufficiently diluted the blood. He assumed it had been sufficiently soaked into the grass to not be identified as the location of Joe's death. Any blood that remained would be washed away by the rains over the next week.

Fred cleaned up the area inside and outside the cabin, at-tempting to remove any trace evidence he had been there. Hav-ing satisfied himself that he sufficiently cleaned up the cabin and the surrounding area, Fred started the climb back over the moun-tain and back to the highway leading to Helena. The only con-cern he had left was figuring out what story he was going to tell his boss. How was he going to explain what happened to Joe? How was he going to explain another kidnapping failure?

CHAPTER FIVE

The Investigation

June 2020, Helena, Montana
Police Station

"Do we have the coroner's report on that sand and gravel body?" asked Duke, the lead detective, directing his question to Jill.

"Not yet," was her response, "but he promised we should have it shortly. Should be go talk to Morton?"

"Yep, let's go down and see what he's got so far."

The two walked off toward the staircase that led down to the basement where the coroner's office was located. Entering the facility, Duke approached Morton Mararac, the coroner, and asked, "What do you have on the body from the gravel pit?"

"Just wrapping it up," explained Morton. "Looks like you might have a murder investigation. He has a couple sharp hits on the head which occurred before his death, and then he has sev-eral wounds and scrapes on his body, but they all appear to be after his death. I suppose there is a chance the head wound was accidental. Maybe he fell into the dump chute. But there doesn't seem to be any reason for him to be up there. My guess is he was hit from behind and then thrown into the chute."

Jill jumped in, "Why would anyone want to haul his body onto the chute belt and run it all the way up to the top of the chute to dump his body in there. That seems like a lot of trouble."

"Only to temporarily hide the body or mask the wounds with more cuts and scrapes. To make it look like an accident," suggested Duke.

"But you're in a sand and gravel pit," added Jill. "Wouldn't it be easier to just dig a quick hole in the sand and stick him in there?"

"That would make more sense," commented Morton. "Except you're expecting sense to come from criminals, and I've found they have very little common sense. When they get into panic mode, they make mistakes, and that's what we as criminal investigators look for; mistakes."

"Looks like we're going to have to treat this as a murder for now," responded Duke. "We should keep tight control on the evidence. If we find out later it was suicide or an accident, which I doubt will happen, we can always back off, but we need to be vigilant for now."

"Anything else you need from me?" asked Morton.

"Not for now," replied Duke. "Just keep tight control on the evidence and send me the detailed, final report. Jill, let's you and I go out to the gravel pit one more time and have a look around."

"What are we looking for," she asked.

"Don't know," he replied. "Just want a closer look, this time from the perspective this is a murder investigation."

The detectives departed out the side door of the police sta-tion, heading for their police cruiser, climbed in, and took off for the Falcon gravel pit.

Arriving at the gravel pit they drove up to the front office. The pit office was located at the edge of the pit, which went down between ten to twenty feet lower than the roadway. The office was arranged so its back side allowed employees to view into the pit to see what activities were in process. In front of the office was a wide-open parking area at street level which included an in-ground scale for weighing trucks, and the area around the scale had lots of room for parking the company's gravel and cement trucks.

The detectives drove right up to the front door, climbed out of their vehicle, and entered the office. Judy, Roger's wife who ran the office, saw them drive up, walked to the front door to meet them, and asked, "How can I help you guys?"

Duke responded, "We just want to take a closer look around and get a better understanding of how someone could end up in the dump chute. Is there someone who could walk us around and show us the equipment? Hopefully, someone who was there when they found the body."

Judy responded, "Eric is out there in the pit. I'll call him up here and he can show you around. It was his truck that was involved. He was the one that found Bud." She walked over to the counter, picked up a walkie-talkie, and radioed Eric. "Eric, we need you up here in the office. We have some people waiting for you." Then turning to the detectives, she said, "You can have a seat over there on the couch if you want to wait for him."

"Can we just walk around and take a look while we're waiting for him?" asked Jill.

"Of course," answered Judy. "Look around. Let me know if you have any questions."

The detectives walked to the back of the office and looked through the viewing window at the gravel pit below. Off to the right they could see the blending and loading equipment that was used to fill the cement trucks. Judy walked over to the window and pointed to someone walking towards the building, "That's Eric down there coming towards the building."

Less than a minute later Eric entered the building at the lower, pit level and came up the stairs to meet the detectives. Judy provided an introduction, "Eric, these are a couple detectives, and they have some questions about when you found Bud in your truck."

Eric turned toward the detectives and said, "Sure. What would you like to know?"

Jill was momentarily stunned. This is what a gravel pit worker looks like? He doesn't look or act cowboyish. Her mind was momentarily blank, and so Duke spoke up, "Can you walk us through what you think might have happened. We'd like to see the exact locations where everything happened. Like, where you found Bud, and how you found him, etc."

"Sure," replied Eric. "But I already did all that with pictures and everything on the morning I found him."

"We have all that, but there are a few points that we need to go over. We just want to make sure we understand everything correctly."

"What kinds of points? Maybe I can answer them for you," responded Eric.

"We'll get to them as we go through everything. For starters, can you walk us through what you were doing at the time the body was found?" said Duke.

Eric took the detectives to his truck and explained how the loading process worked. He pointed the way so he could follow behind. They started walking in that direction, but Eric wanted to get a better look at Jill without letting anyone know he was looking. Or at least that's what he thought, but Jill was hoping he was doing exactly that. She was hoping he was looking. But in her mind the chaos continued. In her mind she thought, "Why do I care whether he's looking? He is so stinking cute. Judas, I'm no good at relationships, and this will most likely just be another disaster. Pull yourself together and be professional. You are a detective for goodness sake. Quit looking at him and start think-ing about the murder."

Eric was going through his own battle. His eyes were glued to Jill. She was wearing uniform shorts and her legs were incredible. She had the body of an athlete, straight and strong, without the oversized boobs so many women think is a requirement for sexiness. And a strong, firm ass, which showed no sag. "She is superhot," was all he could think.

Eric, trying to compose himself, explained the process. Gravel, sand, and cement were poured into the chute that was at the back end of the truck, set higher than the drum. This was where the materials were poured into the drum as the drum turned, mixing the materials together.

Then he took them to the filler chute and explained how the trucks were loaded. The bottom of the filler chute was at the same level as the top of the cement truck chute, which was about 15 feet off the ground. The truck's chute was positioned directly under the filler chute. Materials were released from the filler chute and poured directly into the truck.

The top of the filler chute was about 35 feet off the ground. It contained the correct quantity of each of the materials that were going to be dumped into the truck.

Above the filler chute was a conveyor belt which transferred materials from ground level up to and into the chute. The ground crew was responsible for making sure the correct quantities of gravel, sand, cement, and drying chemicals were run up into the chute. The conveyor was then used to dump these materials into the filler chute.

There were foot-hold steps attached to the legs of the filler chute frame that allowed individuals to climb to the top of the filler chute and inspect it as needed. Duke climbed to the top of the chute and looked inside. He took several pictures which he would send to the coroner, allowing him to assess the possibility some of the injuries were accidently inflicted.

Duke questioned, "So someone had to climb all the way up that ladder carrying the body in order to throw him into that filler chute?"

Eric added, "Yes, or else he was alive when he went up there and fell in. Or there is a third option and that is that he was somehow placed on the conveyor belt and then dumped in."

"Is there any way of knowing if the equipment was turned on after work on that evening?" asked Jill, trying to maintain her cool and not be too obvious. She decided she was going to get to know Eric better.

"No. Sorry," Eric responded. "It's a manual switch. Someone would have to turn the switch on and after Bud fell into the chute, they would have to turn it off again. It would have been intentional."

"If he was going to commit suicide, would he go through all the trouble of climbing up there?" asked Duke.

"The conveyor wasn't running in the morning, so if it was suicide, he would have had to climb up there," replied Eric. "But there are easier ways to commit suicide. And besides, no one would even think of going up there. We rarely go up there, even for work. It was probably two months since anyone has bothered to go up there."

"Let's assume suicide for now and that he climbed up there. How would he kill himself? By jumping in the chute?" quizzed Duke.

"That really doesn't make sense, does it," responded Eric. "There's nothing up there to kill yourself with. And he didn't have a gun or any weapon with him."

"Then let's go to accident," continued Duke. "Again, the belt option is out because someone would have had to turn it off. Would there be a reason for him to climb up there in the middle of the night?"

"No. That doesn't make sense either," said Eric. "And about the only thing that would kill him would be to fall off the ladder onto the ground, which didn't happen. The chute is usually pretty full, ready for the next mix, so he would not have far to fall inside the chute."

"Then unfortunately we're left with the only remaining op-tion, which is murder," commented Duke. The three looked at each other in shocked understanding.

"Has anyone been up there since all this happened?" asked Jill.

"No," responded Eric. "We found him when he was in the truck. We didn't spend a lot of time considering the chute as a problem."

"So," Jill continued, "if we go up the ladder, we wouldn't find any footprints on the dust which has accumulated on the steps."

"There definitely should not be any footprints on the steps," responded Eric.

Jill went to work photographing each of the steps on the ladder up to the chute. She slowly climbed the steps and took pic-tures as she ascended. Eric and Duke just watched, waiting to hear if she discovered anything. But Eric was observing her more closely than Duke. After she reached the top Duke yelled out, "See anything?"

"Yes," she responded. "It's weird but the top three steps have footprints on them. The remaining steps up to here are clear of dust. Someone has definitely been on the top steps."

"That's weird," was all Eric could think to say.

"But weren't you up here when you pulled out his body?" asked Jill.

"No! I was on the ladder that's attached to the side of the truck. The ladder you're on is rarely used. We only go up there if there's a problem with the loading chute."

Jill continued, "Then how do you get footprints on the top of the ladder and not on the bottom?"

Eric was thoughtful and then commented, "That doesn't make any sense, no matter how you twist Bud's death." Then he yelled up to Jill, "Do those steps, with the footprints have dust settling in on top of where the footprints were?"

"Yes," she replied. "The footprints probably weren't made in the last couple days. They must have been made several days ago. Or maybe even a week or more. I can't tell for sure. But I guess it doesn't really matter when they were made since he obviously didn't come up here this way."

Duke yelled up, "Come back down. You're scaring me up there. We'll have our CSI guys check it out again and see if they can come up with anything more. It's probably nothing. Espe-cially if it predates the murder. Now get down from there!" Duke placed a call to the CSI team and instructed them on what he wanted them to do. Then he used sawhorses to place a barrier around the chute ladder and wrote a sign that he stuck on one of the sawhorses which said, "Crime Scene. Keep Out."

Jill, after having looked down, and seeing how high up she had climbed, now felt an urgency to get down as well. And she descended the ladder quickly.

Jill, Duke, and Eric continued their discussion about what happened to Bud after he mysteriously ended up in the loading chute. "When you found Bud, he was head down in the back end of your truck?" asked Bud.

"Yes," replied Eric. "His body was turned somehow so that he came through the loading chute headfirst and jammed down into the chute on the truck. However, the chute on the truck takes a sharp turn and dumps everything into the rotating drum on the back of the truck and Bud's body couldn't make that sharp turn. He jammed up the works right there, causing the re-maining gravel and concrete materials to spill out over the top of the truck."

Jill continued, "And when you tried to pull him out, he was imbedded in the midst of the gravel?"

"That's correct," responded Eric. "We had to scoop away gravel which was jammed around his body in order to free up his body enough, so we could pull him out."

They continued discussing the details of the event, but there weren't any new discoveries. They waited around for the CSI team to arrive, making sure that the ladder wasn't disturbed. They instructed the CSI team to do a thorough fingerprint search, not expecting to find anything because this was an active working pit, and everything that the killers touched was probably touched a dozen more times since then. But on the off chance that there are any fingerprints that can't be eliminated by the local work crew, they felt that they should give it a try. After the arrival of the team, Duke and Jill left, heading back to the police station.

CHAPTER SIX

More to Investigate

June 2020, Helena, Montana
Police Station
(Two Weeks Later)

It's been two weeks since their visit to the Falcon Sand and Gravel outfit. Duke was sitting at his desk when Jill came over to him and asked, "Anything new on the gravel pit case?"

"Nothing. The CSI guys went over there and did a more thorough search, but they didn't come up with anything new. Between the wind and the dust, it's hard to come up with anything meaningful," said Duke.

"What about the footsteps on the ladder?" asked Jill.

"Apparently they believe that the footprints predate Bud's murder. That turned out to be a dead end."

"Fingerprints?"

"That's a dead end too. They were actively working the equipment the morning after the murder and anything that the killers touched was touched by the workers. We found some partials that were tough to identify, but that's nothing that we can use."

"How do they explain that there are only footprints on the top few steps?"

"It seems that one of the tricks they use is to drive the cement truck up against the ladder, and climb up the cement truck, then go over to the ladder in order to finish their climb. Eric and Roger weren't too happy to hear about that since it's a good way to damage one of the trucks."

"Interesting," responded Jill. "I've visited more of the rela-tives and asked them about any enemies, but they make Bud sound like the nicest guy on earth. No enemies and lots of friends."

"I don't know where to go next with this case. It's a big fat dead end."

Just then Duke's cell phone rang, and he answered it with, "Duke here. How can I help?" Duke listened for a minute and said, "I'm leaving now. We'll get there as soon as possible."

Jill questioned Duke after he disconnected the call, "What's up?"

Duke replied, "There's been another murder. Two within a couple weeks. That's unusual for Helena. We need to get going."

"Good enough. Let's go."

"We'll need to take one of the CSI guys with so he can map out the scene in case this really is a murder as reported," re-quested Duke. "And we're meeting some state cop who has been assigned to this case, primarily because it is rural, which means the state gets involved."

"I'll grab someone from the CSI team and meet you at the car," responded Jill.

They drove out to the freeway, Interstate 15, and took the north on-ramp toward Great Falls. It was about a 35-minute drive to Wolf Creek where they took the exit to Holter Lake. It was another ten minutes before they arrived at the Holter Lake campground where a forest service boat was waiting to take them up the river to the crime scene. Holter Lake was a dammed off section of the Missouri river which started at the Gates of the Mountains in the South and ended at the dam next to the camp-grounds. It had numerous cabins along the lake, most of which were only accessible by boat. The crime scene was at one of these cabins.

At the docks they met Ranel Marinduque. He was the state trooper assigned to assist in the investigation. "Hello," he yelled out. "Are you the Helena detectives that I'm working with on this crime scene?"

"Yes, we are," explained Duke. "What do you know about this crime."

"Actually, I'm not even sure it is a crime," explained Ranel, "That's one of the things I'm here to determine."

"Let's go find out what we have," explained Jill as the three of them climbed into the forest service speed boat that was waiting for them.

The boat ride took another thirty minutes before they finally arrived at a cabin that was simply described as "two cabins to the left of Robert's Roost." Robert's Roost was a bar that had become a hangout for the Walleye fishermen that came to catch their limit on the lake. The Fish and Game boat that the officers were riding in also included a Forest Ranger who explained, "We were called by the owners of Robert's Roost who complained that there was a strong smell coming from the cabin, and when we investigated we found a dead body lying on the side porch. It looks like a suicide, but we can't be sure. Anyway, we tried not to touch or move anything until you guys arrived. We have a couple officers at the cabin making sure no one messes with the scene in case there's more to this than we suspected."

Duke asked, "Do you have any idea who the victim is?" He had to yell over the sound of the boat engine.

"No idea. The body is too decayed to tell. It's really grotesque," responded the officer.

"I'm sure I've seen worse," commented the CSI tech.

"I haven't," said Jill as she squinted her face. "I'm not looking forward to this at all."

They arrived at the cabin and pulled up to the small private dock which held three boats. The cabin was a two-story a-frame building with a front lawn area and a redwood deck out front. Two boats were in the dock and one dock space was left empty for the arriving police officers. The smell was immediate and apparent. They climbed out of the boat and were met by another officer. "We have been waiting for you. It's not a pretty site."

"Where do we go?" asked Duke.

The ranger pointed to the left side of the cabin and said, "There's stairs up that side of the cabin and the body is lying on the deck at the top of the stairs."

The three detectives and the CSI investigator walked around the side of the cabin and quickly found the stairs that led to the second floor. The smell became steadily worse as they ascended. At the top of the stairs they could see the bloated corpse of a man appeared to have been laid out with his arms and legs outstretched.

Suddenly Duke's face turned white and was flushed. He appeared as if he was going to faint. He leaned against the wall and slowly sat down. Jill immediately noticed that something was wrong and asked, "Are you feeling okay?"

"I'm okay," replied Duke, attempting to compose himself. "It must have been something I ate or the boat ride over here. I just suddenly felt faint."

To Jill, there was obviously more to Duke's reaction then he was telling. He was feeling good just seconds earlier. Something happened to him when he saw the body. This wasn't the first dead body Duke had seen, so it wasn't that. There was some kind of recognition that occurred when Duke saw the body and Duke wasn't going to share what he recognized. But Jill would remember this reaction and often wonder it meant.

"You see anything obvious," questioned Duke of the CSI tech, trying to recover his composure. "It's strange that the body is laying all sprawled out on his back."

"This is what you would expect to find at the current stage of decay," explained the tech. "As the body bloats it spreads out but that's not necessarily how he was laying when he died," replied the CSI tech. Taking a closer look at the body he continued, "I don't see rope burn marks around the neck which should ob-viously be there and should be caused by the rope if he really did hang himself. And I see a knife puncture wound on his upper arm. I'm guessing there was some type of struggle. This was staged to look like a suicide."

"Why do you say that?" asked Jill. She was struggling hard to keep from gagging. The site of the body and its smell made her want to vomit. She wanted to leave the scene, but she didn't want to appear weak. She wanted to be tough, like the rest of the guys.

"See the rope hanging from the roof?" he responded. "I think that was staged to look like he was trying to commit suicide. I don't think his head was ever tight in that noose. It was placed there after he was laying here, already dead. I think whoever stag-ed this was hoping that the rope around the neck would suggest a hanging, but it doesn't look like that to me. The neck wounds aren't there which should have been there if he really did hang himself. My initial guess was that something else killed him, but I can't be specific without an autopsy. The stab wound on the upper arm must be postmortem because I just don't see any indication of a sufficient amount of blood to suggest that the stab was what killed him." The CSI agent started taking detailed pictures of everything, including the rope and the surroundings around the body. After a few minutes he said, "Looks like you have another murder to work on."

"Are you sure?" challenged Duke.

"Preliminary analysis says there may have been a conflict and this guy lost. Afterwards his death was staged to look like a suicide," responded the tech.

Duke turned to Jill and Ranel and said, "Let's look around and see if we can find evidence of a fight."

"Good idea, except that if this was staged, I'll bet they cleaned up the area where the fight occurred," responded Jill. She was anxious to leave the dead body. "It may be hard to identify where he was actually killed. But we better make sure before the site gets used by someone and evidence gets lost." The two went off in opposite directions around the outside of the cabin while Ranel stayed with the body, looking for some sign which would help to explain the death.

"Find anything?" Duke asked Jill after they met up again on the back side of the cabin.

"Nope," she answered. "Let's check the inside."

"Before we do, I saw something that looked like recent activity on the side of the hill. I'd like our tech to have a look."

They returned to the site where the CSI tech was still examining the body and Duke asked, "Can you come with us? I want you to look at something."

"Sure," responded the tech and the four went up the ravine past the outhouse.

Duke pointed to what looked like some footprints leading up and out of the ravine. "What do you think?" he asked.

"Looks recent," responded the tech. "I'll document it and take a cast of the shoe."

Ranel added, "At the state crime offices we have a data base of statewide crime evidence and it might be worth comparing that shoe cast with the data base. You never know what might pop up."

"We might want to run all our evidence from both murders against that data base," added Jill. "Just in case there is something serial going on here. We wouldn't want to miss something obvious."

"Excellent," replied Duke. "I agree. In the meantime, Jill and I will check the cabin inside." They put on gloves and shoe cov-ers in order to not disturb any evidence.

They tested the door. "It's locked," said Duke as he tried turning the doorknob. "But I have no plans to come back later so we're going in." He pulled a screwdriver out of the tech's toolbox and slipped it behind the door stop, jamming the lock open. Then the two detectives entered the cabin and started touring the upstairs three bedrooms, and the downstairs kitchen and living room. After fifteen minutes of looking around, Duke went to the CSI tech and instructed him, "Can you do a search of the inside of the cabin as well? Maybe your ultraviolet lights will identify blood or something else that we can't see with the naked eye. We didn't find anything in our search but maybe you can find some-thing."

"Sure," replied the tech.

"How long until you're done?" asked Duke.

"I'll need another hour," replied the tech. "Then we can go. They can start removing the body now. I'm done with that."

Duke instructed Jill, "Tell the officers to bring up the body bag and have them put the body in the bag and haul it down to the boat."

"Sure thing," replied Jill as she started down the stairs.

The officers were not happy about getting stuck with the job of hauling out the body. They thought that the police should be doing that, but they did it anyway. After another fifteen minutes the tech came out of the cabin and informed Duke, "I found a large splotch of blood in the middle of the living room. But I'm not sure it's human. I tested for human blood and it came up weak, like it was mixed somehow with animal blood. Anyway, I cut out the section of carpet that had the stain and I'll be able to take a closer look at it back at the lab."

"Show me where you found it," requested Duke.

"Where the carpet is missing," replied the tech pointing in-side and in the direction of the living room. "I'm sure it's animal blood, but we'll have to test it to make sure."

Duke and Jill went into the living room and looked around for other clues of a struggle but found nothing until Jill looked up at the ceiling. She pointed upwards and said, "Look at that."

Duke responded, "What are you seeing?"

"Footprints."

"Go get our CSI tech and have him check if these footprints on the ceiling are old or recent. I wonder if they are related to the struggle somehow," instructed Duke.

Jill brought in the tech and told him what was needed. He went to work analyzing the footprints on the ceiling. "These are recent. Possibly caused during the struggle."

"What does it mean?" asked Jill.

"Beats me," replied the tech. "That's your job. However, I do see a similarity between these, and the footprints found out back going up the hill."

Duke paused for a moment thinking, "Jill. Can you go ask the officers if there was a boat out here when they arrived. I can't believe both the killer and the victim hiked in here. It's a long hike over those mountains." Then turning to the tech, he asked, "Were the footsteps on the side of the hill going down or up?"

"Both ways," replied the tech. "Two sets of footprints coming in and one going out. And one of the sets coming in and going out wore the same shoe. The other footprints, the ones coming in and not going out, belong to our victim's shoes."

"I assume the ones on the ceiling don't match the shoes of the victim," asked Jill.

"Not sure. I'd give it about a 50% chance that the shoe of the individual that came in but didn't leave is the shoe print on the ceiling. It's pretty close, but I won't be hundred percent sure until I get back to the lab."

"I'll check if there was a boat here," responded Jill as she left to go talk to the officers who were still waiting at the boat dock. She was back in less than a minute with the answer, "No boat when they arrived."

"So, the killer was a single individual, probably male, who came in from off the hill and returned up the hill," summarized the tech. "And we think that the victim arrived from the hillside as well. But I wish I could be certain that no one else was around at the time. It seems like a lot of trouble for the two of them to come all this way just to kill one of them and then return over the hill again. Something is missing in this scenario. What are you planning to do next?"

"Actually, those aren't the only possibilities," added Jill. "Your options assume there were only two players in all of this. What if there was a third? What if a third person came in on a boat, along with the person that was killed, committed the murder, and left by boat. What if the tracks up and down the hill do not have anything to do with the murder?"

"I guess we'll know more once I'm back in the lab. For example, if the footprints on the ceiling match the footprints on the side of the hill, then we know that the individual who came in off the hill was involved." asked the tech.

Jill continued, "It's possible that the hill climber was involved, but I'm just suggesting that a third person with a boat would help solve the mystery of how and why our dead person happened to be at the cabin."

"Or even a fourth or fifth person," added Duke. "We really don't know much at this point."

The tech replied, "We'll know more once I get the body back to the lab and take a closer look. Maybe there was more than one person involved in the murder."

Jill added, "So many questions and so few answers."

Ranel spoke up, "There are several things that we still need to do. For example, we need to talk to the neighbors. And we need to send someone up the hill with a dog to follow the footprints. Jill, you seem to be getting along with the officers better than any of us. You go talk to them about possibly having someone with a tracking dog go up the hill. And the rest of us should go and visit some of the neighbors."

Ranel, Duke and Jill went to the lake side of the cabin and approached the officers. Jill started the conversation with, "Do you have access to a tracking hound? We see footprints leaving the cabin and heading up the hill, but we need a dog to try to track them before the scent is completely gone."

"We do have a tracker," replied one of the officers. "We'll send for him to come here with his dog."

"Excellent," replied Jill.

CHAPTER SEVEN

The Mystery Deepens

June 2020, Holter Lake, Montana
Cabin Area

Ranel, Duke and Jill coerced one of the rangers to give them a ride over to the dock of Robert's Roost, the rest-aurant and bar two cabins over from the murder scene. These were the owners which had originally reported the smell, which in turn triggered the current investigation. The distance was less than one hundred yards, but the steep hillside made it nearly impossible to walk from the cabin to the restaurant. A boat was the only way to get between the two locations. Arriving at the dock the three climbed out of the boat and walked up the stair-case to the restaurant / bar at the top of the incline.

Entering the bar Duke asked, "Is the owner here?"

"I'm the owner," replied the person behind the bar. "What do you need?"

"We're detectives investigating the death two cabins over. Are you the one that made the report?"

"Yes, but all I reported was the smell. I didn't know anyone had died over there at the Falcon cabin," replied the owner.

That comment caused Jill and Duke to look at each other with a questioning look. Duke spoke up, "You say that's the Fal-con cabin. Do you know the Falcons?"

"Of course," replied the owner. "Everyone knows them. They own a Sand and Gravel business in Helena. I'm sure you heard of them before."

Jill jumped in, "Have the Falcon's been up to their cabin recently?"

"I haven't seen any Falcons over there in over a month."

"How about anyone else. Any boats?" asked Jill.

"Nope. Nothing," replied the owner.

Just then his wife walked in from the kitchen in time to hear the last piece of the conversation, "I saw a boat over there about a week ago. It wasn't the Falcon boat, and I didn't watch to see what was going on. The Falcons have lots of friends and they let people use their cabin to clean their catch, so I didn't pay a lot of attention to what was going on. As far as I can remember, the boat was only there a short time."

"Did you see who was on the boat," asked Jill.

"Nope. Sorry. Like I said, I really didn't pay a lot of attention to it," replied the wife.

Duke continued, "When the Falcons do come up, who is it that comes?"

The wife continued, "It's usually the kids and sometimes the wife. The husband says he's not much of a water person, so we don't see him much more than once a year, maybe at the 4th of July. And they always have friends come up with them."

"Just to confirm, we're talking about Judy and Roger Falcon," asked Jill. "That A-frame cabin over there is theirs."

"That's right," answered the owner.

Duke asked the wife, "Can you describe the boat that you saw over there?"

"It was a blue inboard-outboard ski boat, like the fifty that you see going up and down the lake every weekend. Except it wasn't a weekend. It was the middle of the day in the middle of the week," she replied.

"Do you remember exactly what day it was?" asked Duke.

"No," she replied. "Wait. I can remember it was Wednesday, and week and a half ago, because it was foggy and misty. It was a kind of weird day. Yes, I remember now, it definitely was on Wednesday."

"Thanks," answered Duke. "Is there anything you can remember that might help our investigation. For example, was anyone else up here on that day?"

"Can't think of a thing," the owner responded as the wife also shook her head negatively. "I remember it was a miserable weather day and no one came up to the lake."

Then Duke handed him a business card and said, "Let me know immediately if you think of anything."

"Will do," responded the owner.

Duke and Jill returned to the dock and they were shuttled back to the Falcon cabin. Upon arrival they found that a tracking dog had been located. In addition, a ranger which was of American Indian descent had also joined the group because he was the dog's trainer. The two of them had achieved a statewide reputation for being excellent trackers. They immediately went to work and started up the hill.

June 2020, Holter Lake, Montana, The hill behind the Falcon Cabin

Namid, a Cheyenne Indian whose name means "Star dan-cer", started working his way up the hill behind the cabin follow-ing his dog Tucker. Namid was a tall six foot two and very well built. The climb up the mountainside normally takes over three hours, but Namid was in excellent physical shape and with Tucker, a brown Labrador Retriever, pulling him along he would probably make it in less than two hours, that is if the trail led all the way to the top. That's the main reason why they almost always went alone. No one else was ever able to keep up with the two of them. Namid ran behind the dog for about thirty minutes, at first going straight up the side of the mountain, and then the trail veer-ed off in a southerly direction. It became obvious that the trail was heading over the top of the mountain to the south rather than going straight up the hill directly behind the cabin. This route would lead them toward the freeway. Unfortunately, this southern peak was significantly higher, and the trip would take even more time.

The two trackers continued following the very easy track of the individual which had come to the cabin. It had become ob-vious that the individual had come in using the same route that he was now using to leave. Whoever it was, he had come across the mountain specifically to visit the cabin. The trail was in a straight line, with no deviation. This individual knew exactly where he was headed.

As Namid rounded a ridge and started to work his way down the side of a small ravine and up the other side he was met with a surprise. Two girls were hiking up the side of the mountain wearing nothing but underpants and boots. He waved to them and they waved back. One of the girls yelled out, "Sorry to embarrass you. We lost a bet on a game we were playing, and this is how we have to pay it off. We have to climb to the top and back dressed like this."

"No problem," responded Namid. "It's great seeing you." The comment made him feel silly, but he recovered quickly. "I mean it was good meeting you."

"I'm glad it was, for your sake," replied the other girl. She could tell where he was looking, and it wasn't at her eyes.

Namid wasn't bothered by the scenery that the girls offered. He wanted to take it slow and enjoy the view. He wasn't in a hurry to press forward, but Tucker wouldn't let him rest. So, he was forced to push ahead. "Hope you enjoy the view," he said as he continued tracking.

"Hope you did too," replied the second girl sarcastically.

The girls headed toward the east, up the lower hill while Namid continued his climb over the southern mountain. He reached the top of the mountain about two hours after he had started. From the top he could see the highway running along the other side of a large wheat field which was at the bottom of the mountain. It was

Interstate 15 which ran from Helena to Great Falls. It seemed obvious that the person being tracked came from the freeway and returned there as well. But Namid had to make sure so he continued following the trail. He started the long climb down the south side of the mountain toward the free-way.

Eventually he learned that his assumption had been true. The trail led to the freeway. He gave a call to the Duke and reported, "I found where the trail ends. It stops at Interstate 15 and I can see where there was a car parked."

"Stay there," responded Duke. "We're driving towards you and we'll stop so that our CSI guy can investigate the area."

"Will do," responded Namid.

Thirty minutes later Duke and Jill arrived with their CSI investigator, who immediately went to work searching the area for clues.

June 2020, Helena, Montana
Behind the Local Wal Mart

Fred and two of his fellow criminal grunts pull up behind Walmart. It was past midnight, and the place was deserted. There were a couple piles of wooden pallets and several dump-sters, but other than that the area was dark and empty.

"What are we doing here?" asked Fred, slightly nervous about the intentions of his comrades.

"We're supposed to meet someone here and collect a pay-ment for protection services that we have been rendering. It should only take a few minutes," responded Ricardo, the indiv-idual who had been driving.

"We need to get out of the car," responded Alfredo, who had occupied the passenger seat. Fred had ended up sitting in the back.

"Why?" asked Fred suspiciously.

"Because this guy gets nervous about people sitting in a car," answered Alfredo. "He thinks they're pointing a gun at him the whole time, and he doesn't feel comfortable. If he sees you in the car he'll drive right by."

"That's stupid," responded Fred. But he was satisfied with the explanation and started to climb out of the vehicle.

The three stood in silence, close to the car, waiting. After another ten minutes, a police cruiser came around the back side of the store and drove up close to the three. Because of the dark-ness they couldn't see inside the cruiser's window. After the cruiser came to a stop, the driver side window rolled down and the driver asked, "Which one of you is Fred?"

Alfredo and Ricardo both pointed at Fred. Then there were three silenced rapid shots fired in quick succession. Alfredo and Ricardo jumped to the ground and Fred fell over backwards. Before anyone had a chance to react, the police cruiser sped off.

"Is anybody hurt?" asked Alfredo.

"I'm okay," replied Ricardo, "but I'm not sure about Fred."

Alfredo and Ricardo both stood up. Neither had been shot. They walked over to see how Fred was doing and they saw blood oozing from between his eyes and from two places in his chest. They checked for vital signs. It was too late. Fred was gone.

"What the heck was that about?" questioned Ricardo.

"Obviously, this was a hit on Fred," respond Alfredo.

"Why would they put a hit on Fred?"

"Because he screwed up his last two assignments, and now the police are looking for him," responded Alfredo.

"Then why did the police shoot him?"

"That police officer was obviously not on a police assignment when he came here. His assignment was to take out Fred."

"This is a crazy business that we're in," responded a nervous Ricardo.

"No kidding!"

"So, what do we do with the body? We can't put him in the car. We don't want any forensics tests on the car to find anything. And I don't want to get rid of this car. I like this car. It purrs like a kitten."

"Fine," answered Alfredo. "Let's put him into one of these dumpsters. But let's make sure he's covered up good, so no one sees him in the morning when they start using these dumpsters again."

"Good idea," replied Ricardo. "Let's hurry up and get this done and get out of here. Obviously, we're not collecting any protection money tonight."

"You're right about that," answered Alfredo.

Chapter Eight

Some Assumptions

June 2020, Helena, Montana
Police Station
(The Next Day)

Duke, Jill, Ranel, and Bridger Blakeslee met in Duke's office to discuss their findings up to this point. Bridger was an FBI agent whom the FBI called in to assist, since there was now the possibility of a serial killer.

"What have we learned so far," Duke asked.

Jill gave the three of them a status update. "For the murder at the cement factory, the coroner has decided that Bud was indeed murdered and that the murder was committed before the body was dumped into the loading chute. It appears that someone, probably more than one individual, killed him by hitting him over the head several times with a heavy object, put him on the loading ramp, ran him up into the loading chute, then shut everything down and left the scene. They have gone out and searched for footprints and tire impressions in the area that don't match any of the Falcon Gravel Company equipment and they did find a set of tire tracks that come from a smaller vehicle, like a car. Nearly all the other tracks are from trucks."

Bridger jumped in, "Do we have anything that suggests a motive?"

"Bud and his wife went through some divorce squabbles a few years back," responded Jill, "but that's old news and does not seem relevant. Bud didn't seem to have an enemy in the world. His friends are suggesting it might be mistaken identity, because there are plenty of other shady characters working there at the gravel pits."

"How about gambling or affairs?"

Duke jumped in, "We had all those angles checked out. He's a clean as a whistle. Almost too clean."

Ranel suggested, "Being too clean raises suspicions too. Is someone hiding something?"

Jill responded, "I don't think so. There are just not that many angles that we can twist in this case. We're not finding a motive. That's why mistaken identity might be a possibility."

Duke explained, "What's curious, and apparently the reason why the FBI insists that you be brought in Bridger, is because there was a second murder. It also seems random and unexplain-ed. But what ties the two together is that they were both commit-ted on Falcon property. Jill, why don't you give us an update on the cabin case."

Jill started, "The second murder was committed at a cabin on Holter Lake. This individual has been identified as Joe Basig-liano and based on our background check he has a history of working with organized crime. We were able to track the killer back over the mountain and onto the main road. We were able to make a tire impression of the vehicle that picked him up and, another coincidence which ties these crimes together, is that the tire impressions are a match with the tire tracks we found in the gravel pit. Right now, we're guessing that Joe was involved in the first murder and that something went wrong. And what we think might have occurred at the second murder scene was that he was accidently killed or killed to silence him. It's also interesting that there were two sets of fresh footprints that came down to the cab-in and only one departing. The set of footprints that came down but didn't leave matches the shoes of the victim."

She continues, "We've tied Joe to a partner that he seems to work with in his exploits. His name is Fred Fartner, and we put out a 'person of interest' arrest warrant for him hoping we can get some answers. We are still waiting on forensics and the autopsy report. That's where that particular investigation stands at this point."

Bridger spoke up, "If he's tied to crime, then there may be a syndicate which had a reason for his execution."

Ranel explained, "Why would they drag him over a moun-tain, at least a 5-hour effort, just to kill him. I don't think he was the intended victim. I think something went wrong and he be-came the second accidental victim. And maybe that's what hap-pened at the gravel pit too. Maybe the wrong guy got killed both times. Maybe these were two attempts at the same crime and they both went wrong."

Bridger questioned, "Then what were they attempting to do? What was the crime that didn't get committed? Just because they are both committed on Falcon property, we cannot automatically assume they're connected. I think we should pursue your theory, but we should not stop looking at the possibility that these were two independent crimes, and maybe the coincidences, like both locations being owned by the Falcons, are just coincidences. There's also the possibility that they're trying to throw us off track."

Duke continued, "Of course you're right. I wasn't intending to drop any option at this point. I was just trying to make sense of the coincidences under the assumption that the crimes are related in some way. I think we need to list all our options and then, since we can't investigate everything at once, we need to prioritize our options and attack them that way."

Bridger added, "I totally agree. Let's break down the options and maybe we can at least have two or three teams working the top priority options, and as they dead end, we work our way down the list."

Ranel jumped in, "Is there any way we could get more FBI support? We're not staffed as heavily as we would like to be for an important case like this one."

Bridger said, "Of course. I will have at least one agent and possibly two on each team. Tell me how many teams you think we need, and I'll see what support I can assemble to join us."

Just then there was a knock-on Duke's door. A detective was waving through the glass to get permission to enter the office. Duke waved him in.

Duke asked, "What's so urgent?"

The agent replies, "They found Fred Fartner. Unfortunately, he's dead. His body was dumped behind Wal Mart in one of the dumpsters. It looks like it was intentional. They say he was shot three times at close range. We'll know more after the coroner has a chance to look him over. CSI is on their way over there now to do a thorough search for clues, but it's a heavily travelled area, people are throwing out garbage into those bins all day long."

Bridger jumped in, "How did they miss seeing the body if it's a heavily travelled area?"

The agent answered, "Apparently he was down in the bottom of the dumpster and no one noticed him until it came time to unload the dumpster. Then someone saw him fall out of the dumpster as they were dumping it into the truck. If it wasn't for that, he may never have been found."

Duke responded to the agent, "Thanks for the report and let us know the minute you learn anything new. We'll head out there as well and join you as soon as we're done here."

"Will do," replied the agent as he left the office.

Jill spoke up, "I guess we call off the search for Fred. We're not going to learn anything from him. But this looks more and more like these events are not random and like there is a mastermind behind all this. I'm starting to think that Joe and Fred were eliminated because they failed to complete their assignments. And maybe our putting an arrest warrant out for Fred ended up sealing his fate."

Bridger suggested, "I definitely agree. I am now convinced we have something much larger here than a couple random acci-dents or even random killings. This smells of organized crime and I'm going to bring in more agents to work this case. It has the potential of blowing out of proportion. There are probably activit-ies going on right now that we have no clue about. I'm going to make a few calls and then let's work on that list of alternative scenarios that we are going to investigate."

Ranel jumps into the conversation and suggests, "I better do the same. I better see if we can get any additional state trooper support for this case. It's definitely getting out of hand."

Bridger and Ranel leave the office and each goes into an empty interview room to make their calls to the local FBI office and to the state police. When Duke and Jill are alone in the office Duke speaks up, "I hope we don't find any more random bodies floating around. This is getting out of hand."

"No kidding," Jill said. "All of these events feel completely connected to me. I don't see randomness here. I see intent and a focused effort. A master plan. But I can't imagine what it is. And I'm afraid it's probably a lot larger than these three deaths."

"I tend to agree with you. Let's follow Bridger's suggestion and start listing options."

Jill and Duke work on listing all the possible scenarios on the board. Jill would write, and both Jill and Duke would dictate ideas. The list started getting quite long and it included:

Bud was killed accidentally unknown to anyone and fell into the chute (this alternative was temporarily placed on hold because the chute was turned off after he fell in)

1) Bud was killed intentionally and dumped into the chute

    a. For the insurance money

    b. By his wife or his wife's lover

    c. By the husband of one of his lovers

    d. By someone angry at him because he owes something

2) Bud was killed accidentally and was dumped into the chute by someone involved in the accident who didn't want to be caught or connected with the accident

3) Bud committed suicide (this alternative was put on hold because he was dead before he was dumped into the chute)

4) Joe was killed accidentally (this alternative was put on hold because of the faked broken noose around his neck)

5) Joe was suicidal (this alternative was put on hold because of the stab wound – the suicide was staged)

6) Joe was killed accidentally by Fred

7) Joe was killed accidentally by someone other than Fred

8) Joe was intentionally murdered by Fred

9) Joe was murdered by someone other than Fred

10) Joe and Fred were the ones that killed Bud accidentally and they went to the cabin to finish a job, whatever that job was

11) Joe and Fred were there during Bud's killing but weren't involved in the murder

12) Fred was killed execution style by his boss because of the two failures, one at the gravel pit and the other at the cabin

13) Fred's murder has no connection with Bud's or Joe's murders

All three murders are connected in some grand master plan, possibly instigated by organized crime

Just then Bridger and Ranel walked into the room at the same time. Bridger, looking at the list, joined the discussion, "I can have more agents coming in to join us and help us out with this case if you think it's needed. I'll have to do some fancy talking to my boss in order to get him to agree. I just learned that what we're seeing here also parallels some organized crime activity that we've seen going on in Boise, and there is the strong possibility that this is all connected. The FBI has listed this as a Priority One case. Depending on how many resources you can provide, we're going to attack this case with several teams. The teams don't all need to be of the same size. In fact, I would prefer they aren't be-cause some options are easier to investigate. Let's look at your options and organize teams around common themes."

"When can your agents arrive?" asked Duke.

"It will take a couple days. At least one is coming from Boise, bringing those experiences with. Any others are coming in from Denver and even New York."

"Excellent," commented Jill.

Then Ranel added, "I may also be able to provide additional resources. I'll try to have more individuals join us as early as to-morrow."

"That's excellent," Jill blurted out excitedly.

Duke added, "We only have two detectives that we can bring in from this office, but I'm going to request additional support from some of the surrounding cities."

"Good," answered Bridger. "Let's get to work analyzing our options." The three walked over to the whiteboard and started drawing groupings that looked like:

> Options "Discarded for now" – 1, 4, 5, 6
> Options grouped as "Bud murdered independently" – 2, 3
> Options grouped as "Joe murdered independently" – 7, 8, 9, 10
> Options grouped as "Fred murdered independently" – 14
> Options grouped as "Murders all linked together" – 11, 12, 13, 15

There were additional options that were not considered at this time, like two of the murders being linked together but not all three. That would come later if the initial analysis did not work out.

Bridger spoke up, "So it looks like we have four teams, and we'll try to put at least two detectives on each team. I vote we keep the FBI guys with the organized crime teams because of their experience in that area and they should be placed where they can do the most good."

Duke commented, "I'm OK with that because I have a feel-ing the first three teams are going to find out that there are strong cross connections and, in the end, we'll all end up on the fourth team."

Jill said, "I agree, but we do need to check out all options."

Bridger suggested, "Then let's put names next to each of the four teams." The four proceeded to assign agents and detectives to each of the teams. Then they called everyone who was available and who would be assigned to this investigation into the office to discuss the plan of attack."

Once everyone was assembled Duke started the conversation, "As you know, we are faced with three murders that may or may not be connected. We just don't have enough information to know for sure. But there is an urgency here because they happen-ed so close together and there seems to be a lot of commonality. We're going to have to look at these murders both ways, as inde-pendent crimes, and as linked crimes. We have defined four teams, as you can see on the board. The teams will be a combination of Helena detectives, Montana state detectives, and FBI agents. Each team has specific assignments, as you can also see from the numbered items on the board. We have our theor-ies about what's going on here, but I don't want them to taint your investigations. I want each team to take the assignment that you see on the board and perform your own thorough investiga-tion. Don't leave any rocks unturned. Follow every lead. We have a murder spree going on here and we can't let it get out of control. We know about three murders, but there may be a lot more that we don't even know about. Do you have any ques-tions?"

One of the detectives spoke up, "So you have one of us on each of the first three teams and the rest are on the last team. When will we get the rest of the members of our teams?"

"The FBI agents are arriving over the next few days and Ranel needs to make a few calls to get the Montana detectives identified and down here to Helena. But that shouldn't keep those of us who are already here from starting work on our speci-fic assignments. Any other questions?" Everyone shook their head negatively, and then Duke wrapped up the meeting with, "Okay then. Let's get to work." And the room emptied out.

Bridger spoke up, "I'm going to personally work on the last team because I'm convinced that's how this is going to end up."

"Same here," said Jill. "But Duke, shouldn't you need to stay neutral and sift and share information between the teams. We need someone to keep a 'big picture' perspective on all of this."

"I totally agree," responded Bridger, and Duke just nodded his head.

"And where do you want me?" asked Ranel.

"Why don't you and I work together overseeing the teams and looking at the big picture," suggested Duke.

"Okay," responded Ranel. "I think we will work well together."

Everyone exited the conference room.

Chapter Nine

Is the Killer Serial?

June 2020, Helena, Montana
Police Station
(Three Days Later)

The police station conference room was filled with agents and detectives, all sitting around the table or along the back wall. Duke started the meeting by once again reviewing the crimes that had been committed, the options under consideration, the teams that have been organized to address each of the options, and the assignments of who is on which team. He then turned the meeting over to Bridger.

Bridger spoke up, "I will be extremely angry if I hear that one of my agents is not working side-by-side and as an equal partner with their Montana counterparts. There will not be anyone-up-manship here. This crime spree is too critical for us to waste time trying to claim credit. If we solve this there will be plenty of credit to go around for everyone's resume. But if competitiveness gets in the way, we'll end up with nothing. Do I make myself clear?"

Not getting the reaction he was hoping for, Bridger said it again, with twice the emphasis, "Do I make myself clear?"

This time the whole room responded with, "Yes sir."

Bridger continued, "Through FBI channels we have learned that the events that are happening here in Helena have parallels to similar events in other cities. That doesn't prove a connection. It may just be coincidental. But if there is a connection, we decided to make this case here in Helena the proving ground for getting to the bottom of what's going on. We want to get a better understanding of why these murders are occurring, so we can eventually get to the root of the problem and put an end to it. This means we need to find MOTIVE people!" Then he turned to Jill, "Do you have anything to add?"

Jill spoke up, "Does everyone understand their assignments? Who they're working with? What their goal is?" Looking around the room all the heads were giving a positive nod. Then she continued, "Duke and Ranel will be working together and they will be the central communication point for all activities. Anytime you have any breakthroughs or questions, go to them. They'll track and decide how to handle each of the communications. Bridger and I will be joining team four and work directly with boots on the ground, so don't come to us. We have our own problems to deal with. Always work with Duke and Ranel."

One of the FBI agents spoke up, "But what if our issue is an FBI issue?"

Bridger responded, "Come to both of us. I will handle the FBI issues and Duke and I will work together on case related issues. Duke and I will decide how every piece of information is to be handled."

The agent continued, "But that's a breach of traditional FBI protocol."

Bridger responded, "You have your orders. We are a team and that's how I want this whole thing handled, as a team. No secrets from each other."

With that Bridger dismissed about half of the agents and de-tectives by saying, "Team four stays in the room and everyone else can leave. I have a few more things to discuss with my team."

When only the team four members were left in the room Bridger explained, "I wanted to discuss the various possibilities that exist here. First this could just be an unrelated series of mur-ders and have no connection with events in other cities. The second option is that this is a copycat activity imitating some other crime spree, which we would investigate in much the same way as the first option. But then we get to the third and fourth options which suggest that there is a connection with some of the other crime sprees. The third options is there is criminal intent to con-trol a market here, like a drug market. That would parallel what we've seen in other places like Boise and Reno. In that case we would need to investigate organized crime syndicates in the area, especially territorial syndicates, who might be attempting to gain control of the market. The fourth possibility, and this is one we strongly suspect in the FBI, is that this is a travelling road show. It seems to happen in one city, then it stops there and starts up in another city, and so on."

An agent spoke up, "Why would anyone do that option? Is it for power?"

"We believe it is an extortion ring. Then, when they have emptied the local coffers, they move on to another area where the pickings are richer. It never lasts more than a few months in any specific area. But we're thinking it's here in Helena now and we want to figure it out before it moves out of the area."

The agent spoke up again, "Then let's go get them."

Bridger continued, "We can't just lock in on that fourth option and ignore the others. We need to work on all of them simultaneously and let the evidence lead us. Right now, there really isn't much evidence for any of the options."

Bridger and Jill, the lead detectives in team four, made assign-ments to the remainder of the team. Some were to go out to interview and re-interview witnesses. Others were to investigate the backgrounds of the victims and everyone in their lives. Still others were assigned to study the crime scene along with the CSI team and to work with the coroner. The meeting ended with everyone going out to work on their assigned duties.

June 2020, Helena, Montana
Duke's Car

"What is going on?" challenged Duke who was talking on the phone. "Now we have three dead people and we still haven't accomplished anything. All we've done is to make this mess bigger and bigger. I understand why you took Fred out. He knew too much. But Bud and Joe weren't necessary."

The voice on the other end of the phone responded, "Don't challenge me on what I'm doing. You're not my boss and that's not your role. Bud and Joe were both accidents, and you are cor-rect in saying that Fred had to go because he knew too much, and he created this mess."

"Did you need to let his body be found?"

"That was another accidental screw-up. He wasn't supposed to ever be found. But a nosey garbage man spotted him as he fell into the garbage truck."

"Every action you've taken has been a screw up. Are you ever going to accomplish your mission?"

"Of course. But now we have cops crawling around everywhere. Even the FBI is here in force. We're going to lay low for a couple weeks and hopefully the heat will blow away."

"Probably a good idea. We don't want to leave any more clues. Is there anything we could do to keep suspicion off of me? Maybe we can create a distraction of some sort that will send the investigation off the track of what we're trying to accomplish. It won't be long now before we've accomplished our goal. If we can derail the investigation for a few days, then we can disperse and the whole process will quickly become an unsolved dead file."

"I'll get back in touch with you as soon as possible," responded the voice on the phone and then the phone line went dead before Duke could respond.

CHAPTER TEN

Threats

June 2020, Helena, Montana
Jill's Home
(Seven Days Later)

Jill was exhausted and discouraged. It had been another long and frustrating day and now she was finally able to come home at her usual time around 10 PM. She had been working this case for two weeks and she felt as though no headway had been made. No one knew anything that was helpful. There was nothing, other than that two of the murders were on Falcon prop-erty, and that two of the victims were close friends, that tied all of this together. That just didn't seem to be enough to draw any conclusions.

She drove onto the driveway of her small suburban home and parked the car in the carport on the side of the house. She enter-ed the house through the side door, going through the wet room which doubled as a laundry room, and then on into the kitchen.

She flicked on the kitchen lights and started unloading the bag of groceries that she had purchased on her way home from work. Some of it went in the refrigerator and some up in the cup-boards.

Having finished that task, she left the kitchen, crossed through to the dining room and into the living room without turn-ing on any lights. She reached for the light switch on the wall to her right and instead of finding a wall she found a hand, which grabbed her hand tight. Before she knew what was happening she felt someone step around behind her, put their knee behind her, and flip her over their knee in one quick judo move which sent her legs flying through the air and landed her facedown flat on the floor. Before she could even think about what to do next, she felt her hands get zip tied together and then the zip ties were zip tied to the leg of the coffee table in the center of the room.

Finally, she was able to adjust to what was happening and she started kicking and screaming, twisting, and gyrating her body around in an attempt to break free and do damage to her assail-ant. But her attacker was quick. One of her legs was zip tied to the couch leg leaving only one limb, her left leg, free. She tried kicking with that, but her assailant was prepared.

She was finally able to take a close look at her assailant. He wasn't exceptionally tall or strong. But he apparently was skilled in martial arts. He wore jeans and a t-shirt, Teflon gloves, and a ski mask. It was too dark to make out the color of his eyes, or much of anything else. She wished she had one arm free, so she could pull off that stupid ski mask. But that wasn't an option.

Without saying a word, he cut her pants away, starting at the belly button, and down each pants leg. It was just seconds and her pants were completely gone. Next came her shirt and bra. Within just a couple minutes her assailant had her stripped completely naked laying on her floor, with three limbs disabled.

"What are you doing to me," she screamed.

"What does it look like?" asked the assailant. There was something different about his voice, causing Jill to want him to talk more in the hope that she might be able to identify him. There was an accent which was vaguely familiar, but she couldn't place it. She was in too much of a panic to think.

Jill started crying, not so much out of fear, but out of a small hope that she might be able to get some sympathy. "Please don't rape me. I hurt and bleed terrible when I have sex."

"Sure," was the non-sympathetic response. Then he said something that sent shivers down Jill's spine. "If you weren't sticking your nose into places where it doesn't belong, then I wouldn't need to stick any of my body parts into places where they don't belong."

Jill screamed out, "You animal. How can any human be so brutal and cruel? When I find you, I will cut your balls off and stuff them in your mouth. I'll treat you like the animal you are."

Jill now realized that this rape was about intimidation. This assailant wanted her to quit working the case. That's why the voice sounded familiar. It was someone she had had a conversa-tion with recently. But she still wasn't able to place it.

The assailant finished the rape, got up, and pulled up his pants with a final comment, "This will happen again, or maybe even worse, if you can't get your team to quit working the case." The assailant left the house through the back door and disappear-ed.

Now Jill, although scared and frustrated, was able to slightly relax and think. She used her free leg to push the coffee table up, thereby allowing the zip tie that was holding her hands to slide out from under the table leg. Next, she was able to use her hands to lift up a corner of the couch and free her remaining leg. She went to the kitchen, grabbed a knife, and cut off the zip ties.

True to her prediction, her crotch hurt terribly because of the forced entry. She double and triple locked all the doors of the house, turned on all the lights, and went off to the bathroom where she sat on the toilet and cried. It had been an enormously traumatic experience, even for someone as strong as Jill.

She knew she should call the CSI unit, but she just wasn't ready for that yet. First, she had to get over the shock of what had just happened to her. She called a female CSI agent that she had worked with in the past and explained what had happened to her. The CSI agent came immediately to her house and collected all the necessary samples from Jill's body. There wasn't a semen sample, so the assailant must have been wearing protection, thereby preventing his DNA from becoming evidence. Shortly after that, the full CSI team arrived to go through the house and search for fingerprints or any other evidence.

Jill went off on her own. She felt the need to stand in the shower for a long time in order to flush off the grossness of the assailant's smell and touch. And then she had to just think. What did all of this mean? How should she react? Finally, when she was comfortable and confident with herself, she touched base with Duke, telling him what had happened. She was sure he would come right over and comfort her. She had to try to flush away the horror of everything that had just happened to her.

June 2020, Helena, Montana
Duke's Home

Duke had a late night as well. Being the head of the Helena detectives made him feel a level of responsibility and commitment. If his detectives had to work late, then he should be right there with them.

He felt the need to put on a show of frustration and disappointment that the investigation wasn't further along. There were lots of leads, but no new information that added anything of real significance to the case.

He walked into the house and his wife was waiting up for him as usual. The kids were all tucked in bed and she was left by herself watching Downton Abbey for what seemed like the 400th time. One of the main characters had just died and she was in tears, so Duke sat down beside her, wrapped his arms around her, and just held her while she sobbed. He couldn't understand how, after seeing this show so often, and knowing what was going to happen next, she could still be so emotional. But he had re-signed himself to the fact he would never be a smart enough de-tective to understand women's emotions. Some things were sim-ply beyond understanding.

They sat there for about 15 minutes when suddenly a beer bottle, with a burning wick attached, came flying through the front window. Duke reacted quickly, realizing that the bottle most likely contained gasoline or some other flammable liquid. Luck-ily, the bottle hadn't broken so he jumped up, grabbed the bottle, and threw it as hard as he could back out the broken front win-dow and out into the yard, where it immediately exploded. He had come within seconds of his entire house exploding into a burning inferno.

Duke ran out the front door, nearly tripping on a rock on his front porch, and out into the street to see if he could spot any-thing, but the assailant was long gone. Coming back to the house, he saw the rock that he had nearly tripped over and picking it up he read a note which said, "Quit this case or next time I will be successful."

Realizing that he was tampering with evidence Duke dropped the rock and the note and called the CSI unit. In spite of it being late at night the CSI team was on site at Duke's in less than 30 minutes. But there was nothing to be found. The rock and notes were clean of evidence, and the beer bottle had been badly scorched to where there was also no visible evidence.

A cardboard piece was placed over the hole in the front window to temporarily seal it. But that wasn't enough for Duke's wife. She had reacted by waking all the kids, packing an overnight bag for all of them, and packing them into the minivan. Before Duke realized what she was doing she was rolling out of that place. As she drove off, she told Duke, "When you're done here, you'll find me at the Holiday Inn. I'm not leaving the children in this dangerous situation." And she was off before Duke could argue with her. But Duke never had any intention of arguing. He felt the same way. He assigned two local police officers to keep watch on the house and was about to leave for the Holiday Inn when he received a call from Jill.

June 2020, Helena, Montana
Jill's Home

It was nearing midnight when Duke arrived at Jill's house. He had also placed calls to Bridger and Ranel and the four of them were assembled in Jill's font yard. The CSI team had followed Duke and they had the run of Jill's house, which was now taped off as a crime scene.

Duke commented, "I'm so sorry Jill. I can't imagine what it's like to get raped, brutalized, and manhandled like you were. No one should ever have to go through that."

"I agree," sympathized Bridger. "The idea that someone uses their strength to dehumanize you like that makes my blood boil."

Jill explained, "I always thought of myself as a strong person. I thought I could handle any situation. But that experience made me feel helpless. I felt like an animal being butchered. The whole thing made me feel less than human; dirty. I felt like crawling in a hole and literally dying. But I know that giving up is not a solution either. In spite of the threats, I am not quitting."

"Tell me about the threats," questioned Bridger.

"He said that if I didn't get the team to drop this case, the same and possibly even worse would happen."

Duke responded, "I would love to tear that guys eyeballs out."

Jill responded, "That's not all I'd like to tear out."

Bridger interjected, "I know you guys are just blowing off steam, but don't do it in front of me. I don't want to have to testify that I heard you guys threaten this guy."

Duke responded, "You have to be kidding me. You'd really testify against us?"

"No. But your comments do make me feel a little uncomfortable."

"Sorry to make you so uncomfortable Agent Bridger!" Jill said sarcastically. "I am mad as hell now".

"Don't get me wrong," apologized Bridger. "I am incredibly sympathetic to your situation, and if I was ever alone in a room with this guy, some *stumbling accidents* might occur, like him accidentally running into the door. I'm sorry for even saying any-thing. I feel kind of stupid now."

Duke answered, "Good enough. We need you on our side. Now back to the case. I think we can throw away any question about whether these murders were unrelated events. The big crime, whatever that is, is apparently still in play, and these mur-ders were either intentional parts of that, or missteps and fail-ures."

Ranel suggested, "Missteps is my vote."

"Me too," included Bridger. "Let's get the team together first thing in the morning and rethink our strategy."

"Agreed," answered Duke.

"First things first. I'm not going to be in early tomorrow," said Jill. "I have to get through some emotional baggage, and then I have to get some sleep. Start without me and then update me when I get there."

"Will do," answered Duke. "Do you want to ride with me to the hotel?"

"Yes please," answered Jill. "I'm still a little jittery."

"Understood," answered Duke. "And don't feel the need to come in at all until you feel ready. I'd prefer it if you take the time you need to get over this. I explained the situation to my wife earlier and she has volunteered to spend the night with you if you feel that would be helpful."

"That would be wonderful," she said.

"Then let's get going," answered Duke. And turning to Brid-ger and Ranel he said, "See you in the morning."

"Whenever you get in," replied Ranel. "Don't rush. Get sett-led in as well."

"Thanks," answered Duke as he and Jill walked off to his car.

CHAPTER ELEVEN

The Serial Option

June 2020, Helena, Montana
Falcon Sand and Gravel

Did you get the samples?" questioned Roger Falcon on the phone. He was sitting at his desk in the main office, with the door closed.

"Yes," was the response over the speaker phone.

"Where are they now?"

"In route to Montana via San Diego. We had a little trouble finding a way to get them through customs. But we found a way to smuggle the samples in as part of a fish shipment from Guate-mala. We're smuggling them inside the fish. We're doing some-thing similar for the samples coming from Mexico. But it takes a little longer when we have to smuggle them in."

Roger questioned, "Why do we need to smuggle them in?"

"Because they are pieces of historical significance. They are archeological treasures. Customs officials would recognize them immediately and stop us in our tracks."

"We are anxious to investigate their significance and compare them against our samples here. Is there any way to speed up the process?"

"You could fly down to San Diego, which is where the containers will be arriving and pick the samples up there if you're in a hurry. They'll arrive tomorrow afternoon."

"I'll be there," responded Roger as he ended the call. Next, he called his secretary and instructed, "I need a flight down to San Diego for tomorrow morning, with a return on the following day. And I'll need a hotel and rental car while I'm there."

"I'll get right on it," responded the secretary over the phone.

June 2020, Helena, Montana
Falcon Sand and Gravel
(One Day Later)

Jill, still emotionally torn by the rape, decided that she need-ed to get back to work. She needed the distraction. She had al-ready driven to Falcon Sand and Gravel before she decided to call in and report. She called Bridger, who had taken on the role of the lead for team 4, and suggested, "I'm going to go back to the Falcon cement location and interview the employees."

"Take it easy," Bridger suggested. "Don't rush the process."

"I need the distraction. I need to get my mind off the anger and hate I'm feeling. Doing some interviews might help."

"Good enough. But your health is important. FBI protocol would suggest that you be removed from the case since you have been emotionally compromised. But you don't work for the FBI, so I guess you can do whatever you want."

"Thanks. I'll spend some time at Falcon and then get back to you." The call was disconnected, and Jill climbed out of the car. She entered the Falcon offices and spoke with the receptionist. She presented her credentials and requested to talk with Roger Falcon.

"I'm sorry," was the receptionist's response. "He departed for San Diego early this morning and he won't be back until tomor-row evening."

"I have some additional questions about the murder," Jill requested. "Is Eric around?"

"I'll call him on the intercom and have him come to the of-fice. He's somewhere out there in the pit. He could be just about anywhere. Let me call him in." With that she picked up the intercom system and announced, "Eric, there's someone here from the police to see you in the office. Can you come in ASAP?"

"I'll be right there," was the response back on the intercom. "Have them meet me in Roger's office."

"Will do," answered the receptionist. Then, turning to Jill she said, "Follow me down to the office." Roger's office was on the lower floor of the two-story structure, where the upper floor was level with the parking lot, and the lower level, on the back side, was level with the ground floor of the gravel pit. It was at the same level where the trucks drove in to get loaded with gravel or ce-ment.

Jill followed the receptionist down to Roger's office and was shown into the office. "Have a seat and Eric will be right with you. He shouldn't be too far away."

"Perfect," replied Jill as she sat down on one of the office chairs.

Jill started to feel strange. She had some conflicting emotions. She had spent the last night with Duke's wife in the bed next to her at the hotel, but she couldn't ask her to stay with her again. This meant that Jill would be alone tonight. She didn't want to be alone. But she didn't want a man to be with her. That thought repulsed her after what had happened to her. Just the thought of the rape made her feel like crying. She would have to fight back the tears as she did this interview.

Then she thought of her married sister who lived in the area. The sister had three children, but maybe she would be willing to spend a night or two with her. She sent the sister a text saying, "I am having a really tough time of it right now. Any way you could come and stay with me tonight at a hotel in town. I will tell you all about it when you come. Within five minutes she had received the hoped-for response, "Of course. What hotel and what time?"

"Holiday Inn. I should get there around 8 PM. Thanks a lot."

"No worry. I'm there for you sister."

Five minutes later Eric arrived at the door of Roger's office and held his hand out to Jill. "Great to see you again," he said. "Are you making any progress on finding out who killed Bud?"

"Sorry," she replied. "I'm not allowed to share any of the details of the case. But I would like to ask you a few more questions."

"We've gone through the events a dozen times. What do you think you're going to learn this time that you haven't learned before?"

"The way it works," Jill said, "is that we collect evidence and as we learn more, we get more questions. Sometimes there are discrepancies, and sometimes questions come up that we just didn't think of asking before. Do you mind?"

"Got it," replied Eric. He was still fascinated by Jill and enjoyed having to meet with her, but he felt a slight coldness com-ing from her. He couldn't understand why since she had seemed so friendly in the past. "What new questions have you come up with?"

"I'm trying to understand the connection between the two murders. They were both committed on Falcon property. They seem random enough, but police don't believe in coincides. Give me your perspective on why there were two murders, both on Falcon property, but many miles apart."

Eric sat back in his father's chair in thought. "I don't have a quick answer for that. I just wrote it off as bad luck." After some thought he said, "I really have no idea. There isn't any connec-tion between the two individuals that I know of. Both murders make no sense to me. I have no idea how Bud got into that chute. And the murder at the cabin was some guy we never heard of. It seemed completely random, like he was a vagrant using our property without permission. I just figured someone was using our cabin who didn't belong there."

"Tell me about Bud's personality. What was he like?"

"Quiet. Only spoke when spoken too. That kind of guy. He wasn't the type to get into an argument with anyone. He worked totally on his own all the time. That's why the whole thing doesn't make sense. He had already left to go home for the night, along with everyone else in the crew. I just don't understand what happened."

Jill explained, "That's where we're confused as well. His behavior that night wasn't his normal behavior. And we have to wonder if that's what got him killed."

"Are you saying that there must be criminal activity going on here after dark and that's what got him in trouble. Do you think that he interrupted something that he shouldn't have?"

"I'm not saying anything for sure. I'm just looking at options or possibilities."

Eric explained, "Since the murder occurred, we've put up surveillance cameras all around the place. If something's going on, we should be able to see it in the cameras." He pushed some buttons on his dad's computer and turned the screen so that Jill could see it. "I'm playing back last night from about 8 PM till about 6 AM when everybody starts showing up for work the next day. I'll run it through at high speed and let's see if there is any activity out there."

After going through the tape of the previous night, Jill responded with, "I guess there's nothing to see for last night. Let's go to the night before."

Again, there wasn't anything on the tape.

"One more night," Jill requested. Again nothing.

"People kill for a reason," Jill asked pointedly and directly. "They don't just randomly kill someone for no good reason. Why do you think Bud was killed?"

"It has to have been a mistake. Maybe mistaken identity."

"If it was mistaken identity, don't you think the intended victim would have also been killed by now?"

"You'd think so wouldn't you. I really didn't think this through, but you're right. The intended victim should also have been killed."

"Because of that I have to think that Bud was the intended victim," reasoned Jill.

"Maybe. Or maybe they backed out of doing the real murder because they were scared off."

"I guess that's possible. But not likely. Because they wouldn't get paid if they didn't complete their contract."

"I give up," stated an exasperated Eric. "I have no idea what happened."

"Let me ask you a different question," continued Jill. "Let's assume he was the intended target. Is there a message or some symbolism in the way his body was found?"

"You're asking if there was some message in the way he was killed. That's a strange question. I'll think about it, but I really can't make any sense out of the whole mess. Sorry."

Jill could see that this conversation wasn't getting her any new information, so she asked, "Can we walk around the area where all this occurred. I'd like you to explain the process to me again. Maybe there is some magical insight that we can get just by going through the process one more time."

"Sure," was Eric's response as he shrugged his shoulders. He found Jill interesting, so he didn't mind spending a little more time with her, even though there was lots of work that needed to be done around the gravel pit.

The two of them walked out to where the concrete trucks were loaded, and Eric explained the process to her. He discussed how the mixing occurred following a computer-generated formula specific to the weather conditions of the day. He described the loading of the truck using the chutes.

Jill asked, "So there is really no way this could be anything but an intended murder. The belt to the chute needs to be turned on and off for Bud to have ended up in the loading chute."

"That's it," responded Eric. "There's no accident here. It doesn't make sense." He continued to explain the process to her, and Jill let him talk. She didn't feel like doing much else. It was strangely comforting to be talking to Eric, but she didn't really understand why. She decided to burn the rest of the day at the gravel pit before returning to the hotel.

As Eric explained the process, one of the other employees joined in on the conversation, "I remember that evening and have been replaying it several times in my mind. I think Bud forgot something and had to return to pick it up, and he just happened to be in the wrong place at the wrong time. Nothing else makes sense."

Then Jill asked, "What would you guess would have been occurring here which would make this the wrong place to be? It almost seems boring around here at night. What could possibly be happening that would result in someone getting murdered?"

The employee suggested, "There have been mornings when I've come to work and there had obviously been a lot of activity around here the night before."

Eric gave him a glare, and the employee backed off the comment he was making.

"Why makes you think there was a lot of activity around here?" asked Jill.

The employee knew he had to respond so he answered her question as abruptly as possible, "Tire tracks."

"Did you see anything else? Was there any sign of a strug-gle?"

Now Eric jumped in, "Sometimes the kids from the local high schools will come here to the pit to race cars or to have gang fights. We have tried to stop it by posting guards in the evenings. It's only occurred during weekends. More recently we put up cameras which record activity all week long. But Bud's death was during the week before we had cameras, and we didn't have any guards posted at that time."

"That's unfortunate," responded Jill. "It could have been tremendously helpful. Have you heard about anyone getting hurt in the past?"

"No. But that's our biggest concern. We don't have insurance coverage for random events outside of the working environment. We've checked every night since we installed the cameras, as you saw earlier. I personally have been checking the recordings daily, just out of curiosity, but I haven't seen much. However, now that you mention it, there was something strange that didn't make sense. I know we checked the last three nights and didn't see anything. But this conversation reminded me of something I saw about a week ago which didn't make sense to me. Do you want to see it?"

"Definitely," replied Jill. The two of them walked back to the office to view the video. After arriving at the office, they played the video back and what Jill saw left her stunned.

CHAPTER TWELVE

The Conspiracy

June 2020, San Diego, California
Shipping Docks

Roger Falcon arrived at the docks on schedule and met with his contact. "Do you have the samples?"

"Do you have the money?"

"Right here in this backpack," responded Roger.

The two swap backpacks and each of them opened their bag, searching the contents. Roger was the first to speak, "It looks like everything is in order."

"Agreed," responded the contact as they both zipped up their bags.

They shook hands and each left heading off in different directions. Roger placed a quick call. The person he was calling answered the phone with, "Hello."

"Roger here," he said in an excited voice. "I have it."

"Excellent. I'll get everything ready here so that when you get back, we can go right to work."

"Perfect," Roger responded. It was late and there were no more flight connections that day back to Montana, so Roger headed for the hotel. Early the next morning he caught a flight back to Montana.

June 2020, Helena, Montana
An Office In A Warehouse In Northeastern Helena

"You're telling me Roger was able to get the samples. How do we get them away from him?" questioned Gerd, the boss, sitting at his desk with three of his lieutenants sitting across from him.

"Our original plan to kidnap him and keep him from getting the samples didn't work," one of the lieutenants, Doug, said.

"Darn right it didn't work," stressed Gerd. "We ended up with three dead bodies and I'd hardly call that a successful oper-ation. I'm not sure Roger even has a clue that he was the intend-ed target. No one should have been killed. We obviously didn't want Roger killed because he has the information, we're after. But apparently that message did not get through. I was contracted to intercept Roger and his activities, not to kill or hurt anyone. The people that are hiring us want his research, not his life."

"What do you want us to do?"

"At this point, since we didn't prevent him from getting this far in his efforts, I think we should let him continue his work and then, when he gets close to accomplishing his objective, I think we should take it away from him."

Doug continued, "It may get rough. There may be more bod-ies."

"I don't care. We're in this pretty deep already. I don't know how it can get worse. We just need to make sure we get the infor-mation. I don't think you guys realize how important this is. It may sound trivial to you, but this will revolutionize how the entire world works. Can you imagine no more destruction from earth-quakes or other natural disasters around the entire world? This will be earth shattering and the owner of this technology will be able to set his own price for this knowledge."

"Somehow that doesn't seem right, one organization control-ling it all, when it's something that would help everyone."

"Who cares about right. This is about might, not right."

"How will we know when the time is right to steal Roger's work?"

"We'll have to get into Falcon Sand and Gravel and keep an eye on what's happening. There will be a significant change in atmosphere when they're successful, and in the way they are doing things. Guess what? The three of you are all going to apply for jobs and try to get in there. I want at least one and preferably all three of you to go to work there." Gerd was adamant.

"Yes boss," was Doug's response.

With that the conversation ended and Gerd dismissed everyone.

June 2020, Helena, Montana
Falcon Sand and Gravel
(One Day Later)

"We have three good candidates that might be considered for replacing Bud," Eric was giving Roger an update on what transpired while Roger was in San Diego.

"How'd you come up with three. We've always had trouble finding anyone willing to work in a gravel pit. It's hard work and this new generation seems to think they can just play computer games all day. Most of this newer generation is looking for sluggish computer jobs," suggested Roger.

"They're not young," responded Eric. "Late 30's and early 40's. But they seem willing and interested in doing the work."

"It almost sounds too go to be true," suggested Roger. "It sounds like you want to hire all three."

"There is an advantage to grabbing them while the iron is hot. We need to replace Bud and we were one hand short anyway, which gives us two. And the third might be early but sometimes you have to move when the opportunity presents itself."

"You're probably right, Eric, I'll leave it to you but make sure there isn't anything fishy about these guys. When things seem too good to be true, they often are."

"Got it. I'll make sure we check them out thoroughly. By the way, how did it go in San Diego?"

"I have what I need to move forward. I'll be working with my boy at the warehouse later today to hopefully move forward in learning what we can from the samples," explained Roger.

"Excellent. Let me know how I can help."

CHAPTER THIRTEEN

Confusion

June 2020, Helena, Montana
An Office In A Warehouse In Northeastern Helena

Gerd was the first to speak up, "What did you learn when you were at the gravel pit the other night?" He was speaking to the two other individuals in his office, Doug, and Karl.

Karl spoke first, "We didn't learn much. It was obvious that the belt up into the chute had to be turned on and off manually, and that's why the police concluded that this was an intentional murder. Those two clowns, Fred and Joe, couldn't have messed this up anymore if they tried."

"How about the samples," asked Gerd.

This time it was Doug who spoke, "We did manage to sneak into the office area using a bathroom window that was left slightly cracked open, but we couldn't find anything. I'm sure that the samples have already been delivered to whoever is working on them."

"How are we going to find them?"

"We need to grab Roger and force him to reveal their loca-tion to us," suggested Karl.

"Or we could just follow him?" suggested Gerd. "Then he won't know that we are after the samples."

"We could do that too," responded Karl.

"We'll attach a tracking device on his car, and we'll see where he goes.

"Do it," insisted Gerd.

"What are these samples all about anyway," asked Doug. "Why are they so important?"

"First off, it's none of your business. But even if it was your business, I wouldn't have a clue why they are so important. The guys that are hiring me to get these samples away from Roger don't explain the why. They just tell me to do it; and they pay well so I do it. But I do know that apparently what he's working on is revolutionary and can change construction around the world. I get the impression that whoever controls this technology will be raking in a lot of money."

"Can't they just get their own samples of whatever they're do-ing?" asked Karl. "What's so special about the samples that Roger is getting?"

"Don't know and don't care," replied Gerd. "But I do know if we keep screwing this up, the guys that are hiring us are going to find someone else to do the job and we get nothing."

"Got it," responded Doug. "We'll get it done and we'll do it right."

"Did the attacks on the cops do anything," asked Gerd.

"Not much," answered Karl. "It caused them to move to a hotel and it chewed up a bunch of resources investigating their homes, but other than wasting a couple of days of their time, they seem to be back at it in full force."

"That's disappointing," answered Gerd. "But we can't have them interfering with our efforts so we're going to have to find something else to divert their attention away from this. Any sug-gestions?"

"We could kill one of the cop's kids and leave a threating message that there's more to come if they don't lay off," suggest-ed Doug.

"These guys are stubborn," answered Karl. "Killing a cop or one of his family will just result in bringing in more cops."

"You're right about that," responded Gerd. "We need some-thing that would be more distracting."

"How about a series of arson fires?" suggested Doug.

"How about we burn down the Falcon offices?" added Karl.

"I like that," responded Gerd. "It adds confusion because the Falcons are brought back into the picture, which will drive these cops crazy. If we can't scare them off, maybe we can at least keep them running in circles until we complete our job here."

"You've got it," replied Karl. "Tonight, the Falcon offices go up in smoke."

Just then a phone call came in on Gerd's cell phone and he answered with, "Who's this?" He listened for the response and then he made a confused remark, "You're kidding? How did that happen? Do they know who did it?" There was another delay in the conversation as Gerd listened and then he said, "Thanks for the update. That's confusing information, but it definitely wasn't us."

The phone call ended and then Gerd turned to Karl and Doug and said, "Something else is going on here. Someone just shot up the Falcon offices. It was a drive-by shooting where some-one sprayed bullets in their offices and one of the secretaries was killed and Roger's wife was shot in the shoulder. We better stay away from the Falcon offices for now because it will be under tight police security. No fires tonight."

"What's going on?" asked Karl.

"No idea," answered Gerd. "I'm going to check with the guys that hired me and try to find out if there is a second team that's been asked to get the Falcon samples. But why would they be shooting up the place? Why would they want that type of visi-bility? I don't understand what's happening here. I'm going to make a few calls. In the meantime, maybe you guys can at least get a tracker on Roger's car."

"Who made that call to you?" asked Doug.

"I have an insider who keeps me informed about what's going on, but I'm not going to tell you more than that. The fewer people that know about him, the safer he is."

"Now, I need you to do one more thing for me."

"What's that?" asked Doug.

"I need you to dispose of the van," instructed Gerd. "They have pictures of it and the police are actively looking for it. They know they've seen it before and they saw it at the gravel pit the other night, so they're convinced that they're going to find it. We'll need to burn it up so that there's no trace of evidence left in it that they can use. Can you two take care of that without any screw-ups?"

"Not a problem," responded Karl.

With that, Doug and Karl left Gerd's office and went off to find a way to track Roger's vehicle and to dispose of the van. As they walked Doug said, "I hope that the shooting at the Falcon gravel pit wasn't done by who I think it was done by."

"That's what I was wondering too," responded Karl.

"And what's with this insider?" asked Doug. "Insider with the police or with the Falcons? He's keeping secrets from us which I don't like. I don't want to end up like Fred, dumped off in a dumpster somewhere."

"I agree with that too," answered Karl. "We're going to have to watch our backs."

"I feel like starting that fire to burn down the Falcon offices anyways, just to prove we can do it right under everybody's noses."

"Let's do it. But let's do the van first, just so that's out of the way."

= = = = = = = = = = =

Back in Gerd's office, Gerd was placing a call. When the call was answered, the greeting was, "Hello. Is this Gerd?"

"Yes. I wanted to talk to you because something strange is going on out here."

"Like what?"

Gerd continued, "The Falcon offices just got shot up and we didn't do it so I'm wondering who did."

"And you're thinking I had something to do with it?"

"The thought did cross my mind."

"The command didn't come from me. But if someone else is interfering in what we're doing, I want to know."

Gerd continued his questioning, "So you definitely didn't have anything to do with the shooting?"

"No! But I want to know who did! They may be going after the same prize that we're after. I need you to figure out who is doing this. Now we have a fourth body lying out there and we're still no closer to the prize. Get your butt moving and figure out who did this and get back to me as soon as possible."

"I'll do my best, but it may not be easy."

"Do it anyway!" demanded the voice on the phone.

The call was disconnected, and Gerd sat back in his chair. Suddenly he jumped up and said, to no one in particular, "How'd he know another person has been killed? I didn't mention it."

CHAPTER FOURTEEN

Still Another Murder

June 2020, Helena, Montana
Falcon Sand and Gravel

Falcon Sand and Gravel was swarming with police and emergency vehicles. It seemed like the entire police force had turned out for the occasion. The large picture win-dows at the front of the building were riddled with bullet holes, and the windows in the back of the building were also filled with holes, showing that the bullets had travelled completely through the building. One person lay dead on the floor with a sheet cover-ing her. Roger's wife, Judy, had been whisked away by an ambu-lance to a nearby hospital. There were several other employees in the office, but they escaped unharmed because they were quick enough to drop to the floor before a bullet found them. Each of them was individually being pulled aside, one at a time, and inter-viewed by the police detectives.

The report of the attack was bare. No one saw the vehicle, which became apparent because one witness identified it as a van, another as a car, and a third as a pickup. Luckily, there were now surveillance cameras surrounding the building and they recorded a pickup driving by slowly and a passenger with a weapon that looked like an Uzi spraying the building with bullets. The pickup had no distinguishing marks, and it was turned sideways to the camera, so the license plate was not visible. The individuals in the vehicle wore ski masks, so they could not be identified.

For the police, this was another frustrating murder, with minimal evidence and even less clues. All it offered was a fourth, random, dead body and lots of bullets to be analyzed. An APB was put out for the pickup, but the limited description made it impossible to locate. There were too many similar pickups in Montana.

Duke turned to Jill and said, "Another murder connected with Falcon. Who has it out for that company?"

"I'm at a total loss," she responded. "None of these people are related to each other. I'm not sure there is a connection, oth-er than the Falcon's. At least the first and the fourth murder don't seem to be connected to anything. The second and third murder victims were at least friends. This is nuts!"

"I've been wondering if the different murders were diversions from the actual murder. For example, the second and third murders weren't connected to the other two, but there also seems to be no reason for those murders unless it was an internal organ-ized crime cleanout. I wonder if they were just a diversion, and either the first or the fourth murders were the actual intended vic-tims."

Jill continued, "We haven't had a chance to analyze the background of this most recent murder, but it seems random, not targeted. It could have been anyone in that office. And the research we've done on the first murder hasn't turned up anything either. It's hard to see how Bud was a target."

"Maybe the real victim is still going to be murdered," sug-gested Duke.

"That's a gruesome thought."

"Bottom line is that we really don't know anything, do we?"

"Nope."

June 2020, Helena, Montana
Falcon Sand and Gravel
(Later That Night)

Doug and Karl are driving slowly past the front of the Falcon facility. Doug spoke up, "I see a cop car there, and a couple individuals in the car. They must be guarding the property."

Karl suggested, "Is there a way we can sneak around the back side and come in that way?"

"The son, Eric, lives in a house right next to the property and we might be able to drive up his driveway and get to the gravel pit that way. But I would think our safest bet is to park a little way down the street and walk. The car makes too much noise, both with the tires and with the engine."

Karl continued, "That would be quieter, but it also makes our escape more challenging. We're going to have to run for it and be quiet about it at the same time."

Doug suggested, "We'll start the fire and get out of there before it becomes very large. By the time they raise the alarm, we'll be long gone."

"Good enough. We'll do it your way. I just don't want to get caught."

"Neither do I, you jerk."

Down the street was a marine repair shop which had a parking lot filled with cars and boats. They pulled into the parking lot and parked the car amid other vehicles, so it didn't stand out. They put on ski masks, exited their vehicle, and made their way back to the Falcon property where they snuck between trees and behind rock piles. They worked their way around to the back side of the office building, which was on the level that was lower than the front side of the building were the police guard was park-ed. They carefully and quietly constructed a small wood teepee against a wooden section of the building and stuffed it with paper and wood shavings that they found on the ground. Then they lit the shavings on fire and slowly made their way back towards their vehicle.

Once inside their vehicle Doug commented, "That went smoothly. It would have been fun to watch the place go up in flames."

"The best thing we can do is get the heck out of here," commented Karl as he started to drive off the parking lot and headed down the road away from the Falcon pit. They had successfully made their escape long before the heat of the flames started to creep up the wall of the two-story building.

By the time the officer on duty realized that the building was on fire, the fire had become intense and any effort to put it out was a waste of time. Within minutes of the call made by the offi-cer, the fire department and police department were on site in force. But the building was a total loss, including any recordings from the security cameras. The fire department trucks, and crew stamped out any footprints or other evidence that might have helped the police. Any clues that would have helped find the arsonists, were gone. It would be another frustrating day for the police.

June 2020, Helena, Montana
Police Headquarters Conference Room
(The Next Day)

The entire team was assembled for the briefing on the events of the previous day. As usual, Duke started the conversation, "As I'm sure you already know, the Falcon headquarters property was shot up during the day and was burned to the ground last night. There are a lot of theories why this happened, but if we add the first and fourth murders into the mix, it's starting to look like the Falcons are the targets. We need to investigate them closely and see if there are any clues as to who might be attacking them and why."

Ranel spoke up, "The attacks on the two police officer homes need to be mixed into all of this as well. Obviously, they are try-ing to discourage us from continuing this investigation. They're trying to keep us preoccupied with their attacks. My guess is that burning the Falcon property was a way of hiding evidence and we need to include the Falcon's as suspects in the burning because they might have been trying to hide something as well."

Duke spoke up again, "I think it's time to reorganize our teams. We need a team focused on the shooting attack and burn-ing of the Falcon property, and another team focused on the Fal-cons themselves. We need to keep a team focused on the attacks on myself and Jill. And the team that is working directly on the murders and treating this as a conspiracy should continue with this fourth murder."

"Agreed," commented Ranel. "Does anyone have anything else relevant to report to the team?"

No one spoke up. New tasks were assigned, and the meeting was dismissed.

CHAPTER FIFTEEN

Assassination

June 2020, Helena, Montana
An Office In A Warehouse In Northeastern Helena
(Early The Next Morning)

Doug and Karl entered Gerd's office and before they had a chance to sit down Gerd spoke up, "I thought we weren't going to burn the place down? What happened?"

Doug answered, "We took it as a challenge to see if we could do it. It was fun sneaking in there right under the cop's noses and setting the place ablaze. We didn't stick around to watch but I hear it was quite a big fire."

Gerd responded, "I don't want you taking those kinds of risks. I understand that you had fun doing it, but I don't want to end up with anyone getting caught and the finger getting pointed at me."

Karl tried to change the focus of the conversation and asked, "Did you learn anything about the shooting? Who did it and why?"

"Everyone's denying involvement," answered Gerd. "I don't believe any of them. Someone's behind this and I think someone is after the same thing we are after. We just can't let that happen."

Karl responded, "That's right boss. We need to find out who was behind those shootings."

Gerd continued, "My inside source tells me that the cops are wondering if the Falcon's intentionally started the fire to hide evidence."

Doug said, "Good. Instead of looking for us, they're going to waste their time investigating the Falcons."

Gerd added, "Actually that's not all that good. If they start investigating the Falcon's they may find the thing that we want, and that will complicate our taking it away from them. We can't have that. We need to throw the cops off track."

"What do you suggest?" asked Doug. "Do we do another attack on the lead cops and try to discourage them."

"It didn't work last time, so I don't have a lot of hope for it working this time," responded Gerd. "All that did was add more cops to the investigation."

"Do you want us to shoot them?" asked Karl.

"That might work," replied Gerd. "Let's think about who we should shoot and when would be the best time."

Doug spoke up, "I don't like that Duke guy. He's pretty arrogant."

Gerd responded, "Yes. That might work. He's the head of the entire investigation and that would throw the entire process temporarily into chaos until they get a chance to reorganize. It would also put fear into the rest of the detectives."

Karl asked, "Would that leave that FBI guy in charge? I'm not sure that would be good. Or worse yet, the Filipino guy who works for the state troopers."

"I think they would have to put another local cop in charge and the FBI would just be support. At this point the FBI hasn't taken over the investigation, which they might do if the local pol-ice office doesn't find someone else to replace Duke," suggested Gerd.

"I wouldn't be surprised if they put that girl in charge," inserted Doug. "Now that would be a disaster waiting to happen, wouldn't it?"

"That might work in our favor," suggested Gerd. "Do it!"

"You bet boss," replied Doug, and the two left the office.

"Do we have a tracking device placed on Roger's car?" asked Gerd.

"You bet!"

As they were walking Doug asked Karl, "When and where should we do this? He doesn't go to his home anymore and we don't want to do it around the police station or the hotel because there are too many people around."

"I say we tail him and when the opportunity presents itself, we make sure we're ready."

"We do it by pulling up next to him in the car."

"That might work," answered Karl. "Let's hang out at the police station and wait for him to come out."

The two drove over to the police station, parked across the street from the police parking lot and waited. Their wait wasn't long, about an hour, when they noticed Duke driving out of the parking lot. He had a male passenger with him that they did not recognize. They slowly pulled out behind the police car and started following, staying back a few car lengths to not be too ob-vious.

"What are we going to do?" Karl asked Doug. "Should we pull up beside him and take a shot, like we discussed earlier?"

"I don't have any better ideas, so let's give it a try."

They started driving a little faster to catch up with the police car. They didn't want to be obvious, so they moved up slowly. Eventually they caught up with the police car, and they switched into the right-hand lane. They came upon a stoplight and used that opportunity to pull up next to Duke's vehicle.

Karl was ready and Doug had rolled down his window, so when the opportunity was right Karl raised his pistol and fired three quick shots into Duke's vehicle. Doug jammed down the accelerator and flew through the intersection, not waiting for the light to turn green. They raced quickly back towards their ware-house headquarters, taking a route which allowed them to make sure they were not being followed. As they raced forward, ano-ther vehicle, a pickup, rushed up behind them and rammed the back of their vehicle. The pickup was too close behind them and looking through the back window all they could see was the grill of the pickup. Doug tried to stick his head out of the window and take a shot but each time he tried to get into position, the pickup would ram the back of the car, knocking Doug and forcing him to miss his shot. On his third try, the hit by the pickup was so hard that it knocked Doug backwards, forcing him to reach for the frame of the car and knocking the pistol out of his hand.

Doug had a second pistol, Karl's pistol, and decided to take one more try at shooting the driver of the pickup. The chase was now close to 60 miles per hour on city streets. He climbed partially out of the window, and sat on the frame of the door, holding on to the frame with one hand and the pistol with the other. As he started to take aim, the pickup again rammed the car extra hard, this time knocking Doug out of the car and sprawling on the street. No one, neither the car nor the pickup, stopped to see if Doug had survived the fall. They continued racing onward with the pickup in hot pursuit.

The driver of the pickup had placed a call to 9-1-1 and had informed the police that he was chasing the shooter's car. The police had arranged for a roadblock. They were waiting for the car and were ready for it. A second police vehicle had also been dispatched to the location where Doug had fallen out of the car.

As Karl's vehicle approached the blockade, Karl slowed the vehicle down and suddenly came to as stop. He jumped out of the vehicle and started running. A police cruiser quickly drove up to the location where Karl had started the chase and two police officers chased after him. They yelled at the driver of the pickup to stay in his vehicle in case there was any shooting. The good Samaritan had experienced enough of an adrenaline rush for the day.

The police chased Karl through gates and into back yards, then over fences and into other back yards. Eventually a helicop-ter was able to join in the chase and it kept a spotlight on Karl. But Karl ducked into a house through an unlocked back door. The helicopter kept the spotlight on the back of the house where he entered, while at the same time keeping an eye on the front of the house to make sure he didn't sneak out that way.

When the foot cops finally arrived at the back door of the house where Karl had taken sanctuary, they could see through the window that Karl was holding several members of the house at gunpoint. Fortunately, one of the cops was a sharpshooter. He took careful aim, and with one shot, put a bullet into Karl's head.

Doug also lost his life. The fall out of the fast-moving car was headfirst and cracked his skull open, causing him to die instantly.

Duke and his passenger didn't fare well either. His partner, an FBI agent that had been assigned to work with him, was killed instantly from one of Doug's shots to the head, and Duke was severely wounded as well, having received a shot to the bottom of his chin. Duke was shielded from being killed by his unfortunate FBI partner. Duke was immediately rushed off to the hospital in an ambulance.

When Jill, Ranel, and Bridger arrived on the scene, all Jill could say was, "Three more dead and it looks like we have another assassination attempt gone bad."

Bridger responded, "I'm sure Duke was the target here. My agent was just in the wrong place at the wrong time and ended up being Duke's shield."

"That's incredibly unfortunate," responded Jill. "Is there any doubt in your mind that this event is connected with the other murders?"

"None whatsoever. This case gets messier by the second." Then, turning to leave, he said, "Let me know if your CSI team finds anything."

"Will do. Thanks."

CHAPTER SIXTEEN

The Trap

June 2020, Helena, Montana
An Office In A Warehouse In Northeastern Helena

Gerd was pacing around in his office in frustration when he received a knock on the door, "Who's there?"

Pablo walked into the room and said, "What are we going to do now boss?"

"Sit down. Let me think about this mess. I'm losing guys faster than the enemy. This just isn't right. Do I have nothing but idiots working for me?"

Pablo shut the door to the office and walked over closer to Gerd's desk. He sat down. "Do you still want to kill Duke?"

"Yes. I don't like it when I look like a failure. I've lost four members of my team, all of them good at their jobs. They were the best of the best. Now Duke is in the hospital under high security. We're going to have to wait a few days before we can get access to him and finish the job. But even then, the score is three to four and we're losing. Seven murders so far and there was never supposed to be any. This is an unbelievable disaster."

Just then a large piece of machinery started up out in the warehouse making a large screeching sound. Gerd, still pacing, stopped to look out the window at the back side of his office. Pablo stood up, pulled out his pistol, and said, "Duke was our informant and now he's out of commission. You've become a liability." Pablo unceremoniously shot Gerd in the back of the head. "Now the score is three to five," he said as he walked out of Gerd's office, locking the door behind him.

June 2020, Helena, Montana
St. Peter's Hospital
(Later That Evening)

Jill, Ranel, and Bridger were in Duke's hospital room. Duke had just come out of surgery and was still a little groggy from the drugs, but he was eager to get updated. His mouth and chin were taped up with bandages covering his entire head. He was unable to speak so they provided him with a computer, and he typed his messages on the keyboard so they could communicate with him. "I feel like Steven Hawkings," was his first comment. "I have to type everything out on a computer."

There was a chuckle from Jill and Bridger and then Jill said, "You look a little like him too."

Duke came back with, "Don't make me laugh. It hurts too much. Tell me what happened. Tell me what you know."

Bridger explained, "Two individuals attacked your vehicle and we're convinced that it was an attempt to assassinate you, Duke. The unfortunate FBI agent that had been riding with you was killed. He was the shield that saved your life. Also, unfort-unately, both assassins were killed so we can't learn anything from them except what we can glean from their cell phones and ID's. The team is researching the background of those two killers right now to see what they can learn. There seems to be no question that is was all connected somehow with the other murders, but we don't know how or why."

Duke typed, "Another failure to acquire any evidence. That's too bad. My priority is to make sure my family is protected. Are they being guarded?"

Jill responded, "We immediately sent four officers over to the hotel to make sure they were safe. We had the same concern, that if they couldn't get at you, they may try your family next, so we took care of that right away."

Duke typed, "Thanks."

Jill responded, "I can't help but think the common thread is still somewhere in the Falcon Sand and Gravel works. I'm going to go over there and just hang out and observe. It sounds like a waste of time, since the offices were burned to the ground, but they now have some temporary trailers they are using as offices and business seems to be back to normal. Besides, everything else we're doing seems like a waste of time. We're just spinning our wheels."

Ranel interjected, "I have no problem with Jill following up her hunch. At this point hunches are all we have."

Jill continued, "I went through some recording tapes with Eric a couple nights back and saw something that was both interesting and confusing. I'm not sure it has any significance to the case."

"Tell us about it. Why didn't you report this 'a couple nights ago' when you came across it? Don't keep us in suspense," demanded Bridger.

"What I saw on the video recording was Gerd and Roger having a conversation out in the gravel pits. What's curious is that Gerd is a known criminal element here in Helena. What would Roger be doing having a chat with a gangster?"

"That's strange," responded Ranel. "Did they seem friendly or was it contentious?"

"It seemed very friendly," answered Jill. "And then a third person showed up. At the time I didn't recognize him, but now I know who it was. It was the FBI officer that was killed when the assassination attempt was made on Duke. All three seemed overly friendly and they even seemed like they were joking with each other. They seemed like best buddies."

"What? This is significant! Did you copy the recording before it got burned?" typed Duke.

"Yes," responded Jill. "Luckily I made several copies that I was going to give each of you. You should watch it for yourselves and see what you think."

"I have no idea what all that means," commented Ranel.

"I don't either, but I'll keep working on it to try to find out," added Jill. "Maybe I'll play Gerd a visit and ask him and do the same with Roger."

"Be careful," typed Duke.

Bridger added, "I can have extra men come in if needed. FBI headquarters is really upset that we lost one of our men. I have teams working on this latest attack on you, and other teams working on the attack on Falcon headquarters. So far, they have nothing. Maybe one of them can help Jill in her interviews of Gerd and Roger. I find it curious that an FBI agent is having a con-versation with a known gangster. There have been no under-co-ver assignments. I would be curious to find out what that little conversation was all about."

Duke typed, "We may need the additional resources. I feel bad that I'm of no use right now. It looks like I'm going to be laid up here for a while. But please keep me informed about what's going on. It may bring something to mind that could be useful in solving this mess."

"Will do," said Jill and Bridger simultaneously.

Just then a nurse entered the room, "Times up. You need to let him rest now. You can come back tomorrow, but that's enough for today."

Bridger answered, "We were just wrapping up anyway."

With that Bridger, Ranel, and Jill said their goodbyes and departed.

June 2020, Helena, Montana
Falcon Sand and Gravel
(The Next Morning)

Bright and early the next morning Jill went over to the Falcon facility. She arrived at 6 AM and found the cement operation already in full swing. Without announcing herself, she drove up to the edge of the hill overlooking the operation, next to the burnt-out headquarters building, and just sat and watched. She wasn't sure what she was looking for. But she hoped she would recognize it when she saw it.

Jill saw workers scurrying around, using the chute to load their trucks with sand, gravel, and cement. She saw truck drivers enter and leave a small trailer which she knew housed the com-puter systems that calculated the mix. After the truck was loaded, they drove off and the next truck would pull in, repeating the ritual of calculating, loading, and leaving for their ultimate des-tination.

There were eight trucks that went through this routine. She paid extra close attention to Eric, who was the fourth truck in the sequence. There was something about him that fascinated her.

After the last truck was loaded and departed, Jill climbed out of her vehicle and started walking around, with a camera in her hand. She took lots of pictures. Different people would recognize her and wave to her and she would wave back. She wandered through the burnt remains of the headquarters where the CSI team was still busy trying to identify clues. She spoke to the lead CSI team member, "Find anything?"

"The only thing we found that's disturbing is that someone must have come here last night and rummaged through this crime scene. I'm not sure what they were looking for, but a lot of the scene was disturbed. However, one item that mysteriously disap-peared was the recording equipment for the security system. But I don't think that's the only thing they were looking for because several other areas were searched."

"Interesting," commented Jill. "What were they searching for?"

"I don't know. We did find the source of the fire. It was obvious. No one tried to hide it. It was on the back side of the building. We did get some fingerprints, but we haven't processed them yet to see if there was anything interesting."

Jill responded with, "This is an urgent priority. People are dropping like flies. Please put a rush on it and let me know as soon as you learn anything."

"Of course."

Jill continued strolling around the area, taking pictures, and making notes. But nothing jumped out at her as being unusual. After a couple hours, the cement trucks started returning to the Falcon facility, having made their deliveries. They each had their assigned parking slot at the top of the ridge. Eric was one of the earliest to return. When he saw Jill, he headed directly to her and struck up a conversation, "How are you doing? Have you found anything helpful?"

Jill answered, "I guess your cameras weren't working when this fire was started."

"I'm sure they were working, but all the recording equipment was stored inside the building and I'm sure it was destroyed."

"It looks like it might have been removed after the fire. Would you know anything about that?"

"No way," blurted out Eric in a surprised voice. "Someone stole the recording equipment after the fire. That's crazy. I just assumed it was destroyed or else you would have already found whoever did this. I'll bet that whoever stole it did so just in case there was anything incriminating on the video. But I would suspect that it was all destroyed anyway."

Then Eric got up enough nerve to ask, "By the way. I wanted to ask you. Are you busy tonight?"

"Why?" asked Jill, hoping for an invitation of some type. She was still hesitant about mixing work and personal life, but since spending time with Eric seemed strangely comforting, she was eager to spend more time with him.

"Do you want to go out to dinner with me tonight?" It took every ounce of nerve for Eric to ask. He didn't understand why it was so hard. It's not like it was the first time he asked someone out. But this time it seemed more challenging. Jill did something to him. Just being around her made him feel like he was a teen-ager again. He knew it was ridiculous, but she unnerved him.

She was thrilled but in shock, "Sure. When?"

"I have some cleanup to do but we could go as early as four or five?"

"Let's make it five. I'll be hanging out around here all day today, so I should be easy to find when you're ready to go. And I'll be starving by then, so you better make it good!!"

"Excellent," said an excited Eric. "I'll see you then." He headed off to the trailer which had been brought in as a temporary office.

Eric walked in the door and headed to the small office of his father, Roger, who asked him, "How'd it go?"

"It went great. We have a date tonight. I'm looking forward to it."

"Excellent," answered Roger. "Let me know what you learn."

"Will do," responded Eric.

CHAPTER SEVENTEEN

Change in Leadership

June 2020, Helena, Montana
Lucca's Restaurant

Eric arrived with Jill at the door of Lucca's, the top end restaurant in Helena. He opened the door for her, acting the role of the perfect gentleman. They were greeted at the door and escorted to a table. Once seated, Jill said, "This is the first time I've eaten here. I heard good things about this place, but I've never been here. I feel totally out-of-place since I didn't go home to clean up and change. But thanks for the invitation."

"My pleasure," responded Eric. "I don't come here very often, mostly because I rarely have a reason to come here, but bringing you here was special occasion enough. Thanks for hang-ing out with me tonight."

"What big plans do you have for after dinner?" she asked. She hoped that they would be spending the evening together. She didn't want to go home, but she also didn't want to end up with something intimate. She decided to find out what he had planned so she could be ready. She didn't want things to go too far.

"After dinner I was hoping we could do some country dan-cing at a dance club close to here."

Jill was excited, "Wow, not many men want to take me out dancing. But I love to dance, and it's been forever since I was out dancing. I'd love that."

The two spent the meal getting to know each other. They learned each other's background and history, their likes and dis-likes, and what they hoped to see in their future. Eric explained how he hoped someday to take over his father's business and expand it to other locations. His dream was to have gravel pits in every major city in Montana. Jill, in turn, hoped to someday earn the rank of Chief of Police. She realized that in a cowboy town, a female Chief might cause some people to turn up their noses, but that just meant she would have to prove herself, and she felt she was up to the task. Both Jill and Eric saw Helena as their long-term home, which fueled the idea that maybe there was hope for a long-term relationship between them.

Eric enjoyed the conversation. Jill was cute and he liked her friendly, out-going personality. He was attracted to the "police-woman" qualities. She was strong and independent. He had never dated anyone like her. He usually ended up with the at-tractive, needy women. The kind that had fake boobs, fake fin-gernails, fake eyelashes, hair extensions and on and on. Every-thing was fake on them, but ironically, they were always looking for a "real man." These girls were annoying to Eric. But Jill was different. Maybe this could turn into something more than just a single date.

They ordered their meal, both having steaks, which were pre-pared perfectly. Then they left the restaurant for a short five-minute stroll to the dance club. Eric, again being the perfect gentleman, got them both drinks and a table where they sat and waited for the perfect song to dance to. Eric decided to ask the question that had been troubling him, "Tell me how the case is going."

"Slowly," said a sad and disappointed Jill. "We just can't get a break on this one."

"People around Falcon are seriously worried. In the last couple weeks two people have died at the gravel pits, and a third at the cabin, and my mom has been seriously injured, and add to that, the place has been burned down. People want to know what's going on and we don't have any answers."

Jill continued, "Neither do we. I wish I could tell you we were on the verge of putting the bad guys in jail, but it would be a lie. We're really not sure who the bad guys are."

"Can you give me anything that I can tell the guys back home?"

"Nothing. Our CSI guys have been digging through every-thing and they are as frustrated as we are. You may not know all the details, but I'll tell you a few things that the newspapers haven't printed. For example, we now have a dead FBI agent and Duke was seriously injured and will be spending months recov-ering. Also, his house was shot up and he is living in a hotel. I was attacked and beaten in my home and I'm now living in a hotel with a police guard as well. No one seems immune from being attacked." Jill's eyes were watering up as she remembered the attack on herself and how scary that night was. She just couldn't tell him she had been raped. It was still too unbelievable, and she just couldn't face it yet.

"Oh my gosh. I'm sorry to hear that happened to you. I only heard the story from a Falcon perspective, but you've defiantly had some trials of your own."

"I have my sister staying with me every night at the hotel, or I wouldn't be able to sleep. It's really rattled me. I'm supposed to be a tough cop."

"Not meaning to be offensive, but now you've probably developed a lot more sympathy for the crime victims that you deal with," added Eric.

"That's for sure. And you're not being offensive. I thought I understood how they felt before this incident, but it's nothing like how I feel now."

"I don't want to be forward, but I live in a house by myself and I have extra bedrooms that my family uses occasionally for company. You're welcome to stay there if you get tired of the hotel.

And maybe it would give your sister a break as well. Don't feel any pressure but consider it an open invitation."

"Actually, I might just take you up on that. I fear that I'm putting my sister in danger by having her stay with me. I would never be able to live with myself if she ever got hurt because of all of this," Jill responded thoughtfully. "It's a lifestyle that I chose, and she's now gotten sucked into it."

"Are you saying that you'd rather put me at risk?" Eric said jokingly with a smile on his face.

"You know that's not what I meant. But I need to be blunt and put this on the table. If I were to stay with you, there would be nothing physical between us. I've been rattled by all this and the thought of anything physical would be enormously offensive to me."

"I absolutely understand. That wasn't my intention. It was just a friendly invitation to a friend in need. I do like you, but I wouldn't be much of a friend if my only goal was to take advan-tage of you."

Eric picked Jill's phone up off the table, handed it to her, and said, "Call your sister and tell her she has the night off. We'll leave here in a little while, go by, and pick up your stuff at the ho-tel, and you're staying with me tonight. In fact, tell your sister to take her stuff with her as well because you're checking out of the hotel, at least for the next few days. You're going to be under my guardianship for a while."

"There's something wrong with this picture," stressed Jill. "We now have the victim of a crime guarding and the cop who is assigned to the crime. That just sounds wrong no matter how you twist it."

"Twist it all you want," stressed Eric in a firm tone, "that's what's happening."

"Thanks," was all Jill could say.

Shortly after Jill sent the message to her sister one of Eric's favorite songs, Little Big Town's "Pontoon" started playing and he pulled Jill out of her seat and onto the dance floor. They stay-ed on the floor for the next few songs. Once they got started dan-cing it was hard to get Jill to stop.

Jill and Eric stayed at the dance hall a couple more hours. Then Eric drove Jill to the hotel, helped her get her belongings to the car, checked her out of the hotel, and drove her to his house on the Falcon Sand and Gravel property. Once in the house Eric said, "This is going to be your bedroom, and the bathroom here in the hallway is totally yours. I have my own bathroom connected to my bedroom."

Jill responded, "Thanks again. I hope you don't mind, but I'm really tired. It's been a long day."

Eric answered, "Don't worry. Just make yourself at home. I'll see you in the tomorrow."

"Don't worry about me. If I have to get going, my car is still here at the Falcon works and I can do whatever I need to do."

"That's good because my day starts at five AM, and I'll probably be up and out long before you. Feel free to rummage through the kitchen and find whatever you can for breakfast."

"Will do and thanks again. Please don't be offended if I barricade the door. It's not about you. It's just about making me feel comfortable."

"I don't mind at all. I'll do you one better. I'll install a couple security locks on the inside of the door during the day tomorrow. That should help as well, and you won't have to move furniture around."

"I'm very grateful that you're so understanding."

"Don't worry about it. I'm interested in being your friend. I want you to trust me. I'm glad to do it."

They each headed off to their respective bedrooms, said goodnight, and shut their doors.

Jill barricaded her bedroom door, not because she was afraid of Eric coming into her room, but because it just made her feel safer. She knew this was somewhat foolish because if someone was after her they could easily break through the window, but it just felt better. The following morning Jill was awakened by the sound of Eric getting ready and leaving for work. She stayed in bed and ended up falling back asleep. She got up at 6:30 AM, took a shower, and got ready for the day. She walked over to the Falcon gravel pit, got in her car, and drove off to the police sta-tion where a new meeting had been called by Ranel.

The meeting was being held in the conference room and nearly everyone was already in attendance when Jill arrived. Ranel, started the meeting by saying, "Now that we're all together, let's get an update from each of the teams."

Each team made their reports about their recent activities, but there was very little new to report. After the meeting, Ranel dismissed everyone, but he asked Jill to stay behind. Once the room was emptied, and the door shut, Bridger started the conversation with, "I understand that you spent the night with Eric at the Falcon Sand and Gravel works. Is that true?"

"Yes," was Jill's response. "Are you having me followed?"

"We have a couple cops doing protective detail on you and YES, they followed you to the Eric's house. What's the story there? I understand that you went on a date with him and then spent the night with him. Tell me what's going on."

"Nothing's going on. He offered me a place to stay that would allow my sister to go home and have a break from babysitting me. We had separate bedrooms and bathrooms. What's the problem?"

Ranel jumped in, "The problem is that your objectivity has been compromised. You're no longer neutral in this case. I need you to remove yourself from working on this case."

Jill was taken back as if she was attacked, "I have not been compromised. I can be neutral in spite of the date." She was bothered by the fact that now both she and Duke, the two original detectives on this case, were successfully removed from the case.

Bridger said, "I've already discussed this with your chief, and he agrees that you need to be pulled off the case and that Lemery will take your place as the local police detective representative."

"But Lemery hasn't been working on this case. He's not familiar with it," Jill protested. Now she realized that he had just been in the debriefing that had occurred, and this explained why he was there.

Ranel added, "We'll get him caught up quick enough. With the permission of your chief, I'm taking over Duke's role along with Bridger as the leads in this case. Bridger has appointed Matthew Christ from the FBI to take over his former role on the FBI team."

Jill was frustrated and troubled. What had seemed innocent enough had now completely backfired on her. Now she would be relegated to some minor burglary case and would no longer be able to investigate the case that had consumed her life for the last month. She was furious, at herself for accepting Eric's kind invitation and at her colleagues for pushing her out.

Jill left the conference room telling herself that since she was now staying on the Falcon property, she would still work the case, with or without Ranel and Bridger's approval. She would take advantage of her stay at Eric's house. During the day she would work on her new assignments, but when she was on her own time, she would still focus on the case that was now known as the "Falcon murders"

.

CHAPTER EIGHTEEN

Samples

June 2020, Helena, Montana
Helena Police Station

Ranel and Bridger were in their element. Neither had local jurisdiction, but the two of them had taken over the case and they loved being in charge. Duke and Jill were out of the picture, as far as they knew. They didn't have to answer them or even check with them. And Lemery didn't know what was going on so Bridger and Ranel could easily control him by only giving him as much information as they wanted. Lemery would always be kept partially in the dark allowing the other two to maintain leadership of the case. Matthew was an FBI subor-dinate and would also be easy to be controlled by Bridger, his FBI superior.

Bridger was eager to announce his leadership, so he had call-ed another short meeting of the entire team that was working this case and during this meeting he informed them that he was now in charge along with Ranel. He explained that Duke would be out for some time recuperating and Jill was no longer on the case. He would be taking Duke's place, Lemery would be taking Jill's place, and Matthew would be taking on Bridger's old role. Ranel would continue to be second in charge under Bridger.

Bridger's first act in this new leadership role was to reorganize the teams, placing one team in charge of investigating the Falcon Sand and Gravel works and the Falcon family members with Lemery in charge. A second team would focus on the attacks on Duke and Jill. Bridger would be the de facto leader of that group. And a third team would focus on the big picture, trying to find the common link between all the attacks and murders with Matt-hew in charge. It all seemed logical enough and no one resisted the changes. Ranel would maintain his role as the focal point for interactions between the teams.

June 2020, Helena, Montana
Falcon Sand and Gravel

"Don't tell me you already got her in the sack," blurted Roger as Eric entered his temporary office in the trailer.

"Of course not," replied Eric, but he could see that his father didn't believe him. "It's all very innocent."

"Don't bore me with the details of your exploits. Tell me what you learned from her."

"The cops don't know anything," responded Eric. "They're totally in the dark about what's going on and how all these murders are connected. And as long as I have her staying in my house, I'll be able to get daily updates."

"Excellent. Keep me informed."

"By the way," Eric continued, "How's your little enterprise going?"

"Really good," responded Roger, "lots of trial and error, but we're moving forward. It shouldn't be long before we have something to show for all our efforts."

"And you're convinced that what you're doing is causing the attacks that are behind all these murders and the burning of our offices?"

"Almost one hundred percent sure," responded Roger. "Have you been out to visit mom lately?"

"I was out there yesterday and I'm going by the hospital again today. It looks like she should be out of there in another day or so."

Roger expressed his concern, "It will be nice to have her back, but I don't want her coming out here to the gravel pit for some time. I don't want her to be at risk anymore. I need your help with keeping her at home."

"I agree, and I'll do my best to keep her away," answered Eric. Just then there was a knock on the door. Lemery and two other detectives entered the room. Eric was about to leave but they insisted that he stay.

"What can I do for you?" asked Roger.

"We're confused about a few details," suggested Lemery. "At this point we've had three deaths and two vicious attacks on your properties and we still don't have a connection between them. Why was Bud killed? Why were your offices shot up giving us another murder? And why were your offices burnt to the ground? And how is that connected to the guy that was murdered at your cabin? What is the piece that we're missing? What con-nects each of these items?"

Roger responded, "You think the murder at the cabin is related to all of the rest of this?"

"Yes. The tire tracks for the drop off vehicle for the guys that went to your cabin are the same tire tracks that we found on the night Bud was killed."

"Wow," replied Eric. "I didn't realize all of that was connected."

Lemery stressed the question, "So what is the connection?"

Roger spoke up, "You're seriously asking us to solve these crimes? I was hoping you would be able to figure out what that connection is. You're the experts."

Lemery said, "We just know they're connected because there are common elements. For example, all of these activities occurred on Falcon property, but beyond that we have no idea what triggered any of them let alone all of them. Tell me again about any enemies or disagreements that you or your organization has had recently."

Roger responded, "I wish I had something to tell you, but unfortunately, I have nothing. We have the occasional unhappy customer to deal with but nothing would trigger this kind of angry response to where someone would resort to murder or arson. How about you Eric, can you think of anything?"

"Nothing," was Eric's response. "We have very few unhappy customers. And usually it's because of a misunderstanding, not something blatant which would cause this level of anger."

Lemery jumped back in with, "Is there any competitive jealousy going on here? I know there are other cement companies in the area and they probably resent your taking some of their business."

Roger answered, "Competition exists, but not at the level of murder. No, there's no way that could be it."

"Any marital issues between you and your wife? I see you went to San Diego recently. Tell me again, what was the pur-pose?"

This question angered Roger, but he wasn't going to let his temper show. At least not in front of the police. "It was strictly a business trip. Not unlike any other business trip I take occasionally."

"What kind of business?"

"I had to pick up some cement samples that one of our customers wants us to match."

"I thought you were picking up fish?"

Roger continued, "The samples came with a fish shipment, but it was the samples I flew down there for."

"Couldn't they have been shipped to you?"

"Yes and no," responded Roger. "There was a level of urgency that required a quick response. Also, if these samples were to get lost during shipment, it would be disastrous for us. We wouldn't be able to match the quality of the existing struct-ures." Roger was giving some information out which amounted to half-truths, but he wasn't about to reveal the big picture.

"I'll need the details about this customer and what they are expecting."

"I'm sorry, but that's impossible. Our contract specifies secrecy, or we lose the job. I can't give you those details. Besides, I'm not sure how any of this is relevant to the case we're discus-sing."

"Do I need a court order?" asked Lemery.

"By the time you arrive with a court order I will have warned the customer and he will have cancelled the order." Roger acted frustrated so he continued, "I'm not sure why you're wasting your time running off on this tangent. I'm not having an affair in San Diego. There's nothing wrong with my marriage. And my wife isn't having an affair because she works in the office 14 hours a day, by my side. Of course, now we don't have an office and she's in the hospital, but that's the way it's been in the past. I was down in San Diego doing my job and servicing a customer."

"I don't see why you would lose the order just by telling us the name of the customer. It looks like we might have hit a nerve," responded Lemery.

"What you've hit is my point of frustration. This isn't an inquiry; this is a witch hunt. I wish you guys would actually come up with something meaningful in your investigations; something that would actually uncover an arsonist and a killer."

"That's what we are trying to do. We need cooperation and not sarcasm. Don't tell us how to do our job," scoffed an angry Lemery.

"You've just been telling me how to do my job, so I feel I have a right to tell you how to do your job."

Lemery stood up and in frustration commented, "Well I can see that this conversation is going nowhere. We'll be back with a court order so be ready to give us the details about your customer and your activities in San Diego." He turned and headed for the door.

After the police had left the room Roger waved to Eric to go shut the door.

Eric stated, "I'll work on fabricating a customer and coming up with some fake samples that they can analyze."

Roger responded, "Good. Thanks. I guess we better do that quickly. They may come back at us as early as tomorrow. That's what I get for being partially honest."

"I'll get right on it."

CHAPTER NINETEEN

More Confusion

June 2020, Helena, Montana
Eric's Home
(That Same Evening)

Jill arrived at Eric's house around 6:00 PM and knocked on the door. Eric answered with, "You don't need to knock. You live here for now. It's your home too. Even if it is just temp-orary. Feel free to come and go."

She handed him a takeout bag of Kentucky Fried Chicken, enough food for several meals. She said, "I thought I'd cook tonight. Hope you don't mind."

"This is great. Thanks. I'm not sure how it will compare with Lucca's, but it smells great."

Jill and Eric went to the kitchen table, sat down, and emptied out the food box. Eric grabbed some plates and a couple sodas from the refrig and the two dove into the food like it was their last meal.

Eric said, "Thanks again for cooking tonight. I wasn't in the mood." Then he got up, walked to the other side of the table to where Jill was sitting, put his arms around her and went to give her a kiss on the cheek. Instead Jill turned her face so that Eric kissed her on the lips. He was about to pull away when Jill put her arms around him and pulled him back closer to her. She was finally getting over the dark feeling of the rape and kissing Eric made her feel as though she could be loved. She somehow felt less dirty. Maybe Eric was exactly what she needed in order to open up again.

The kiss finally ended with the two of them still holding each other and looking into each other's eyes. Eric said, "Thanks."

Jill let him go and he stood up, thrilled at what had just happened. But he wanted more so he bent back down and kissed her again, this time just a quick kiss. Het felt comfortable with Jill, like it was the most natural thing in the world, to kiss her. The two did a quick cleanup. Then Jill spoke up and said, "I brought a couple movies with me. Do you want to watch something toget-her?"

"I'd love it," was Eric's quick response. "What do you have? I have some too, but I'm not sure you'd like any of mine."

"The same may be true in my case. I have lots of chick-flicks, but you might like either *Salt* or *Gravity.*"

Eric responded with, "I love both of those, but I'm going to pick *Salt*. Go get it and I'll get the DVD ready for us."

"Will do," Jill said as she got up from the table and went to her room.

The evening started with the two of them sitting separately on the same couch. Soon Jill was lying down with her head on a pillow and her feet on Eric's lap. From Eric rubbing her feet it soon went to Eric lying behind her on the couch with his arm wrapped around her midsection. He kissed the back of her head and her neck, which caused her to move his hand up to her breast. Unfortunately for Eric the movie ended shortly after that, and Jill got up, said good night, and headed off to her room clos-ing the door behind her.

Eric was concerned that he might have overstepped his bounds. He hoped he hadn't made Jill angry. He hadn't felt this way about any woman, and he didn't want to blow it. He decided he would try to keep himself in check and not scare her away.

June 2020, Helena, Montana
Eric's Home
(The Next Morning)

Jill woke up around 7 AM. She had completely missed Eric's departure. The day before he had made so much noise getting ready for work. She must have been enormously tired to have missed all that this morning. She got dressed and ready for the day. She walked out into the living room and her eye was caught by a bookcase filled with books. She went over to the bookcase and perused the books, finding a lot of books on ancient cultures of the American continent. Eric seemed to have a strong interest in Inca, Kiche, Aztec, Mayan, and other similar North, Central and South American native cultures. His library also included books on the Aztec and Mayan calendar, and on religious books which focused on this same region, like the Popol Vuh and the Book of Mormon. She decided she would have a conversation with him about his strong interest in these ancient American civil-izations.

Then she saw a book which surprised her and caused her to take it off the shelf to page through it. It was titled, *Lost and Forgotten Ancient Technologies of the Americas*. She flipped through the book and found discussions of large carvings, rocks that fit together so tightly we can't slip a razor blade between them, iron that didn't rust, and strange construction materials that we are unfamiliar with today. The corner of a page was turned down, so she flipped to it and found a discussion of ancient cements. After browsing through the book, she returned it to the shelf and spent a few more minutes looking through the remain-ing book collection. After that she headed out the door.

The garage was a separate building, connected to the house by a roof that allowed passage between the two buildings without getting snow or rained on. Jill decided to be nosey and looked inside. It had a couple jet skis, a couple snow mobiles, and a bunch of tools that were most likely used to repair the equip-ment. But then she saw something that caught her eye. On one of the work benches was a burnt DVD player, and she was left wondering if this unit had been pulled out of the burnt-out office building. She remembered how Eric had denied knowing who took the DVD player out of the burnt-out office building.

She checked to see if the recorder had a DVD in it and it was gone. Apparently, it had already been taken out and reviewed. She decided she would confront Eric about the recorder and see what he had to say. It was too coincidental to not be pursued.

June 2020, Helena, Montana
Falcon Sand and Gravel

Eric entered Roger's office and sat down, "What's up," asked Roger.

Eric answered, "I'm ready for the police just in case they show up with a warrant."

"What customer did you come up with?"

"I found someone that went out of business just this last week in San Diego and used their name, but there's no one left there for them to talk to in case they want to tie something down. And I came up with some samples from an old project of ours that we did a few years ago. I also created some paperwork showing a purchase order. They can have all that and good luck with it. It should keep them busy for a while."

"That works, and we can say we just found out today that they are out of business, so my trip and all our efforts were a complete waste of time."

"Perfect," was all Eric could say. "Do you think the cops will buy it? It seems like a stretch, but for now it's about the best we can come up with."

"As for the real effort, it's moving along like gangbusters and we should have something to look at in the next couple weeks."

"Excellent."

"I understand that you were able to pull the security recorder out of the burnt office. Were you able to get any information off that unit?"

Eric handed Roger a picture, "Not much that's very helpful. It looks like the guys that started the fire were the same guys who were killed during the attempted assassination of Duke."

"We don't really know much."

"Well, what we do know is who these guys worked for. They worked for Gerd, the leader of the Liroza family, a local group of gangsters."

"I know Gerd Liroza. Is he the one behind all these killings and the arson?" asked Roger. "He's an old family friend. I wouldn't call him a good friend, just an old acquaintance."

"I'm not sure if he's behind it all, but there does seem to be a connection with his flunky," answered Eric.

"I'm going to go pay him a visit and find out what's going on."

"Let me know what you learn."

With that Eric got up and left the office, heading out into the gravel pit to see how the day's work was progressing. When he was outside, he ran into Jill who was just heading for her car. "How are you today?" he asked.

"Doing great," she responded. "How about you?"

"Everything is on track today. Are you going to find out who murdered Bud and our secretary?"

Jill didn't want to tell him that she was no longer on the case. In her mind she was still working the case, even if it was unof-ficial. She sarcastically replied, "Yep. We're going to solve every-thing today."

"Beautiful. I can't wait to hear all about it." They each went off in their own directions, Eric toward the gravel pit and Jill to her car. Then Eric yelled back, "Can I buy you lunch?"

"Sure," replied Jill.

"Meet you at Burger King around eleven."

"Perfect," she said as she climbed into her car. She would take the opportunity to confront him about the DVD recorder at that time.

June 2020, Helena, Montana
Helena Police Station Conference Room

Ranel was holding the morning debriefing session. He didn't have anything new to add but he wanted to see if anyone else had any new information. "Let's have each of the team leads update us on what they have been working on."

The Falcon team was the first to report, and they shared, "We put a tail on Roger and followed him. He went to a ware-house in Northeast Helena and spent about four hours there. We haven't been able to look in through a window because the only windows are too high. We're not sure what was going in there but considering how much time he spent there we will definitely need to find out more."

"Definitely. What do you plan to do?" challenged Bridger.

"We can't get a search warrant because we don't have probable cause. We thought we'd knock on the door accom-panied by the fire chief and just say we are there to do an annual fire safety inspection. We'll look around while we're there."

"Excellent," said Bridger. "Let's get it done as soon as possible. Of course, nothing will be admissible without a search warrant, but at least we can find out if there is a cause for getting search warrant. Anything else?"

"We have a bit of a concern about Jill moving in with Eric Falcon. That seems a little strange and bothersome. Isn't there a conflict of interest with that?"

"Yes. That's why you no longer see Jill on the case, and we need to be careful about sharing any information with her. We don't want to compromise our case by having something leaked to the Falcon family."

"Understood. Should we continue to keep a security guard watching her?"

"Yes," confirmed Bridger. "Since she's been attacked, she deserves the protection, at least for another couple weeks."

"Anything else that you'd like to share with the team?" asked Ranel.

"Only that the search of the burnt-out office building yielded nothing. It was searched by someone else before us and we're not sure what was taken other than the security recorder. Whoever was searching the burnt out remains knew what they were looking for and seemed to go straight to it."

Just then Jill knocked on the door of the conference room. Ranel waved her into the room. He stressed to the team, "No more conversation about the case for now." Then turning to Jill, he said, "What do you need?"

"I just wanted to share a little information with the team."

"What's that?" asked Ranel.

"I found a burnt-out DVD recorder in Eric's garage. I'm going to confront him later today and see how he explains it."

Bridger was indignant, "You're off the case. You shouldn't be looking at anything related to this case."

"Fine. Go ahead and be stupid about it," scoffed an irritated Jill as she turned around and walked out the door. "Do it yourself. I'm going to do what I want. The FBI doesn't control me." She slammed the door behind her.

Once she had left the conference room Ranel instructed the Falcon team, "Go find this recorder and see what we can learn from it." However, Lemery, the leader of the team had already made up his mind to reconnect with Jill and find out what she was learning from her conversations with Eric.

"We can't go charging into Eric Falcon's garage without a search warrant."

"Figure it out," responded Ranel. "We need to find out what they know."

Lemery knew that Jill would be able to get more information out of Eric than a forced police visit would be able to gain and he texted her to tell her so. He knew that his earlier confrontation with Roger and Eric Falcon and his threats to come with a search warrant wasn't going to help him get their cooperation. He was convinced that the Falcons knew more information than they were sharing, and he was desperate to find out what that was. Jill would be the best way to find it out, with or without the support of the FBI and the Montana State Police.

CHAPTER TWENTY

Hidden Evidence

June 2020, Helena, Montana
Burger King

Eric arrived at Burger King shortly before Jill. He waited for her just inside the restaurant. When she arrived, he greeted her by putting his arm around her and asking, "What can I get you?"

Jill asked for a Whopper and a Diet Coke. Eric went up to order as Jill found an empty booth to sit in. When he came back with the order, he sat across from her and asked, "How's your day been going?"

Jill got right to the point and said, "It's been great so far. But I do have a question for you. I stuck my nose into your garage to see the jet skis and snow mobiles, and I noticed the burnt-out DVD player on the bench. Don't tell me you went into the crime scene area and removed evidence."

Eric was taken off guard, but his recovery was quick. "I know it was wrong, but I wanted to see if there were any recordings of who was behind the fire. Unfortunately, by the time I was able to find out who it was, the arsonists were dead. It was the same two guys that attacked Duke."

"And you didn't think to tell me about it? You lied to me about getting the DVD player out of the building?"

"Then I would have to admit I went into the burnt building. I didn't want you thinking I was a total screw-up. Besides, with the two guys being dead, I didn't think it mattered anyway."

"It does matter because it again shows a connection between the various crimes. Do you still have the DVD that you took out of the machine?"

Eric reached into a small bag that he was carrying and pulled out a disk and a piece of paper. "I'll do you one better. Here's the disk, and here's a picture of the arsonists."

Jill eagerly took them and looked them over. Then she pulled out her phone and sent a text to Lemery. She asked, "I have the disk and I have a picture of the arsonists. They were the two guys that attempted to assassinate Duke and they're both dead. Is there anything else I should know?"

Then she asked Eric, "Did you find anything else in the burnt building?"

"Nope. That's all. I just wanted to find out who burnt our building, and now that I know I really don't know any more than before."

It was less than five minutes and two police detectives entered Burger King and walked directly over to Jill and Eric. Jill waved them over and explained, "Here is the disk that came out of the DVD recorder, and Eric printed out a picture of the arsonists. Unfortunately, they were killed in that shootout with Duke."

One of the detectives gave Eric a stern look, as if to say, "What are you doing with evidence," but then he thought better of it. He said, "Thanks," took the disk and the paper, and headed out the door.

"What was that all about?" asked Eric.

"Those guys are working on the burn site," explained Jill. "They needed that information to help re-construct what happened."

"They sure got here quickly."

"I knew they were close by, so I had them come and get the information."

"I suppose they want the recorder too."

"Yes, but not as urgently now that they have the disk," replied Jill. "We can have them come by and get it later. Is there any other information that you failed to tell me?"

"Nothing I can think of," answered Eric.

They finished lunch, but Eric had become leery of Jill's intentions. Was she just staying at his place to snoop around? Or was she really interested in him? He realized that she was just doing her job, but he also realized that he was going to have to be more careful in the future. His attitude had changed slightly. If she was going to use him, then he wasn't going to feel guilty about using her as well.

June 2020, Helena, Montana
A Warehouse In Northeastern Helena

Roger arrived at the Liroza warehouse. He realized that there was a risk in him going there alone, but he felt he had a strong enough relationship with Gerd that he should be able to visit him. He was sure that Gerd would know why two of his flunkies burned down the Falcon offices. He entered the warehouse and headed toward the back where Gerd's office was located. As usual, a couple of Gerd's guards, who were standing guard outside the facility, approached him, and asked, "What are you doing here?"

"I'm here to talk to Gerd," answered Roger.

"Is he expecting you?"

"Nope."

"Hang on. I'm not even sure he's here. I haven't seen him for a couple days which isn't unusual because sometimes we don't see him for a week. Let me check his office." One of the lackeys walked back to the office while the other stayed with Roger. The one at the office yelled out, "There's an awful smell coming from Gerd's office, and it's locked. Do we have an extra key any-where?"

"Nope," was the answer. "You'll have to break down the door."

He didn't have to be told twice. He pushed his shoulder against the door, and it was opened in seconds. Then the same guard yelled out, "Gerd's dead in here. Looks like he was shot in the head."

Several of the guards, including Pablo who was the executioner, came running over to see. Gerd was indeed dead. Roger turned to the man guarding him and said, "I guess he's not available to talk right now."

"You better leave," said the guard in a rough voice, and Roger had no intention of resisting. He headed for the door and departed. As he drove off, he noticed a car that he was sure he had seen earlier in the day, pulling out from the curve as if he was following him.

Roger decided to try to lose the car that was behind him. He made several quick turns, once to the left and then to the right, making it obvious that he knew he was being followed. The car continued to chase him, but the traffic was too thick for Roger to make a run for it. Roger decided to get himself caught in a traffic jam. When he saw that the other car was also caught in the jam, he climbed out of his car and walked back to the other vehicle. He knocked on the driver's window and, when the driver had opened the window, he asked, "Who are you and why are you following me?"

"We're the police and we are a protective detail. Since there have been so many killings on Falcon properties, we have been asked to protect you."

"To protect me or to treat me as a suspect?"

"Both."

"Well, you may want to send someone back to the Liroza warehouse that I was just at. Apparently, Gerd Liroza has been killed."

The officers immediately placed a call, just as the traffic was starting to move so Roger ran back to his vehicle, jumped in, and continued in the flow of the vehicles. Just then Roger received a call. "What were you doing at Gerd's office?" was what the caller blurted out after Roger had said hello.

"Who is this?" demanded Roger.

"FBI," barked Bridger. "I want to know what you are doing with the Lirozas."

"How do I know you're the police. I don't believe anything you're saying. I don't trust anyone anymore, especially you. Why are you having me followed? Why are you treating me like a suspect? When you start answering some of my questions, I'll think about answering yours. And as for this phone call, I have no idea if you're really the police so I'm not answering any questions until I see some ID."

"I'll have you picked up and brought in for questioning, if you prefer that."

Roger was so fed up with the idea that the police were following him and treating him like as suspect, and that they were now questioning his motives, that he just blurted out, "Do what you have to do," and hung up the phone.

Traffic had merged down to one lane because of construction and Roger had finally broken free. He was able to move away. Fortunately, the police car that was following him was still stuck in the merging traffic mess and couldn't keep up with him. Roger got away and, using a confused and round-about route, headed to his Northeastern Helena warehouse where he was able to drive his car inside the warehouse and shut the door behind him. Despite the tracking device that was on Roger's car, the police would have to spend some time searching for him before they would be able to bring him in for questioning.

CHAPTER TWENTY-ONE

Another Death

June 2020, Helena, Montana
Helena Police Station Conference Room
(Next Morning)

Ranel was holding his regular morning briefing. This time when he asked for any new information, he was barraged. The team watching Falcon reported on the DVD and that the arsonists were killed in the attack on Duke. They also reported on Gerd's death and that Roger was at the warehouse when the body was discovered. They mentioned the connection between the arsonists and that they were employees of Gerd. They also questioned why Roger would be visiting the warehouse of the individual who had burnt down his offices.

Bridger raised the question, "We've had four security guards and Gerd himself killed. That's five deaths in the Liroza network that have been killed. What is going on here? Are we looking at a war between two rival gangster families?"

"Who's the other family?" asked one of the detectives. "We only have one family losing lives. Who are they fighting with? The Falcons? They're the only other ones that are losing lives. They aren't "gangsters" by any means. Everything we have learn-ed about them is that they are the typical American middle-class family."

Bridger continued asking questions, "But are the Falcon's trying to break into the Liroza family business? I don't think so. They seem to have entirely different interests. So, I don't understand what the heck is really going on here? Every time we get more information it seems to get more confusing."

Another detective suggested, "If the Falcons were competing with the Lirozas why would Roger risk his life by going by himself to their warehouse for a visit? It doesn't add up. They can't be competing crime families. There's something else going on here."

A third detective chimed in, "I think the key is in Gerd's assassination. Killing the boss' kid is suicide in the crime families. Gerd was one of his father's favorite kids. Killing him is going to bring out the worst in the Liroza family. If we think we have a lot of bodies lying around now, wait till the Liroza revenge begins."

Ranel asked, "But revenge against whom?"

The third detective replied, "That's the million-dollar question isn't it. Unfortunately, we probably won't know until we see more bodies piling up."

Bridger asked, "Is there any additional information that should be shared with the team?"

The lead detective on the Falcon team spoke up, "We went in with the fire department yesterday to check out the warehouse where Roger had spent so much time and we found nothing. The warehouse is apparently used by several different businesses. There is a small lab that they claim is being used to test samples of the food products that are distributed out of that warehouse for another company, which seemed to have nothing to do with the Falcons. We found nothing suspicious in that area. In a separate area they were also working on cement samples, doing some chemical tests on them. But even that was legitimate because it's a government requirement for government contracts. That might be where Roger was spending his time. It all seemed legitimate."

"He's gone there several times. It's a daily routine with him. It's not like he just went there once. I really don't understand what that's all about. It probably has something to do with the cement samples, but I'm not sure what. And then his being at Gerd's office when he was found murdered was also suspicious. I don't know how all of this information fits together."

Bridger added, "We need to keep a close watch on him. There's more to Roger Falcon than we know. Let's have some-one go and interview him about his involvement with Gerd and what he was doing at that warehouse. We also need to start watch-ing the son, Eric. He's got to be involved in whatever Roger is doing. Let's start tailing him too."

"We've had him watched at night but there's not much going on. He occasionally walks around the Sand and Gravel facility, I think just to check and make sure nothing is happening that shouldn't be happening, but he doesn't do anything but walk around the place. Nothing suspicious."

"Let's keep a tail on him during the day as well just in case he's involved somehow. Let's put a tracker on his car too."

"Will do," was the team leader's response.

Then Ranel asked if anyone else had any insights into what was going on with this case. No one volunteered any new inform-ation, so Ranel ended the meeting with, "Well let's get out there and figure this mess out."

<h3 style="text-align:center">June 2020, Helena, Montana
Gerd's Warehouse</h3>

Bridger and his team walked around Gerd's warehouse, not really knowing what to look for. They knew this was one of the main distribution locations for the Liroza's drug ring, but it had obviously been sanitized. Someone beat the police to the location and cleared out anything suspicious. There was nothing that could be identified as being related to drugs.

The CSI team had performed a ballistics review of the assas-sin's bullet, but it could not be linked to any weapon on file. And no weapons were found at the warehouse. Gerd's office was dust-ed for fingerprints but that also yielded nothing unusual. The only fingerprints were members of Gerd's team. It was another frustrating crime scene.

Gerd's dad, Gerrard arrived during the CSI search of the building and went directly up to Bridger, "I understand that you're in charge. Who did this to my son?"

"I have no idea. It would have helped if we would have known about this sooner and if you hadn't sanitized this place be-fore we were able to get our team in here. I have to wonder if someone didn't already know that he was dead and cleared every-thing out before the police became involved. Our CSI team has found nothing suspicious."

Gerrard didn't bother to deny the sanitization of the warehouse. He went on the say, "Maybe they found nothing because there was nothing." Then, with emphasis he said, "I need to know who did this."

"Why?" asked Bridger. "What are you going to do with that information?"

"That's my business," grumped Gerrard. "Do you guys know anything?"

"Like I said, it would have been easier if you hadn't sanitized the place before we arrived."

"I will contact the mayor and make sure he instructs you to keep me updated."

"I work with the FBI, so the mayor won't have a lot of influence over what I do."

"We'll see about that," grumped Gerrard as he stomped off towards Gerd's office.

"Please don't interfere with our investigation," yelled Bridger after him.

"What investigation," answered Gerrard. "You already told me you have nothing."

The conversation ended. Gerrard walked over to a group of Gerd's security guards and had a private conversation with them while Bridger continued walking around the warehouse hoping to find anything suspicious that might help in the investigation. He wondered what influence Gerrard had over the mayor, that allowed him to threaten the mayor to get more information. Suddenly this political twist added another dimension to this case. How was the mayor connected with this crime ring? Was he involved?

Gerrard left the facility acting very intense and focused. He drove off without saying a word to Bridger, leaving Bridger concerned he might have initiated some revenge activity which would result in even more bodies.

June 2020, Helena
Montana, Jill's Car

Jill was working on her new assignments, travelling in her car to investigate a recent robbery at the local 7-11 when she received a call. She answered the call with, "This is Jill."

The caller answered with, "Can you tell who this is by my voice?"

The voice caused her to slam on her brakes. It gave her immediate chills down her spine. Luckily, no one was behind her. Jill paused. She knew immediately that it was the individual that had raped her. She had to think about how to answer the call.

Jill's pause caused the caller to say, "Hello!"

"I'm here," said Jill. "What do you want?"

"I told you what I want. I want this case killed."

"I've been kicked off the case. I have no power or influence in this case any longer. You'll have to threaten someone else if you want this case to die. But murder cases don't die very easily, especially when the FBI is also involved."

"I'm threatening you. I know where you are. Don't think I can't get at you. I know where you spend your nights. You need to get back involved in the case and get it stopped."

"This is a murder case. The public outcry and the mayor will not allow it to be stopped. Things don't work that way. I don't have the power to stop this case. What you're asking is impos-sible."

"Then don't be surprised if you get another visit." He hung up the phone.

Jill was shaken. Instead of going to her crime scene she turned around and headed back to police headquarters. She knew there would be another team meeting and she decided she would barge in and let them know what happened.

Jill tried calling back on the phone number that had called her, but the phone was dead. She would give the number to CSI to investigate, but she knew that her attacker had purchased a throwaway phone and that the number would now be inactive. It would be a waste of time, but it needed to be checked out just in case the caller made a mistake.

CHAPTER TWENTY-TWO

More Hidden Evidence

June 2020, Helena, Montana
Police Headquarters Conference Room

The meeting was already in progress when Jill arrived, but she didn't wait. She barged in on the meeting, no longer caring about Ranel or Bridger's threats and their rude attitude towards her.

"What do you want now?" barked Bridger, as she entered.

"I was just called and threatened by the same individual that attacked me earlier. I need a guard and I need to know what you're doing to solve these attacks. You may not want me invol-ved, but I'm being forced back into this game."

"Well you're not going to be allowed back into the game as long as you have a relationship with Eric. You're compromised."

"I'm also getting threatened."

"What is the threat?" asked Franklin, one of the FBI detectives, which caused Jill to pause. There was a familiar ring to that voice, which caused a chill down her spine. Could Franklin be her attacker? There's no way! He's FBI and how could he be the caller when he is here in this meeting? She dismissed it as a coin-cidence. Still, she needed to find out more about this Franklin guy.

"The caller said that I need to immediately put an end to this investigation. I informed the caller that I am not on the case and even if I was there would be no way a case with this level of visibility could just be dropped."

Bridger chimed in, "Have you had the phone number researched?"

"It was a throw away phone which was immediately discon-nected after the call. He probably discarded it. However, they did check which towers the call bounced off and it was within a block of this police station."

Bridger was indignant, "Are you telling me that the person who attacked you was somewhere close to this office when he called and threatened you?"

"Exactly."

"And how long ago was this call?"

"Maybe thirty minutes at the most," replied Jill.

"So, this guy it is toying with us."

"I'm afraid so."

Now Ranel realized that his efforts may not be having the success he had hoped for he said, "I wish you weren't tangled up with Eric. We could use you back on this case. However, with you staying at his place, that just doesn't work. However, with your permission, I'm going to have someone track your phone and monitor any future calls. Do you have any reason why we shouldn't do that?"

"None," responded Jill. "Go for it. That last attack still has me shaking every time I think about it."

"Do you have anything else you want to share with the team?"

"Nothing," said Jill and walked out. She left the conference room and went directly to her police chief's office, knocked on the door, and when she was invited in, she entered the office.

"What do you need?" asked the chief.

"I need to be put back on the murder case." She went on to explain the phone call that she received. "If I'm going to be threatened, I need to be part of the team that goes after these guys."

"But your relationship with Eric compromises your credibility, as you know it does. If this case was to ever go to court, your testimony is going to be destroyed because of your relationship."

"What if I end the relationship? What if I move back to my house and we keep a guard there?"

"It would require you spending no more time at his house or his coming to your house. No more lunches or dinners. No more anything until this case is laid to rest, which may be a long time. It may be years."

"Understood. I'll make tonight my last night there and that's when I'll inform him that we can't spend any more time toge-ther."

"Okay. It's up to you. Then, after a few days, we can get you back on the case."

"Thanks for your help," Jill said. "I really need to be on this case helping solve these murders."

June 2020, Helena, Montana
Eric's House
(Later That Evening)

Eric was already at home when Jill arrived around 7:00 PM. She walked in and Eric asked, "You want some dinner? I have pork and beans and corn-on-the-cob on the stove. Should I dish you up some?"

"That would be great," Jill responded. "I've had a really long day."

"It sure looks like you've been busy. Have you solved anything?"

"Nope," responded Jill. "We're just spinning our wheels hoping someday to find some magic. Unfortunately, I found out today that I'm going to have to move back to my own house after tonight. I've been chastised for staying here with you when you're a person of interest in this case. Apparently, there are people in my office that think I'm breaking the rules."

"That's too bad," said Eric. "I was getting used to you being here and I was liking it."

"Especially our cuddling and movie time," said Jill teasingly.

"Yes," agreed Eric, "I like holding you and cuddling you. It's been a treat for me."

Eric dished out her dinner and set it at the table. Jill sat down and Eric sat with her, continuing the conversation. They enjoyed visiting and felt totally comfortable with each other. It was a huge breakthrough for Eric. He had never had this with any woman in his life. He hated the thought that it was about to end. "We can still have lunches or dinners together, can't we?"

"Nope. Sorry. I hate it too. But until this case is solved and through the court system, I have to stay away from you. I hope you understand."

"I understand. I just don't like it. And I worry about you. I hope you will make sure you have protective detail on you every night so you can sleep and stay safe. I will do my best to stay away from you, but you have to know it's not going to be easy. Just when I found someone I enjoy being around, I have to give her up!"

"I feel the same way, Eric. Let's just take it one day at a time."

"What do you want to watch tonight?" he asked.

"I vote for *The Princess Bride*," she responded.

"That sounds fun," he said as he got up to go and get it ready.

Jill did a quick clean-up and a half hour later they were both on the couch watching the movie, and it wasn't long before they were laying together, watching the movie with Eric spooning Jill.

Jill fell asleep about halfway through the movie and Eric woke her enough to help her get to her bedroom. He wanted to help her get into bed, but she shut the door behind her.

It was well past midnight and Jill was sound asleep when she felt a hand over her mouth. At first, she thought it was Eric making advances, but then she realized that the hand had a glove on it, and she knew she was in trouble. She took her right hand, formed a fist, and swung hard at where she assumed the assailants head would be, but it wasn't there, and she missed. Then she took her left hand and, swinging as hard as she could, hitting his crotch as hard as possible. This move surprised the assailant and he temporarily lost his grip on Jill's mouth, giving her a chance to let out a scream.

The assailant recovered quickly and once again clamped his hand over her mouth. But it was too late. Suddenly Eric came crashing through the door of the bedroom, coming up behind the attacker. Eric had a baseball bat and hit him as hard as possible. The hit fell on the right shoulder of the attacker and a crack could be heard. The assailant decided not to fight back and made a quick dash to the window. He dove through the open window and out into the yard. Then he got up and started running.

Eric didn't hesitate. He dove through the window and gave the assailant chase. But the assailant was faster than Eric and when he entered a clump of trees, he was able to lose Eric. Eric didn't have a flashlight. He stumbled over a branch and fell flat on his face. He could see that he had lost the chase, so he quickly returned to the house.

Eric went in to check on Jill and asked, "Are you all right?"

"I'm fine," she said. "He wasn't able to do what he came here to do, thanks to you."

"You think he was trying to rape you? Was it the same guy as before?"

"I don't know. He didn't say anything so I'm not sure, and he wore a ski mask just like last time, so I wasn't able to see his face. I'm not sure if it was the same guy or not."

"I'm glad your safe. I don't understand why he's still after you now that you're off the case. He's pretty brazen, to be attacking you when I'm around. Are you sure you want to move out?"

"I have to. Thanks for running him off." responded Jill.

"I'm going to put a board into that window so that it will be impossible to open it," suggested Eric. I'm also going to put a board across the outside of the window, covering the entire win-dow. You won't be able to see the morning sunshine, but it should make you feel safer."

"That would be wonderful," responded Jill. "It will make me feel a lot safer."

Eric blocked the window and then left Jill to try to get back to sleep. But Jill had trouble sleeping, not just because of the adrenaline rush associated with the attack, but also because of what Eric had said about her being off the case. She had told him that she needed to return to her own house to stay on the case, but she hadn't told him that she was off the case. How did he know about that? Why hadn't he said anything earlier if he knew?

CHAPTER TWENTY-THREE

Can't Trust Anyone

June 2020, Helena, Montana
Eric's House
(The Next Morning)

Jill slept in. It took her a long time to go to sleep and when she finally got to sleep, she ended up sleeping in longer than expected. With the window boarded up, she didn't have the sunlight to wake her. When she finally woke up, she checked her phone for messages, and one message made her jump up out of bed with a start. The message read, "Jill and Duke's houses were burnt to the ground last night. No one was in either house so there are no casualties. Arson and CSI teams are on sight looking for clues."

As if her night hadn't already been bad enough, now all her belongings were gone. Without her home, she had nowhere to go. "I guess I'm going back to the hotel," she said out loud to no one.

Jill drove by her house, just to see what was left of it. She didn't cross the police lines because there was no reason to. The damage had been done. Then she drove to the police station and once again barged into Bridger's meeting.

"Now what?" asked Ranel.

"You tell me," responded an angry Jill. She was in no mood for his arrogance. "I was again attacked in the middle of the night, and my house was burnt to the ground. And where was all that protection that you were supposedly giving me? You told me I was getting extra protection after that threatening phone call yes-terday. I guess that didn't work out so well."

Bridger looked around the room and asked, "Who was on protection duty last night?"

One of the agents spoke up, "Franklin and I were there at Eric's house all night. We didn't see anything."

"Were you asleep?" asked Jill. "How could you have missed him?"

"We took turns sleeping," answered the agent.

Franklin's arm was in a sling and Jill asked, "How'd you get hurt?"

Franklin's partner, Mason, answered, "That's my fault. Ap-parently, I left the car in gear and when Franklin was getting out of the car the door flew back and hit him real hard."

Franklin added, "It's no big deal. It should be healed in a day. But to support Mason's comment, we saw no one come or go all night. It was totally dead around there."

Jill didn't buy it. She asked, "What about the two houses that were burnt. There were supposed to be guards on both of those houses because of the previous attacks. Wasn't someone watch-ing them?"

"We had police patrol the area during the day," responded Ranel, "but we didn't think there was any threat at night since no one was staying in either house."

"Well I guess you were wrong," blurted an irritated Jill. "Now that the FBI and the State troopers are running this case, we're seeing nothing but dead bodies and burnt buildings. It's obvious that you guys don't have a clue what you're doing and it's time the local police take over the case again." Jill made these strong state-ments because her chief was in the meeting and she wanted to make a point about their failures in the case.

Ranel and Bridger didn't say anything, ignoring her comments.

"What are you going to do?" asked Bridger, "stay with Eric?" He was being sarcastic and tried to make Jill look bad.

"I'm moving back to the hotel," answered Jill. "I want back on this case and that's what I have to do. And as soon as I'm back, I'm taking over. Duke is gone and I'm next in line. I'm tired of all the screw-ups and excuses."

Ranel spoke up, "You're inexperienced. This is your first murder investigation. You're not in a position to take over this case."

"It's not my first murder investigation. It will be my first lead on an investigation, but I can't do any worse than you! You guys had your chance, and you blew it," replied Jill. "Now it's my turn."

"Right you are," answered Jill's chief. "I want you back on this case starting tomorrow."

"Tomorrow, I run this meeting, and I'm not accepting any more flakey excuses or FBI and State Trooper nonsense," bark-ed Jill. With that Jill left the conference room and went back to her assignments for the day. But she couldn't help but wonder why Franklin sounded so much like her attacker, and why he had his arm in a sling, the same arm that Eric had hit the previous night. In spite of his partner sticking up for him, she had to wonder if Franklin and her attacker weren't the same guy. It was all too much of a coincidence to her, but she was in no position to share her concerns with Ranel, Bridger, or anyone else. They would just call her paranoid. She would do her own investigation of Franklin.

She decided to go to the hospital and pay Duke a visit. Now that she had "pushed" herself back into the investigation as lead detective, she was nervous. She needed Duke's guidance and confidence. It had been a couple days since she had gone by the hospital. She drove to the hospital and went up to his room. "How are you today?" she asked, knowing that he wouldn't be able to reply.

He typed out, "I'm just wonderful," the sarcasm was obvious even though it was written and not verbal. "What's the news on the case? I feel completely disconnected."

"I'm afraid I was removed from the case because of my supposed relationship with Eric. There is no relationship. He just offered to let me have one of his extra bedrooms, so I didn't have to have my sister stay with me or go to a hotel. Now Ranel and Bridger and the FBI boys have taken over the case. They're running the show and I'm not even allowed into the briefings. I'm moving back into the hotel today, so they won't be able to use Eric as an excuse to keep me off the case any longer. The only thing that's new is that I was attacked again last night. I think it was the same guy, but he didn't say anything so I'm not sure. But it looked like the same guy. Anyway, Eric hit him with a baseball bat, and he ran off, so the attack was quick. Also, I suppose you heard that both of our houses are now burnt to the ground."

"Yes, I heard about the houses. I guess my family is stuck in a hotel for a little longer. I hope you get back on the case. I'm dying to know if there have been any developments."

"I'll force myself back on, with the support of the chief who also thinks this case is being mismanaged. And I'll update you when there's something worth sharing."

"You and the chief can't let those FBI and State officers push you around. They think they're smarter, and they do have more information about organized chrime, but no one knows the local environment than we do. We need to push our way back into the leadership of this case and we need to stay there. Give me an update of where we stand right now."

"I wish there was more to share. As you know I've been out of the loop so I'm not current about everything. We have the teams broken down, just like when you were injured, with very little change. The Falcon's seemed to be victims rather than perpetrators, but we're still maintaining surveillance on them. Gerd, whose guards have been involved in several of the crimes, is dead along with a couple of his goons. We have surveillance on everyone, and nothing is turning up."

Duke advised, "It sounds like you're doing everything right. If I were you, I'd push harder on the Falcons. They may not be guilty, but they are at the center of this whole mess and watching them will probably get us closer to the source of this problem than anything else. I'm surprised about Gerd. His death means there is someone higher up that isn't happy with his performance. We're dealing with someone powerful, so be careful."

Jill responded, "Thanks for your advice. I'll keep you informed of any developments so you can help me even more."

The two made a few meaningless remarks about the weather and then Jill departed, planning to spend the day working on her robbery and burglary cases. But as she walked to her car, she had second thoughts. She wondered about Franklin. Was he the attacker? Her gut was telling her that she needed to check him out. She would track him for the next couple days and see what she was able to find out. She would put a tracker on his vehicle and see where he goes. The data from the tracker would be relayed to her computer and it would keep a history of all his activities. Maybe it was nothing, but she was going to find out for sure so that she could put her suspicions to rest.

Jill headed back to the police station and signed out the tracking equipment that she would need in order to place a tracker on Franklin's vehicle. She said she was using it to track a suspect for one of her burglary cases. She went and snuck behind Franklin's car and placed the tracker under the back bumper. Then she loaded the tracking software on her computer and immediately started recording any movement of the vehicle. She also used the surveillance system that was in the police station's garage to see who was riding in Franklin's vehicle, just in case someone else was using the car.

In the evening Jill checked her computer to see what Franklin had been up to and she found that the data for the day didn't provide much tracking information. However, she was surprised to see that he visited Eric during the day, when the Falcon's weren't part of his assignment. She assumed it was Eric he was meeting with since the other Falcons weren't at the pit. She wondered if that was how Eric found out that she was off the case. She decid-ed she would expand her tracking software to include Eric and Roger as well. They already had tracking devices on their vehicles provided by the FBI, but Jill decided to get her own and not rely on the existing trackers. Jill was curious to see if there was a connection between them.

The following morning, after the morning status meeting, Jill acquired two more trackers and went to the Falcon Sand and Gravel pits to mount the trackers. She knew that she was bending the rules. It was illegal for her to track these vehicles without a warrant and that whatever she discovered couldn't be used in court. In fact, she would never be able to reveal anything about what she learned – or at least "how" she had learned it.

After spending her first night at the hotel, she arrived on site at the Falcon property and immediately ran into Eric. "How are you doing?" she asked. "Were you lonely last night without me?"

"I missed our snuggle time in front of the television," was Eric's reply.

"Me too," replied Jill. "You probably heard that my house was burnt to the ground and that I ended up back in the hotel."

"I heard about that. That's terrible. I hope you didn't lose anything valuable."

"Not really," she replied. "However, I am missing a couple earrings. Can I go back into your house to search the bedroom."

"Sure," replied Eric. "I haven't been in the room just in case you came back so if your earrings are there they haven't been disturbed."

Jill wondered why he would expect her to come back. It was almost like he knew about her house being burnt to the ground before she did.

The earring story was just an excuse. She walked over to the house and, when he wasn't looking, she quickly slipped a tracking device under his bumper.

With that mission accomplished, she now wondered how she would be able to do the same with Roger's car. That would be a little trickier. She walked over to the front of the gravel works where the cars were parked. She already knew which car was Roger's. She walked over to the back of his car and bent down behind it, quickly slipping the tracker under his bumper. Eric saw her at the back of Roger's car and yelled out, "Did you drop something?"

Jill responded, "I saw something shiny and wondered what it was, but it was just a piece of glass reflecting the sunlight." She hoped he would buy her story, but she wasn't sure he did. Then she walked back over to Eric to talk to him.

"Did you find your earrings?" he asked.

"Nope," she responded. "I have no idea what I did with them. If you see them anywhere in the house, will you let me know?"

"Sure," replied Eric. "If you get tired of the hotel, come back anytime. The room is yours, ready and waiting for you." Jill wondered what he missed most. Did he miss keeping track of her, or did he like getting updated on the case, or did he just like the physical contact they had when they watched a movie. It did-n't really matter. She couldn't stay at his place if she wanted to return to actively working on the case.

"Thanks for the invite. I'll keep it in mind," she responded.

CHAPTER TWENTY-FOUR

Tracking

June 2020, Helena, Montana
Holiday Inn Express
(The Next Morning)

Jill turned on the computer. She wanted to check the tracking system before leaving the hotel. And she was surprised. Eric and Franklin crossed paths several times throughout the day and on into the evening. It looked like they met up in the late afternoon and travelled together in the FBI vehicle for a period of time because Eric's car remained at the location where they had met up. Later they returned to Eric's car and both drove off separately. When looking at the surveillance videos of the police parking lot it appeared that Franklin and Mason were both travelling together when they left the parking lot and again when they returned. Jill decided that whatever is going on, the three of them, Franklin, Mason, and Eric, were all in on it together.

Jill also found Roger's movements interesting. He travelled to the Liroza family home and spent several hours there. Afterward he went to the funeral parlor where Gerd's body was located. She wondered about the connection between the Roger and the Liroza's.

In the end, Jill felt she had learned a lot, but she didn't know what she would be able to do with this information. She was convinced that Franklin was her attacker. But why would Eric attack Franklin so brutally if they were partners of some kind? She was sad mostly because she knew it was the end of her and Eric. She had hoped that they would be able to continue their friendship, but this was a deal breaker. Or was this partnership between Eric and Franklin something new. And if it's new, how did Eric know that she was off the case prior to this new partnership? There were more questions than there were answers. It was still very confusing.

Jill decided that she would attend and run the morning briefing, and then go out to the location where Franklin and Eric met, to see if this meeting was something they did on a regular basis.

Jill entered the police conference room with the rest of the team members and was immediately attacked by Ranel, "What are you doing here? You haven't been officially reinstated on this case yet. Until then, you can't be in here."

Jill was angered. "The chief put me back on the case yesterday."

"That wasn't official," commented Ranel. "And he's not here this morning. Until it's official, you can't be here."

She left the conference room and, in her anger, decided to put a tracker on Ranel and Bridger's cars as well. She was going to see what they were up to. She didn't expect to find anything. She just wanted to track them out of spite.

Jill decided to work on her burglary case a little while until the meeting broke up and then she would head out to the location where Eric and Franklin met yesterday, just to see if they would be repeating their previous meet.

Once out at their meeting location, she found a place to hide her vehicle, and then she found a convenient hiding place behind some bushes which allowed her a clear view of the parking lot where Eric and Franklin had met the previous day. She sat there quietly, camera and binoculars ready to record anything. She was surprised when, off in the distance, she could see Bridger, also hiding out in the bushes, and watching the parking lot. The only conclusion she could come to was Bridger also had his suspicions about Franklin and that he was watching him as well. This gave Jill the chance to see Bridger, Franklin, and Eric, all in action.

About fifteen minutes later, Eric drove up in his car and stopped in the parking lot near the entrance. Moments later Franklin also drove up and Eric, Franklin, and Mason climbed out of their vehicles and started talking. It seemed like there was an argument, but Jill was too far away to understand what the conversation was about. Eric threw up his arms and started walking toward his car when Franklin pulled a pistol out of its holster and aimed it at Eric. Their voices were raised, and Jill could hear that they were shouting at each other, but it still wasn't loud enough for her to make out what the conversation was all about.

Eric turned and faced Franklin and was surprised to see a gun aimed at his head. He put up his hands, as if to surrender, and was directed to the back seat of the police car. He was handcuff-fed and pushed into the back seat. Then the three of them drove off in the police vehicle.

The turn of events was entirely unexpected. Jill didn't have the time to run back to her car and follow them. She would have to check her tracking mechanism later and find out where they took Eric. She was sure it wouldn't be back to the police station. She decided to stay behind and watch Bridger. She didn't want to give away that she had seen him. He immediately gave up the surveillance and headed back to his vehicle. He didn't seem to be in a rush. Maybe what had just occurred was what he expected. She couldn't tell. He simply returned to his vehicle and drove off.

Jill returned to her car and drove back to the hotel where she had her computer equipment and where she would be able to observe Franklin and Bridger's travels. A half hour later she had the map up. She saw that Bridger had returned to the police station, and Franklin had driven up into the hills around Helena to what appeared to be a house or a cabin. Jill watched for any further activity, and since nothing was changing, she decided to pursue Franklin. She printed a map of the location of Franklin's car, took it with her, and drove off toward what she assumed was a hideout.

The drive took nearly one hour, and Jill became worried that Franklin would be gone before she arrived. But she wasn't disappointed. The house was slightly set back off the main road, but not too far for her to see the police vehicle in the curved drive-way. She drove past the house without slowing down. She found a place to park, a little way down the road. Then she walked back, going around the back side of the house and through the forest and the trees, hoping she wouldn't be spotted. When she started to get close to the house where Franklin was parked, she hid behind the bushes along the fence line that surrounded the property and pulled out her binoculars. She looked through the windows. She could see Franklin and Mason sitting in what she assumed was the dining room. There were also two other individ-uals there that she didn't recognize. But there was no Eric.

Just then, to her surprise, her phone started to ring. She quickly silenced it. She was angry with herself for not silencing the phone earlier. She looked at who the caller was and discovered it was Bridger. Thinking she was far enough away from the house that they wouldn't hear her, she called him back.

"Hello, Jill?" Bridger answered the phone.

"Yes," she responded in an attempted whisper. I'm on surveillance so I couldn't answer right away.

"I talked to your chief and he approved your rejoining the team. I assume I'll see you in the morning at the debriefing in the conference room."

"You bet," she answered. She didn't want to let Bridger know she had seen him earlier. Something was fishy. At this point she suspected everyone, and she was going to keep her eyes opened to see how it all played out. Also, she didn't want Bridger to know she was working the case when she was specifically told to stay off it. "I'll see you then." She hung up the phone and looked up to see two men standing, one on each side of her, each holding a gun that was pointed directly at her. She knew she was in trouble.

June 2020, Helena, Montana
Police Station

Bridger, Lemery, and Ranel met in Duke's office, where Ranel had set up his office while Duke was in the hospital. Brid-ger explained, "I just saw Franklin arrest Eric and I expected them to come back to the office here, but they never arrived. Something is wrong! If it wasn't an arrest, was it a kidnapping?"

Ranel asked, "Is Franklin someone you can trust?"

"I don't really know the guy. The FBI office sent him here for me to use on this case, but that's the first time I've ever laid eyes on the guy. I really can't vouch for him. I checked his file and he and his partner have been working together for a long time"

Ranel continued, "What do you think is going on here. If he kidnapped Eric, where would he be taking him? We need to start tracking Franklin."

"Unfortunately, I agree," responded Bridger. "Let's put someone on a detail to follow him, track his movements using his cell phone, and possibly place a tracker on his car."

Lemery suggested, "Not FBI." Bridger and Ranel nodded their heads in agreement.

Ranel suggested, "I think it should be one of the local cops. We shouldn't have the fox watching the henhouse, so it shouldn't be the FBI. And since the locals have the most at stake here, maybe Lemery should come up with someone."

Lemery added, "I'll have the chief assign someone who isn't connected with this case to keep an eye on him. That way we'll be sure it isn't someone with a vested interest in the case and they can stay neutral."

Lemery commented, "I learned something interesting which may be relevant." Ranel and Bridger turned towards him. "I learned there is an informant, or maybe even more than one informant, within our team who was giving information to Gerd.

We interrogated what remained of Gerd's team at the warehouse. One of the guys told us the informant was within the local police force, and the other informed us that the informant was within the FBI."

"It sounds like they're just trying to throw us off," suggested Bridger.

"I don't think so, because we asked them specific questions, like the make-up of the teams, and what we're working on, and they seemed to know a lot," responded Lemery.

"Great! Now we have to investigate all the investigators! This is nuts!" responded Ranel. "So now we're going to have to do an internal mole hunt across all the investigating units."

Bridger added, "That may become our highest priority. If we have suspects who know what we're doing, they can conveniently stay out of our way, or prepare false alibis. We can't have that going on."

Lemery suggested, "Maybe, if we watch Franklin closely, we may learn who the other moles are." Again, Lemery and Ranel nodded their heads in agreement.

Ranel asked, "What else did you learn from these guys at Gerd's warehouse?"

Lemery continued, "They said that the informants were high up in their respective organizations. They also said that they were playing both sides of the coin. We asked them what they meant, and they said that there was more than one organization that was after Roger. They didn't know why they were after Roger, only that there are competing organizations that are trying to find out some big secret that only Roger knows."

"Wow," interjected Bridger. "That information puts an entirely new twist on this game. We're no longer looking for one killer. We're looking for competing organizations. What organiz-ations?"

Ranel came back to the point he was trying to emphasize, "We need to do a mole hunt right away. We have enough trouble trying to solve this case and tie down who the killers are. But if some of them are in our team, we're defeated before we even begin."

Bridger asked, "What are you suggesting?"

"A trap. Let's put out a false message and see who bites," suggested Lemery.

"Like what?" asked Ranel.

"For example, let's put out the message in our next meeting that we have an informant who is going to meet with us and let us know who is behind this mess. And then let's tell them when and where and we need to be there to see who shows up."

"Why will anyone show up?" asked Ranel.

"Because they will want to know who the informant is," responded Lemery.

Bridger jumped in, "Good enough. Let's do it. It can't hurt. And if it doesn't work, we can always try something else. Are we all on board? I know just the place for the meeting. It has good hiding places and is fairly out in the open."

Lemery volunteered, "I'm game to be the guy out in the open waiting for the supposed informant."

Ranel jumped in, "Good enough. We'll use this trap in our next meeting in the morning."

Lemery asked, "Should we check with Duke to see if he knows anyone that might be our mole?"

Ranel responded, "No. The fewer people know about this the better." But Lemery didn't feel comfortable setting up members of Duke's team without talking to him first.

CHAPTER TWENTY-FIVE

The Mole Hunt

June 2020, Helena, Montana
Conference Room at the Helena Police Station

The meeting was on hold because three key team members were missing: Jill, Franklin, and Mason. They waited an extra fifteen minutes, and made several phone calls, but the three of them were nowhere to be found.

Ranel, Lemery, and Bridger conducted the team meeting as usual, and set the trap for their mole. Franklin had become their prime suspect, but until they knew for sure, they felt the need to continue the mole hunt. The fake meeting was set for early afternoon, at 1:00 PM.

The team meeting was short. There wasn't anything new to report. The only thing they had was a couple coroner's reports, which didn't tell them anything that they didn't already know.

The team meeting was dismissed.

June 2020, Helena, Montana
Wayside Rest Stop On A Hillside Road

Bridger and Ranel were well hidden in the bushes at two different strategic points. They had a good view and were ready to jump in if anything went wrong. They also kept a watch on all the surrounding area, assuming that the mole would observe the rest stop from some hidden location, possibly with a rifle, waiting to shoot the informant. They had no idea how this entire event would play out.

Lemery was parked in the rest stop, acting in his role as the person interacting with the informant. The time had been set at 1:00 PM and that time had passed. It was now close to 1:15 and no one appeared, either at the rest stop or in the bushes surrounding the area. Bridger, Ranel, and Lemery were growing impatient when Bridger noticed movement in the bushes to the north. He quickly signaled his two companions via text that he had spotted something and that they needed to stay alert.

The movement that Bridger had noticed turned out to be a deer, and he was about to let down his guard, when he spotted a man moving through the bushes. All along Bridger was confident that his FBI team was clean and that if there was a mole it would be amongst the local police force. He was extremely disappointed when he noticed that the individual coming through the forest with a sighted rifle was Mason, Franklin's FBI partner. He had identified his mole. He decided to observe him for a few minutes to see what action he would take.

Lemery stood at the back of his car, leaning against the car with his arms folded. Bridger watched Mason as he slowly took aim on Lemery. Bridger assumed Mason was just looking at him through his rifle's sight, in order to get a better view. He saw no reason why Mason would take a shot at Lemery. But he was wrong, and Mason fired a shot which knocked Lemery to the ground.

Bridger quickly jumped into action. He pulled out his pistol and shot Mason. Then he charged over to see how badly Mason was hurt. But it was too late. Mason was dead.

Following FBI procedure, Bridger disabled the rifle by taking out the bolt. Then he went towards Lemery to see what damage Mason might have inflicted on him. Ranel was already there, helping Lemery to a sitting position.

"What happened?" asked Ranel of Bridger as he approach-ed.

"I saw Mason looking through the scope at Lemery, but I mistakenly assumed that all he was doing was taking a better look. I didn't expect him to actually take a shot. And after his shot, I shot him, just to make sure there wasn't a second shot. Unfor-tunately, my shot killed Mason. Are you OK Lemery?"

"Good thing he was a lousy shot - I think he just grazed his back," responded Ranel. "Fortunately, he had on a vest which the rifle bullet was able to penetrate, but the vest significantly reduced the bullet's impact. I've placed a call for an ambulance, and he'll be laid up for a day or two, but he'll be okay."

"Excellent news," replied Bridger. "What a relief. I would hate to learn that my misjudgment of Mason caused Lemery to get badly hurt or killed." In his mind Bridger was disappointed. But he wasn't sure what disappointed him more. His misjudge-ment of Mason, or how Mason, a trained FBI agent, could be such a bad shot.

Lemery was able to speak and he asked, "Did we learn any-thing?"

"Nothing," replied Bridger. "He was dead before I got to him, so I couldn't learn anything from him."

Lemery continued, "How is it possible that Mason, who was not in our meeting yesterday, found out about this meeting?"

Ranel thoughtfully replied, "What you're saying is we didn't clear out all the moles. There is apparently more than one mole in our team. And now we've given away the fact we know there is a mole"

"That's exactly what I was thinking," replied Lemery. "Our mole hunt just became a lot more difficult."

Just then, as if on cue, a shot rang out and crashed through the two side-back windows of the police cruiser. Bridger, Ranel, and Lemery made a quick dash for the side of the car away from the direction where the shot was fired. Ranel yelled, "That takes away all doubt about whether there is another mole in the mix."

They waited a few seconds to see if there would be more shooting. Then they started working their way, from tree to tree, towards the location of the suspected shooter. They searched for some time but found nothing. Giving up the chase they started walking back towards the car.

"The shot that just happened didn't try to hit us," answered Lemery. "I'm sure he could have hit at least one of us if he really wanted to. And then he just disappeared."

"He was just trying to scare us or warn us," suggested Bridger. "I don't think he was trying to hit us. His shot was too far off."

"I'm sure you're right," answered Ranel. "But now what?"

"I think that a natural suspect for the prize of 'mole of the year' has to be Franklin," suggested Lemery.

"You're right, of course," answered Bridger. "It just pains me to think that the moles are in my FBI team. But Franklin is the most likely candidate. But I'm still troubled by the fact that Mason and Franklin were both missing from this morning's meet-ing and yet they still knew about the mole hunt. How many moles do we have in this mess? How can so many detectives be turned against us?"

Just then the ambulance arrived. Bridger told Ranel, "If you don't mind taking care of things here, I'm going to go do a second search for our shooter. There might be some clue or foot-prints we missed. I'm going to see if I can track him. Also, don't forget to have Mason picked up by the ambulance."

"Go for it," agreed Ranel. Bridger headed into the forest in the direction of the shooter.

Bridger first went to where he had left Mason. He found everything just as he had left it, so he headed off deeper into the forest. There was an old dirt road where he had left his vehicle, and he headed towards that to see if the shooter may have also parked somewhere close by. He found his vehicle, and he also found a new set of tire tracks close by where a car had stopped and parked. The shooter must have spotted his vehicle, parked there, taken his shot, and run off.

Bridger wasn't going to disturb the crime scene, so he started walking down the dirt road toward the main road. About halfway back he spotted an unmarked FBI vehicle which he recognized as Mason and Franklin's cruiser. Apparently, Mason had parked there. Mason hadn't travelled far enough to see Bridger's vehicle, so he didn't know anyone else was there. That turned out to be Mason's fatal mistake. But where was Franklin? Mason must have come on his own. Otherwise Franklin would have driven off in the car. Mason must have dropped Franklin off somewhere; but where?

Bridger called for the CSI team to come and investigate the shooting of Mason, his vehicle, and the tracks of the second shooter's vehicle. It would turn out to be a long day of investigations for Ranel. Lemery was on his way to the hospital and Bridger, was now off the case and on leave until his shooting of a fellow FBI agent could be thoroughly investigated. Bridger's departure from the case would leave a big hole in the investigation. It would now require Matthew Christ to take over the role of lead FBI investigator.

CHAPTER TWENTY-SIX

Captured

June 2020, Helena, Montana
The Franklin Hide-Out

Eric was in the basement of the house that Jill had been spying on. Franklin and Mason had brought Eric the day before and tied him to a chair. They took Jill to the basement too and tied her up to a different chair, her ankles were tied to the legs of the chair. Her hands were tied behind her back and connected to the frame of the chair.

Franklin walked into the room and spoke to Jill, "Well, well. What have we here? My old girlfriend came back to visit me. I guess you liked what I did to you last time in your house and now you want a little more. Well maybe I can oblige you. But I have some business to finish up first. Then we can talk more. How in the hell were you able to track me here?"

Franklin and the two guards that had captured Jill left the room and went upstairs as Franklin laughed a sinister, cruel laugh which made Jill shudder. Now she knew for sure that it was Franklin, the FBI detective, that had raped her in her home and had tried to rape her a second time in Eric's house. The thought made her feel sick and she had to hold back the urge to vomit.

With their captors gone, Eric asked, "What the hell are you doing here? Have you been tracking me?" Eric was suspicious of her intentions, even though she still seemed strangely appealing.

"Actually, I was tracking Franklin," she lied. "His voice sounded a lot like my rapist, and I was very suspicious of him. Now I know I had good reason to be suspicious. What are you doing here and why are they holding you hostage?" she asked.

"It's a long story," responded Eric, hoping to get out of trying to invent a lie to explain why he was there.

"I think we have lots of time," replied Jill.

"Well, I was trying to help the FBI, and, in the process, I was asked to meet with them. Apparently, they had other plans for me. But I'm still not sure what they are."

"Were you meeting them here at this house?" Jill asked, hoping to find out if he was lying.

"Yes. They told me to come up to interview me, but they immediately took me hostage and here I am, enjoying the afternoon with you." Jill knew it was a lie because she had watched the process unfold earlier. She knew that whatever else he told her would also not be the truth, so she stopped questioning him.

"Well I guess we're in this together. Do you have any idea what they're after?"

"No idea," lied Eric.

"Then I guess we have no idea how long we're going to be stuck here."

"No idea."

"It's a really bad sign that we know who our captors are. That means that we can identify them. It means that we can count on not getting out of here alive."

"That's not the best news. But as I think about it, I suppose you're right."

"So," Jill continued, "we need to take advantage of any chance to escape. Even if they shoot us trying to escape, it won't be any worse than what they have ultimately planned for us in the end."

"OK, any suggestions?" replied Eric. "You're the policeman. What can we do?"

"You must have known it was Franklin in my bedroom the other night, when you hit him with a baseball bat."

"Actually, I hadn't made the connection at that time and I wasn't sure who it was," responded Eric. "I really didn't expect it to be him."

"Has he said anything about the incident?"

"Nope. But we both know it was him."

"And since I'm asking questions, how did you know I was off the case?" asked Jill.

"You told me," he responded.

"No, I didn't," she replied. Now Jill's level of suspicion had escalated significantly.

"Well I don't know who else I could have heard it from. I wasn't talking to anyone else."

Jill saw no reason to keep up the ruse, so she said, "I know you're lying to me about coming to this house on your own, and at this point I don't know what else you are lying about. I'm start-ing to think you're mixed up in all of this somehow because otherwise, why would you need to lie about any part of it?"

Eric hung his head down. After about a minute of silence he looked up at Jill with a dejected expression and confessed, "I guess it's time for a little honesty. After all, it might be the last conversation we have. I might as well tell you the whole sorry tale of the Falcon family. It started with our sand and gravel business faltering and so we decided to diversify into cement. Our cement business grew rapidly and was, and still is, very successful. But my dad became curious about the various types of cement that are used in the world and he became overly curious about the cement that the Aztecs used, specifically, why their cement didn't decay for more than a thousand years, in spite of erosion and earthquakes. So, he started researching that. Unfortunately, be-cause he shot his mouth off a little too much, his research quickly became a topic of interest throughout the cement com-munity and several large conglomerates who owned cement divisions started to worry that

Roger was going to come up with something that might hurt their business or possibly even put them out of business. They wanted to buy Roger out, which only made him more determined to hang on and figure this thing out. He has a lab where he is doing research on samples of Aztec cement. He seems to think he is near a breakthrough."

Jill was surprised at this response and asked, "So you're tell-ing me that all these murders are about cement?"

"No. Not about cement, about money. Do you realize how much cement is used, just in the United States alone? For build-ings, roadways, etc. Around one hundred million metric tons. And it wears down fast. It's especially susceptible to weather ero-sion in snow and ice. A tree root or frozen water can destroy our hardest cements. So, finding a cement that is more durable against erosion and at the same time pliable which makes it earth-quake resistant, is a big deal."

"I assume that were talking about billions of dollars."

"Trillions," emphasized Eric.

"Roger must be pretty close to an answer if everyone is so hot to find out his secrets."

"Yes. But the story gets even more gyrated. Roger thought if he was involved in a kidnapping ruse, and disappeared for a while, these conglomerates would quit looking for him. He could hide out and concentrate on finding the answer to the Aztec cement mystery. But that all blew up in his face."

"Faking kidnapping is a crime," stressed Jill.

"Well, it didn't happen so that crime was never committed. However, the guys that were supposed to kidnap him ended up accidently killing Bud. And we think that the killing of Joe up at the lake house was also a failed kidnapping attempt."

"Is that where Gerd comes in?"

"Exactly."

"Wow. What a confused mess. Based on what you told me, Fred must have been killed as part of this scheme as well. He was the one at the lake house with Joe, correct?"

"Yes. Our guess is that Fred and Gerd were both killed because of their failure to complete the kidnapping. But we really don't know what happened."

"What about the attacks on myself and Duke. How does all that fit into this mystery?" asked Jill.

"It doesn't," continued Eric. "The attacks on Duke and you, the killing of the FBI agent, the death of the two men that attacked them, and even Gerd's death for that matter, don't fit. There is someone or something else in play here which does not fit. It has Roger scared. And he's going to disappear on his own voli-tion. Since the kidnapping ruse was a failure, he's just going to go away. He's even more scared after my mother was shot and the office secretary was killed. And then our office was burned to the ground. This whole thing is spinning out of control and we have no idea who is doing what anymore."

"What a mess. But I thought the two guys that attacked Duke and killed the FBI agent worked for Gerd."

"That's what we thought too, but they went rogue on that attack. What we think happened is that they were bought out by someone else, but now we'll never know. Or at least we won't learn anything from them."

"I suppose that's true of the fire as well, because they're the ones that burnt down your offices."

"That's our guess."

"It is definitely a confused mess."

"It is a mess. About the only thing we know for certain is that the attempted kidnapping with Gerd didn't work out. It may be that Gerd was working both sides of the coin as well. He may have been working with my father, while at the same time work-ing with the conglomerate that's trying to steal my father's form-ula. Now we have to find out who that other faction is that's at-tacking us."

"Do you still think it's about the cement?

"Definitely. More specifically, it's about the money this new cement technology will generate. We're not doing anything else that would create this much fuss. We're just making cement, like a million other companies throughout the United States."

"Well I don't know why you and Roger kept all this secret. If you would have cooperated with the FBI and police, we would have avoided this whole mess and found the ones trying to steal Roger's technology.

"In hindsight, I can see that would have been better. Now, how are we going to get out of here."

"I do have one more question," continued Jill. "I saw you with Franklin and Mason yesterday. You seemed like you were on friendly terms at that time. What was that all about?"

"They were trying to bribe me into being a stool pigeon for them. When I refused, they resorted to threats on me and my family. I still refused so here we are, sitting in their basement, not knowing what's going to happen next. Now you tell me the truth. Who were you following, Franklin or me?"

"I was after Franklin, but I found you instead," lied Jill.

"I think I preferred it when we were in my house watching a movie, rather than sitting here tied to a chair in who knows whose basement," stated Eric.

"I'd go for that right now as well," agreed Jill. Then the two went quiet, deep in thought.

CHAPTER TWENTY-SEVEN

More Changes

June 2020, Helena, Montana
Conference Room at the Helena Police Station
(Next Morning)

Ranel, Matthew who was Bridger's replacement while Bridger was on official leave, and Lemery wanted to keep the mole hunt a secret, but they also needed to provide an explanation for the shooting on the previous day. They decided to let the team know that they went on a mole hunt and they had found the mole. They wanted to give the impression that they had solved the mole problem hoping that if there were any other moles, they would be put at ease. They wanted any additional moles to think that the mole hunt was now concluded.

Ranel started the daily status meeting with, "I'm sure you all heard the news but just to bring everyone up to date, let me explain what happened yesterday. Bridger, Lemery, and I went on a mole hunt. The story about a meeting yesterday with an in-formant was a ruse to draw out the mole. Lemery went to the meeting point while Bridger and I hid out waiting to see who showed up. Mason showed up and shot Lemery, who was wear-ing a vest and was just grazed and who is in the hospital for another day but should be getting out this evening and will be rejoining us tomorrow. Bridger saw Mason take the shot and in turn shot him before he could get off another shot. Because of that, Bridger is now on leave until the normal FBI internal investigation is over. We probably won't see him for a couple months, and hopefully we've solved this case by then. Matthew Christ is taking his place as the FBI lead. Any questions?"

One of the agents asked, "So Mason was the mole? Was he working alone?"

"That is what we believe," answered Ranel.

Another agent stated, "It's a little unnerving to think you were watching us when we're out there trying to solve this case."

"Unfortunately, that can't be avoided," responded Ranel. "The mole has already seriously damaged our progress on this case, and we needed to get him weeded out."

The first agent remarked, "I see that Jill and Franklin aren't here again. And Franklin was Mason's partner. Which makes their absence very suspicious?"

"Except that a smart mole isn't much of a mole if he's not around to get information," suggested Ranel. "Their absence sug-gests that they're bad at being moles, or that they're not moles."

"Agreed," responded the agent. "But I have to wonder if there isn't something else going on here that we should pay attention to."

"For now, the mole hunt is over," replied Ranel.

"Excellent."

"Any other thoughts or comments?" Ranel asked.

The room was silent and Ranel dismissed the meeting. As they were departing, he asked Matthew and Lemery to wait. When they were alone, he asked, "I'd like to go to Jill's hotel room and see if we can get a clue where she might have disap-peared to. Are you interested in coming too?"

"Definitely," replied Matthew. "This mole hunt has me con-cerned, especially when the moles are in several units including the FBI."

"I don't think Jill is a mole, but I think she might have gotten caught up in the mole hunt anyway. It's very unusual for her to not be at these meetings and not to be seen around the office."

"I'm with you," responded Matthew. "Let's go over there right now and see what's going on with her. But I'm likewise con-cerned about Franklin."

"I agree," answered Ranel. "But I have a lead on Jill. I don't have anything for Franklin. And they seem to have disappeared together so checking out Jill's hotel room might give us a lead on both of them."

"Let's go."

Ranel and Matthew left the conference room and headed out to Ranel's police cruiser. They jumped in and took the short ten-minute ride to the Holiday Inn Express near the freeway. At the front desk Ranel flashed his badge and requested a key and the room number of Jill's room.

"There hasn't been anyone in that room except for the maid for the last two days. We get a daily report on anything unusual in any of the rooms and today I received the same report."

Ranel requested. "Can we also talk to the maid that has been cleaning her room?"

"I'll send her to the room, and she'll meet you there."

They went to the room, entered it, and found it sanitized and organized. The maid arrived right behind them and asked, "Did you have a question for me?"

Ranel asked, "Are you the person that has been taking care of this room for the last couple days?"

"Yes."

"When was the last time that someone used this room?"

"Two days ago. No one has slept in here for the last two nights. Each morning the room is in exactly the same condition as I left it the previous day."

Matthew jumped in, "When you cleaned the room was there any sign of a struggle? Anything unusual or out of place?"

"No. Jill, I know her name because I talked to her when she was moving into the hotel room, is very organized and clean."

"Any signs of a visitor, or someone spending the night with her?" Matthew continued.

"Nothing like that. I saw her come up in the middle of the day and she said she needed to check her computer, but she only stayed a few minutes and then she took off again in a rush."

There was a silent moment and then Ranel said, "Well, I guess we don't have any additional questions for you right now. We'll call you if anything else comes up." Then he handed her a card and said, "If you think of anything else, please call."

"Will do," replied the maid as she departed.

Ranel and Matthew turned their attention to the room. Matthew went directly to the computer and opened it up while Ranel searched the drawers and under the bed.

Matthew spoke up, "Well that was easy. She still uses the same password that the police techies use when they set up a computer. I went right in." He looked around in the computer for a little while and then he said, "Come here. You need to see this."

Ranel looked over Matthew's shoulder at the computer screen and asked, "What did you find?"

"She's been tracking several people. It looks like Eric, Roger, Franklin, Bridger, and a couple others are being tracked."

Ranel suggested, "She must have been suspicious about their movements. Something must not have seemed right to her. I wouldn't be surprised if her efforts got her in trouble somehow."

"She should not have been going out on her own like this. But then again, we're the ones that kicked her out of the investi-gation. I guess she felt forced to go out on her own."

"Can we go back to yesterday, when we had the shoot-out?"

Matthew cycled back on the timeline of the computer and found Bridger and Franklin's cars. Bridger was there for a longer period of time, but Franklin drove up to Bridger's vehicle, stayed there for just a few minutes, and then took off. Expanding the timeline, they were able to see Franklin's car spending the last couple days at a cabin up in the forest south of Helena.

"Cycle back another day," requested Ranel.

They found that Eric's vehicle had not moved for the last two days. They also found that Franklin and Eric's cars were in the same place, about two days earlier, and the Franklin's car departed but Eric's car hadn't moved.

"Everything seems to revolve around this cabin in the woods," suggested Matthew. "I think we need to go up there and check it out. Let's write down the coordinates and head up there."

"Should we have backup?"

"We should, but then we also have a mole, and I'd hate to give Franklin and whoever else is up there a chance to get away before we get there. Let's just have a look around for now. Then, if we feel like we need to strike, then we can call in the troops."

"Good enough," replied Ranel. "We'll do this your way. I just don't want the two of us to end up being victims as well. Let's be careful and play it safe. No cowboying."

"I agree. But let's hurry and get going."

"Do we report that Jill was illegally tracking these individuals without a search warrant?"

"I don't know how we can since we were also illegally snooping around in her hotel room and on her computer without a search warrant. I think we can't ever admit to being here, or we'll make more trouble for ourselves than we will for her."

"Then how do we explain how we found Franklin's loca-tion?" asked Ranel.

"We don't."

"I'm going to write it out on a sheet of paper, and claim we found it in Mason's pocket," explained Ranel. "That's something no one will ever be able to refute now that Mason's dead."

"Wow," exclaimed Matthew. "You can be pretty sneaky when you want to be, can't you."

"I'm just trying to avoid unnecessary problems."

"I'll go for that."

They wrote down the information specifying Franklin's location and took off, heading for the hills south of Helena.

CHAPTER TWENTY-EIGHT

Franklin's Hideout

June 2020, Helena, Montana
Franklin's Cabin

Eric and Jill were still tied up in the basement of the cabin, waiting to learn what their captor's intentions were. "I don't know what they want from us," stressed Jill. "It's not like we know anything. We don't have any answers or any useful information. And expecting to get ransom for us is also ridicu-lous, especially in my case."

"My family isn't rich either," added Eric. "We barely scrape by some months. Everybody thinks we have it made with this big gravel pit we own, but that's not how it works. There's a lot of debt involved that we have to pay on every month."

"Then what are they after?"

Just then they heard the basement door open and footsteps coming down the stairs. Eric yelled out, "Are you coming down to rescue us?"

"Not really," came back Franklin's voice.

Franklin walked towards Eric and Jill and then just stared for about five minutes. Eric finally spoke up, "Let us out of here. We don't even know anything."

Franklin then commented, "I'm going to interrogate the two of you. I'm going to take Jill first."

This brought an immediate chill down Jill's spine, and Eric could see her fear, so he spoke up, "Take me first. Jill has gone through too much."

"No," responded Franklin. "Jill goes first."

"Where are you taking me you piece of crap?" questioned Jill.

"Upstairs," replied Franklin.

Eric could sense that Franklin had more than interrogation planned, and he could see that Jill had the same concern. Eric blurted out, "Leave Jill alone you pervert. Are you so hard up that you can't find a girl willing to have sex with you that you have to force it? Haven't you done enough damage to her. She doesn't deserve you brutalizing her any more you piece of crap."

"How's it your business? She moved out of your place. She's not interested in you. It's you that needs to leave her alone."

Eric was now convinced of Franklin's intentions and angrily yelled out, "I warn you; you better leave her alone."

"Or what?" questioned Franklin.

"You're not going to get away with this."

Franklin proceeded to loosen the zip ties that had Jill fastened to the chair, but he left her hands tied together. Then he put his hand in her armpit from behind and lifted her up out of the chair. He moved her in front of Eric and, standing behind her he reached around and grabbed her two breasts and said to Eric, "Wow, that feels nice." Then challenging Eric, he said, "What are you going to do about it?"

Eric could see that yelling at Franklin hadn't helped. He decided to keep quiet. He felt sick that he couldn't help Jill.

"That's what I thought," edged Franklin. "All talk and no action."

"I'm not done with you yet," stressed Eric, wishing he had the baseball bat.

Jill started screaming, causing Franklin to slap her across the face with the back of his hand and yell, "Shut your mouth. What did you think was going to happen if you're snooping around and following me? You know you want me."

Jill, through her tears, swore at him and said, "You're an evil, cruel, brutal, man. I can't understand how someone like you can feel good about themselves. How can you look yourself in the mirror every morning and feel good about yourself?"

"Don't worry about me," responded Franklin. "I plan on feeling really good."

June 2020, Helena, Montana
Franklin's Cabin Where Eric and Jill Are Prisoners

Matthew and Ranel drove an unmarked police car directly to the location where Jill's computer had tracked Franklin's car. Initially they drove past it and saw that his car was indeed parked at that location. Then they found a convenient place to park their vehicle, along an old logging road, where it wouldn't be seen. Next, on foot, they worked their way around toward the house, Ranel going through the forest and heading toward the back, and Matthew across the road and sneaking through the trees in the front. They used text messaging to communicate, with their phones on silent. Then the waiting game started.

"I think I heard a scream," texted Ranel.

"Did it sound like Jill?" texted Matthew.

"I'm not sure but it could have been."

"Can you get in any closer? Maybe you can see something."

"I'm trying to figure out how many people are in the house, and I'm only counting two. I see one that I don't recognize through the kitchen window. And he is talking to someone so there must be at least one other person," responded Ranel. After a few minutes he texted again saying, "I just saw Franklin dragging Jill through the dining room and back into what must be a bed-room. It doesn't look good."

"I'm going to call in for backup. Then let's go in."

"I agree. Quickly!"

"Here's how we'll play it," suggested Matthew. "I'm going to ring the front doorbell. When you see the guy in the kitchen heading for the front door, you break in through the back. I'll meet you somewhere in the middle."

"Do it," instructed Ranel. He watched the guy in the kitchen, and then noticed him turning around and walking off. Ranel assumed this was the signal and headed for the back glass sliding door. But just then he saw Franklin, charging back into the dining room holding a gun. Somehow, he was tipped off; probably because Matthew called in for backup. He felt he should text a warning to Matthew, but he knew it was too late.

Ranel knew he needed to react. He took a shot and hit Franklin in the upper leg.

Franklin stumbled to the ground, but not before he turned and fired a shot back at Ranel. The shot went wild, because Franklin wasn't able to take a good stance, and then he hit the ground.

Ranel took a couple more shots into the glass, shattering it. Franklin was about to regain his composure as he lay on the floor. He reached for his pistol and was about to take another shot at Ranel. But Ranel was too quick and stomped on the arm holding the gun, breaking a couple fingers in the process. He took away the pistol, checked Franklin's leg for a backup pistol, and took that away as well.

In marched Matthew, holding a gun to the back of the head of Franklin's partner, Is anyone else in this house?" questioned Matthew.

The partner refused to answer. Matthew repeated the question. Still no answer. Matthew hit the man in the back of the head with the butt of his pistol and repeated the question a third time. Still no response. Matthew hit him again, but this time it was hard enough to send the man to the ground, unconscious.

Off in the distance, sirens could be heard. Ranel instructed, "You tie these guys up while I search the house."

"Will do," responded Matthew, and he pulled out some zip ties and tied up their hands and legs.

Ranel went toward the back of the house where he had seen Franklin pulling Jill. He went into one of the bedrooms. Jill was lying face-down on the bed; the back of her pants had a cut down the seam. It was obvious what Franklin had intended, but luckily, they arrived just in time.

Ranel helped Jill up and untied her. "Boy am I glad to see you," she commented. "How did you find me?"

"We invaded your hotel room and found a tracking system. But I won't tell anyone about it if you don't. It saved your life. So as far as I'm concerned, I didn't see anything. Tell me why you decided to track Franklin. You must have had some suspicions."

"He sounded too much like the rapist, and he always seemed to be in the wrong place at the wrong time. You saved my life," answered Jill.

"Well we saved you from getting raped again, anyway."

"No, you saved Eric and my life. We knew who they were, and they would not have let us get away. We knew we were dead. It was just a matter of time."

"Are you saying Eric is here too?"

"Yes. He's tied up and in the basement."

The two headed down to the basement. At this point the backup had arrived and they were starting to help Franklin and his companion out to the police cruiser."

Jill and Ranel went down into the basement and freed Eric.

Ranel instructed one of the cops, "Give Eric a ride home."

"Or maybe you can drop me off at my car," Eric suggested.

"Will do," responded one of the patrol officers.

When Jill, Ranel, and Matthew were finally alone in Frank-lin's house, Ranel spoke up, "You realize we still have a mole to deal with."

"Are you sure?" challenged Matthew.

"I'm positive. Franklin came running out of the bedroom, pistol at ready, the minute you rang that doorbell. He knew you had called for backup. His informant had let him know immed-iately after you made the call."

"It should be easy to figure out who called him," suggested Jill. "Get his phone and check the recent calls or messages."

Matthew ran out the front door to retrieve the phone.

At the car Matthew demanded Franklin give him his phone. The officer in the car said, "We already have it here. It's standard procedure to make sure their pockets are empty before we put them in the car." He handed the phone to Matthew, who walked back into the house to talk to Jill and Ranel.

"What do you see?" asked Ranel.

"I see the phone message that warned him about the raid on his place, but the number isn't identified, so I don't know who it is."

"Call it," said Jill.

Matthew called the number. It rang several times, and then finally it was picked up. The person answering the call said, "Hello Franklin! Did you get away safely?"

Matthew immediately hung up the phone. He turned toward Jill and Ranel and said, "I know who that is. I recognized the voice immediately."

"No doubt?" asked Ranel.

"No doubt whatsoever. I'd recognize that accent anywhere."

CHAPTER TWENTY-NINE

Betrayal

June 2020, Helena, Montana
Police Station, Duke's Office

Jill, Matthew, Lemery, and Ranel were meeting in Duke's office. Duke was still in the hospital and Bridger was still on leave. Matthew represented the FBI, Jill and Lemery the local Helena detectives, and Ranel the Montana state police. Jill started the conversation with, "Lemery, it's great to see you back. I didn't expect you to get released from the hospital so soon. Are you doing OK?"

"I'm doing OK. I ache and I'm on pain meds, but I don't want to lose contact with this case, so I felt the need to get back here as quickly as possible, even if it's only for part of the day. Why are we not meeting with the rest of the team?"

Matthew jumped in, "We need to discuss where we stand on this case, but the possibility of another mole still exists, and we need to decide amongst us how much we should share with the over-all team. Jill has received a significant update from Eric when they were both captives in Franklin's house. Apparently, Roger has been working on a leading-edge cement product that will revolutionize the cement industry and several organizations are trying to either stop his efforts thereby not damaging their incomes or steal his efforts and use them. In an attempt to hide his efforts and drop out of existence, he organized a staged kidnapping with Gerd. But that went horribly wrong and the deaths of Bud, Joe, and Fred, were the result of failed kidnapping attempts."

"That's crazy," stressed Lemery. "We have three deaths caused by a failed fake kidnapping. Are these guys idiots? But then why was Gerd killed?"

Jill jumped in, "According to Eric's theory, he was either in the way of some bigger attempt to steal Roger's formula, or he was executed because of his failures in the attempted kidnap-pings. Someone wasn't happy with his performance. Eric wasn't completely sure why he was killed, but he suspects some larger entity was behind it."

Matthew continued, "Apparently the original problem, of organizations attempting to steal Roger's research, still exists. Eric thinks that these organizations caused a lot of the deaths since then, including the burning of the Falcon offices. Eric expects Roger to go into hiding. In fact, he may have already done that."

Lemery asked again, "So why all the secrecy? Why are we keeping this from the rest of the team?"

Ranel explained, "Because we're confident that we still have a mole in this team. And we may have more than one. Your efforts in the mole hunt didn't put an end to it and our efforts at the Franklin cabin didn't stop it. Matthew called the number that Franklin had been communicating with and he immediately recognized the voice. But we don't want to just get the one individual. We want to trail him and see what other connections he has. We need to get rid of all the moles if possible."

Lemery asked, "Have we questioned Franklin or the other guy that was out in the Franklin cabin?"

Matthew answered, "Both of them have been uncooperative in giving us any new information. Franklin is being tight lipped, and the other guy doesn't know much. He was obviously just a hired hand."

Ranel jumped in, "Here is what I recommend. We tail our mole and try to find out more from him. And we tail Roger and Eric and see what we can learn. For the Falcons this would be as much a protection detail as anything. I'm guessing we should be expecting more attacks on the Falcons, and if we keep close tabs, we may catch someone in the act. Also, I'm sure Eric knows more than what he told Jill. It would be good to bring him in for additional questioning."

Matthew added, "In many respects, this feels like we're starting over. We thought we were working on a couple of simple murder cases, and now we learn that we're working on a national, and possibly international, conspiracy. And this conspiracy involves numerous organizations beyond the reaches of Montana."

Lemery agreed, "Yes. The scope of this case has increased dramatically. But are you going to tell us who this voice is that you recognized? Who is the mole that we're going to follow?"

Matthew continued, "It's curious that he didn't show up today. I think he may be on the run already. But we need to track his cell phone and review all his communications. We may be able to find out who he is working for."

Lemery asked again, "Who is it?"

"Our Australian, Brendt George," answered Matthew.

"You're kidding me," exclaimed Lemery. "You're telling me that one of the state troopers is caught up in this?"

"Did you think it was only going to be the FBI or the local detectives?" asked Matthew.

"I'm just surprised that they got to him," exclaimed Ranel. "Unbelievable. And you say he did not show up today?"

"Yes. Have you seen him around? I see his partner, but I don't see Brendt," suggested Matthew.

"Nope," answered Ranel. "He is definitely missing. And now you see why we need to keep this mole hunt a secret to just the few of us in this room. I'm going to take on the tracking of Brendt through his phone contacts, and I'm going to pull his partner in for an intensive interview. I feel like he is my responsi-bility and that this is a failure in my office."

Matthew responded, "This is a failure for all of us. I think we should do the interview as a team. But I agree that we should track down Brendt's phone communications first. My only con-cern with that is that he may have a second phone that he used for his clandestine work, which is different from his police phone."

Ranel jumped in, "The number I called, when I recognized his voice, was a throw-away phone. It wasn't his police phone. He probably destroyed that phone already, but we can still research his phone calling history."

"I'll leave it to you," responded Matthew. "Just let me know when you're ready to do the interview, because I want to be involved in that."

"Definitely," answered Ranel.

June 2020, Helena, Montana
Warehouse in North Helena

Roger was in his lab working with one of his lab technicians. "How's it going?"

Chase Mitton, the techie, responded, "We had a test today. We are really close. We're just inches away from Aztec gold. The formula for their cement is golden."

"I agree. Can you imagine a cement which doesn't decay for thousands of years? This will be incredible if we can figure it out. What makes you think you're close?"

"The hardness and chemical decomposition are close to the samples you had smuggled in from Mexico. I think we have the basic ingredients correct. We just need to get the correct mixture and we'll have it. And that's going to take a lot of trial and error."

"Well, I have a problem," inserted Roger. "I have guys fol-lowing me all the time. And as you know, my offices have been shot up and burned down. I think we need to get out of here. I think we're getting too close and the guys that are after us are sen-sing it, and they're going to get braver."

"What do you have in mind?" asked Chase.

"I've set up another place for us to do our work, but it's going to require us to go dark. I'm not going to say anything about it in case this place is bugged."

"But if it is bugged, the bad guys now know we're leaving, and they'll come charging in. We have to leave immediately."

"OK, grab what you need and let's go."

"That will be easy. The ingredients that I need are very basic. It will only take me a few minutes."

"Don't leave anything written behind," instructed Roger.

"No worries about that."

Roger wrote a note, so that any listening devices would not be able to hear his plan. The note read, "Don't take any more than you need. Keep the formula in your head. I have a motorcycle stashed behind the building in a storage shed and we'll use that to get away. They won't be expecting that. And then we'll set the place on fire. That will keep everyone distracted and busy as we run for it. Don't take any phones or anything else that's trace-able."

Chase gave Roger the okay sign and a nod for agreement. Chase prepared a small lunch box sized box of materials that he needed to take with, packed it into a backpack, and was ready to go. Roger started a small fire on the back wall of the building, and as the blaze started creeping up the back wall, the two of them snuck out the back side of the warehouse, pulled the motorcycle out of the storage shed, put on their helmets and riding jackets, and rode off in a direction away from the warehouse and out on an old abandoned horse trail. After about a half hour they were able to join a main road, which they used to get them to the freeway. They hopped on the I-15 freeway and headed north out of Helena in the direction of Great Falls.

June 2020, Helena, Montana
Hospital, Judy's Room

Eric had come to visit his mother Judy. They were casually sitting in her hospital room, Judy sitting up in bed and Eric in a chair next to the bed. "How are you doing today?" questioned Eric.

"Great," Judy replied. "I'm anxious to get out of here. I think the only reason I'm still here is so that the police can keep an eye on me."

"How's the bullet wound?"

"My shoulder is doing fine." Judy waved her arm up in a circular motion to demonstrate that she was fully flexible. "It hurts, but it's usable. But what I want to know is, what's going on?"

"Dad has gone dark," responded Eric.

"I expected that. He would visit me twice a day and for the last day he didn't visit, and he didn't even call. Why?"

"I suspect it was because I was kidnapped and held hostage for a few days," answered Eric.

"What!!! So that's why I didn't see you for a couple days too. Tell me about it."

Eric explained his capture and how Jill was also captured and held prisoner. Then he explained how they were rescued.

"Well I'm sure glad you're safe. I'm glad I didn't know about it or it would have caused me a lot of stress."

Just then a text came into Eric's phone. Eric glanced at the text and immediately turned pale. Judy could see that Eric was upset about the text he had received and asked, "What the matter? What's going on?"

"Lizzy has been kidnapped," Eric responded, almost in a whisper. "And they're demanding that Roger turn over his work if we want her back." Lizzy was Roger's sister who was in college in Missoula, Montana.

"Do we have any way of getting ahold of Roger?"

"No," responded an exasperated Eric. "He intentionally left his phone at home so we couldn't trace him."

"But you know where the lab is located right?"

"Yes, but part of his plan for going dark was that he would move the lab. I'll go there immediately to see if there are any clues."

"You're taking me with you," demanded Judy. "If we don't find anything at the lab, we're heading directly to Missoula to see if we can find any clues there that will lead us to Lizzy. They're using your phone to make contact and we'll keep that active in case there are any future messages."

"I'd like to bring Jill in on this," requested Eric. "She seems like someone that can be trusted, and she may be able to help."

"Just because you played house with her doesn't mean that she can be trusted," responded Judy.

"Actually, we talked a lot when we were being held hostage and we shared a lot of information during that time. I think she might be able to help."

"Can we limit police involvement to only her?" requested Judy. "Like you mentioned earlier, there are obviously dirty police are also involved in this mess and we don't need to be be-trayed."

"I'll talk to her and see if she's willing to work with us under those terms."

"Either way, I'm out of here and we're heading to Missoula."

"After we check the lab," demanded Eric.

"Yes," replied Judy.

CHAPTER THIRTY

Lizzy

June 2020, Helena, Montana
Office Complex Near the Capital of Helena
(A Few Hours Earlier)

Venicia was indignant, "What do you mean you had to kill Gerd? Are you intentionally trying to draw attention to us? I know we were just using Gerd, but to kill him means his father is going to be gunning for us." Venicia repre-sented the interests of Intercontinental Cement. She was a private contractor asked to "acquire" Roger's formula "at any cost." And she took the assignment literally, interpreting the "any cost" com-ment to include not just money but any other expense that might arise, including murder.

"Sorry, but it seemed necessary at the time," responded Pab-lo. "He was completely off track and everything he did was a screwup."

Venicia continued, "What do you know about Roger's exper-iments? Have we intimidated him enough to tell us anything?"

"At this point Roger has gone into hiding. We're not sure where he is."

"I thought you had him tailed and had tracking equipment attached to his car."

"He ran off into the back country on a motorcycle, which we didn't know existed. There was no way for us to follow him in our car," responded Pablo.

Venicia paused for a frustrated few seconds and then said, "What are our options?"

"I recommend kidnapping one of their kids."

"You mean you want to repeat the fiasco that you encoun-tered when you kidnapped Eric?"

"Eric was guarded closely by the police. But they've forgotten about the daughter who is attending school in Missoula. I think we should kidnap their daughter Lizzy."

Venicia continued, "But how do we get the message to Roger?"

Pablo responded, "We get the message to his son and wife. We let them figure it out. We make it their problem."

"I like it. Go ahead with it."

The phone call was disconnected, and Pablo explained the plan to Ricardo and Karl, his two remaining companions. "What are we going to do?" asked Ricardo.

"We're going to drive to Missoula, figure out where Lizzy lives, and wait for an opportunity to grab her."

"Then what?" asked Karl.

"We'll drive out of town, find a remote house, and hold her there. Then we let the family know we have her and what our conditions are for her return."

"Let's do it," inserted Ricardo.

The three of them jumped into their van and drove off, on a two-hour drive over the mountain to Missoula. It didn't take long for them to learn where Lizzy lived, using the university's direct-ory. They downloaded a picture of her so they would be able to identify her when they saw her. They located her dorm and waited outside for her.

They ended up waiting about three hours before they saw her coming in their direction, toward the student apartment complex.

"Isn't that her?" questioned Karl who spotted her first.

"I think you're right. I think that's her coming our way," answered Ricardo. "She's hot."

"Keep your mind on the plan," scolded Pablo.

They continued to wait in their van until she got close. Then, when she was walking past the van Ricardo and Pablo jumped out through the side door of the van. Ricardo grabbed her around the waist and her books went flying. She started kicking and scratching at anything she could find. She also screamed, and several individuals heard her and started running in her direction in order to help.

Pablo grabbed her feet and the two of them quickly threw her into the van. They didn't even have the van door shut when Karl started driving off, hoping to avoid a confrontation with any of her would-be rescuers. He successfully escaped any confrontation and raced to the exit of the university as Pablo struggled to shut the van's sliding door.

In the meantime, Lizzy had managed to place a strong and solid kick to Ricardo's groin area causing him to reel with pain. She started to get up, but Pablo came to Ricardo's aid, giving Liz-zy a strong and violent punch to the stomach, causing her to lose her breath and collapse to the floor of the van. As she lay curled up on the ground, Ricardo, angry over being kicked, stood up and kicked her several times on the buttocks, back and head, hoping to inflict some pain of his own.

As she lay there, Pablo grabbed some zip ties and tied her hands behind her back and tied her two feet together. But Lizzy wasn't ready to give up. She rolled over on her back and, with her feet tied, continued to kick out at Pablo and Ricardo. She knocked Pablo over, causing him to stumble and fall, and a well planted kick on Ricardo's side caused him to crash into the driver. The van swerved back and forth several times before Karl was able to take control of it again and continue the drive.

Pablo was angry, and he violently punched Lizzy on the chin, causing her to temporarily black out. While she was out, he pulled her over to the side of the van and zip tied her hands to one of the van's side braces. He used duct tape to cover her screams. When she came too, she realized that she had been defeated. Lizzy was sore and uncomfortable, especially being bounced around on the steel floor of the van as it raced down the freeway.

Karl drove the van quickly but cautiously away from the university and through Missoula, avoiding any police attention. He hopped on the Interstate heading east, but didn't stay on it very long, knowing there would be an All-Points Bulletin placed on the van at any moment. He took Exit 126 and headed south on Rock Creek Road working his way through the Lolo National Forest. He drove East toward Highway 1, and then headed north toward Hall, where he turned left and started his search for a small farm. They found one that was set back off of the highway, which they decided was perfect, and pulled into the driveway.

Ricardo and Karl stepped out of the van and headed to the house. They knocked on the door, and soon a woman answered with, "Hello. What can I do for you? Are you lost?"

Karl spoke up with, "We're here to warn you about a danger to the local water supply. Is your husband available?"

"He's out in the fields," was her reply. "What's supposed to be wrong with the water? We have our own well and the water seems fine."

"Do you have any children in the house?" asked Ricardo.

"Just the baby," answered the woman, and then quickly realized that it was the wrong answer, as Ricardo pulled out a gun and aimed it at her.

"Please step back in the house," commanded Ricardo.

"What do you want?" asked the woman.

"Nothing from you. Just a place to hide out for a few days," responded Ricardo. After a moment he said, "Actually, I could use a paper bag."

Ricardo entered the house, behind the woman, and followed her. She was speechless. One minute later the lady returned with the bag which she handed to Karl. Ricardo was still behind her.

Karl returned to the van where he helped Pablo pull Lizzy out of the van, this time with a bag over her head so she couldn't see what was happening and so she couldn't attack. Pablo unceremoniously drug her into the house and pushed her down on a recliner in the living room.

The lady of the house had regained her voice and asked again, "What do you want? What are you doing with that girl?"

Ricardo turned to her and said, "It's none of your business and unless you want to end up tied up like her, don't do anything stupid."

Just then Lizzy, who had partially worked the duct tape off of her mouth by rubbing it against the shield that was over her head and realizing that there was someone else in the room, yelled out, "They've kidnapped me. Please help me if you can."

Pablo, who had become frustrated with Lizzy at this point, backhanded her across the face, disregarding the bag that was over her head.

Lizzy yelled out again, "I think you broke my nose you pervert. Leave me alone before I smash your balls to raisins."

Pablo pulled the bag off her head in order to take a look, but soon realized his mistake when she jumped up and started trying to head-butt him. He pushed her back onto the recliner and returned the bag over her head saying, "You better stop that, or you really will end up with a broken nose."

Pablo said, "I'm going to go out to the van and make a phone call." Ricardo and Karl knew that the phone call was for the ransom. The prize being Roger's research.

After the phone call, Pablo returned, and they all sat and waited. Earlier, they were told to turn off all their phones and removed the batteries, including Lizzy's, so they could not be traced. They were reluctant to destroy the phones in case they needed to check the contacts at some future time. They threw a movie into the DVD player and waited.

"How long are we going to sit around here?" asked Karl.

"I'm going to call back in the morning," responded Pablo. "Then we'll see what we do next."

The husband came home from the fields around 8:00 PM and was immediately confronted and zip-tied. Everyone was forc-ed to sleep together in the living room that night, with Pablo, Karl, and Ricardo taking turns keeping watch. When morning came around, Pablo went out to check his phone messages and soon returned with nothing to report.

They continued sitting around the living room for another four hours, when Pablo went out again to check for messages. This time there was a message, and it was from a contact in the Missoula police department informing him that he had been located and that there were cops on their way to his location. Pablo ran back into the house and yelled, "We have to get going. The cops are on their way."

"How did they find us?" asked Ricardo.

"Don't know. All I know is that we need to get out of here fast."

"What do we do with these guys?" asked Karl, pointing at the farmer and his wife.

"Forget them and let's get going."

They grabbed Lizzy, ran to the van, pushed her in and jumped in themselves, and were off.

CHAPTER THIRTY-ONE

Missoula

June 2020, Helena, Montana

Eric was driving with Judy in the passenger seat. They raced from the hospital toward the warehouse which Roger was using for a lab. During the drive, Eric placed a call to Jill. "Hello," Jill answered.

"This is Eric. I was wondering if we could meet somewhere so we could talk. I have a proposal I want to make."

"Proposal? Boy you move fast. I don't think I'm ready for that."

"Not that type of proposal. I want to see if we can work together to solve a problem that I encountered."

"Where do you want to meet?" asked Jill.

"At Roger's lab. I'm sure you already know where that is."

"Actually, I'm there right now. The place is on fire. Do you know anything about that?"

"No. Is anybody hurt?" asked Eric.

"We think it was completely empty at the time, but the fire boys are convinced that it was arson, starting in the back of the building. Would Roger have burnt the place down?"

"No! That would have been crazy. I don't know anything about it. We were just heading there because we were looking for him. But I guess you're saying he's not there."

"Is it possible that he rode off in a motorcycle?" asked Jill.

"I have no idea," responded Eric. "We're almost there. We can talk more when I get there."

"Who's we?"

"I'm with Judy, my mom."

"Is she already out of the hospital?"

"Yes and no. I'll explain when I get there."

"Okay. See you soon."

It was about ten minutes later when Judy and Eric pulled up to see fire trucks and police surrounding the remains of the warehouse where Roger had been doing his lab experiments on cement. Jill immediately came walking over and greeted them as they climbed out of the vehicle. Eric asked, "Why did you ask about a motorcycle?"

Jill responded, "Because we see fresh motorcycle tracks leaving from the back side of the building. We wondered if that was his since his car is still parked out in front of the building."

Judy answered, "He's gone dark on us and that would probably have been his plan for escape all along."

Jill asked, "What do you mean he's gone dark?"

"I just mean we can't communicate with him anymore. He would have left all traceable instruments behind, like phones or GPS systems."

Jill asked, "So you have no way of communicating and you don't know where he is?"

"Correct," responded Eric. "He felt that we would be safer if we didn't know what he was doing or where he was doing it."

"Is he alone?" asked Jill.

Judy responded, "He probably took Chase, his lab techni-cian. Chase isn't married and doesn't have a family to worry about and that's one of the reasons Roger liked working with him. They could work together late into the night. Roger and Chase probably snuck off together on Roger's motorcycle."

Jill requested, "Can I get Chase's full name, and his phone number, so I can trace them. Also, can I get Roger's motorcycle plate number, so I can put out an All-Points Bulletin and have police throughout the state watch for him."

"No," replied Judy. "Finding Roger would just put him in danger. He isn't wanted for any crimes."

Jill answered, "He burnt down the building, didn't he?"

Eric jumped in, "That hasn't been proven. That's just speculation. Give him a day before you put out the APB. He deserves at least that much. He's running away to stay safe, not because he's on a crime spree."

"Agreed," said Jill. "Now you have to tell me what you were talking about when you said you had a proposal for me."

"I need this kept in confidence," said Eric.

"If it involves a crime or the investigation of a crime, I can't legally stay quiet. Sorry," apologized Jill.

Eric looked at Judy to see her reaction. She nodded and said, "Go ahead."

Eric continued, "My sister has been kidnapped." He handed his phone over to Jill so she could read the text message.

Jill responded, "Unfortunately kidnappings go immediately to the FBI. Luckily, we have FBI agents working with us already."

"I know you're having internal issues though, like the FBI agent that kidnapped both of us a few days ago, so I'd like to in-volve as few people as possible in this. If your mole learned you were involved it might hurt my sister's chances of survival," ex-plained Eric.

"Luckily, I know an FBI agent who is trustworthy. He's on leave now for shooting one of his own agents who was acting as a mole, so I know he's clean. Do you remember Bridger?"

Eric answered, "Yes I remember him. Can we keep this information between the four of us and not involve anyone else on the team?"

"Let me talk to Bridger and see what he suggests."

Jill proceeded to dial the phone and was soon connected with Bridger. She explained the situation to him and asked him for his recommendation. She explained the need for secrecy, because the family was concerned about a mole in the police department possibly putting Lizzy at risk. Jill said, "Thank you," and disconnected the phone call.

"Here's the situation," she explained to Eric and Judy. "Bridger understands the situation and has agreed to work with us. He is going to meet us in Missoula and the four of us are going to work together. He is officially on leave, so anything he does is unofficial, but his experience with kidnapping cases will be a great benefit in helping us find Lizzy. This is a very unusual situation, where we are working with the police, but at the same time not trusting the police. But I'm not sure how it could be helped."

"Can we leave immediately for Missoula?" asked an anxious Judy.

"I'm going to tell my counterparts that I have to go with you for a little while to investigate something that you want me to see, and then we can leave," explained Jill.

While they were waiting Eric gave Lizzy's phone number another try, but it immediately dropped off indicating that the phone was turned off. Then Judy suggested, "What about trying her work phone. She has a second phone and maybe the kidnappers don't know about that phone."

"But if we call it, then they'll hear it and they will know about it," suggested Eric. "Let's ask Jill if there is a way to trace these phones. Maybe we can learn something before we give away our secret about a second phone."

Jill was quick to return and Eric asked, "Can Lizzy's phones be traced?"

"Let's try," she responded. "It would be stupid of us to not use this opportunity to trace her phones if they are still active. You start driving and I'll make a few phone calls."

Eric jumped into the driver's seat with Judy in the passenger seat and Jill in the back. Jill immediately started making calls, giving Lizzy's two phone numbers for tracing. Then she informed Eric and Judy, "They'll call me back if they find anything."

The drive to Missoula would take them across the mountains on Highway 12, and then on Interstate 90 west. The travel time would be about two hours. They were one and one-half hours into their drive when Jill received a call. After the call she explain-ed, "They found the work phone to be active and they triangulat-ed the location of the call, even though it was difficult because it's up in the mountains south of Missoula. We're closer to their location than the Missoula police, who are also heading down there. We need to take the Drummond exit and head south on Highway 1 until we get to the small town of Hall, where we take a right turn. They're at a small farm building near the end of the road, which is close to the foot of the mountains."

"Excellent," said Eric. "We're about five miles from the Drummond exit. I hope to hell we aren't too late!"

"Don't get too excited," warned Jill. "This may just be the loc-ation where they found out about the phone and got rid of it. But since the phone is still active, there's a good chance that we'll find them there. I'll let Bridger know what we're up to. He was plan-ning to catch up with us in Missoula. I'll have him come down here to where we are."

All three received an adrenaline rush, thinking that they might be able to rescue Lizzy. Jill got back on the phone and asked more questions about the specific location of the farm buildings. She also received a warning that they were not to approach the building until the remainder of the SWAT team arrived. She was told to let the professionals do their job and not put everyone in danger. She passed the message on to Eric and Judy. They didn't care. They were going to save their daughter and sister with or without the police.

They took the turn south at the Drummond exit and drove to Hall where they turned right towards the mountains. Jill placed another call, hoping to get details about the location of the work cell phone, but the police agent at the other end refused to give her any additional information. He explained that he was ordered not to allow Jill, Judy, and Eric to get there before the police.

Eventually they arrived at a T in the road where they had to turn either left or right. "Let's turn around and head back," suggested Judy. "If we go slow, we may spot something that gives us a clue where she might be."

Eric started to maneuver the car around but just then a car came rushing past them and turned left at the T heading south. "Lizzy was in the back seat of that car!" screamed Judy. "I just saw her. Follow that car!"

Eric quickly began following the vehicle. "Guess we didn't avoid the police mole after all," grumped a discouraged Eric.

"That's exactly what I was thinking," responded Jill.

"Do you think Bridger is our mole?" asked Judy.

"No. I think someone in the Missoula police station gave us away," replied Jill.

"Then let's keep them out of this," answered Eric. "Let's not tell them we are going off in a different direction."

"What about Bridger?" asked Jill.

"Go ahead and tell him. If we still see that they're getting information then we'll know that he was the mole," replied Eric.

Jill placed a call to Bridger, letting them know that they were now chasing a suspect vehicle, and that they thought that some-one in the Missoula police station tipped them off. After Jill got off the phone she commented, "Bridger is coming here using back roads, but he is still about thirty minutes behind us."

Eric was cautious in following the suspect vehicle. He would occasionally drop back, and then speed up. There weren't a lot of turn offs so there would be no reason for the driver of the vehicle in front of him to become suspicious.

It wasn't long before the road veered right, again towards the mountains. They crossed a riverbed, and the road took a quick right turn followed by a left turn. This is where the suspect vehicle exited the road, heading north toward a farmhouse that could be seen in the distance. Eric drove on past the driveway and searched for a place where he could park the car. Unfortunately, there was nothing but wide-open fields on either side of the road, so he just gave up and parked the car on the side of the road and hop-ed that no one would find it suspicious.

Jill sent a message to Bridger, letting him know where they were, but warned him not to inform the Missoula police. She mentioned that she had concerns about them leaking informa-tion after they saw Lizzy being rushed away from the previous hideout. Bridger confirmed that he understood and that he was still about a half hour behind them, but that he would put out his flashing light until he came closer so he could rush to catch up with them.

CHAPTER THIRTY-TWO

Roger

June 2020, East Glacier, Montana
Warehouse

Roger and his lab assistant used Interstate 15 north to get out of the Helena area but didn't stay on the freeway long. At Wolf Creek they exited onto Highway 287 to Choteau, where they jumped on Highway 89 and rode it all the way to Browning, on the northern edge of Montana. From there they took Highway 2 to East Glacier, Montana, which was on the Blackfoot Indian Reservation. The trip took about four hours in total, through a series of isolated farms and wheat fields. It was a pretty drive, with the mountains lining the west side of the corri-dor, but it became tiresome after the first couple hours.

During one of the breaks Chase, the lab technician, asked, "Where are we going?"

"I own a small warehouse on the Blackfoot Indian Reserva-tion, and we can work there undisturbed. No one will know we're there. Being on the reservation makes it difficult for the police to come in and investigate," responded Roger. "I hope you don't mind the distance or the drive."

"I don't mind either of those, but I get tired of being splat-tered with bugs."

"I'm with you there."

In East Glacier they drove under the railroad tracks and past the large lodge on the left. They made a right turn off the main road, went one block and turned left. They arrived at Roger's warehouse, where Roger pushed a garage door opener and drove into the garage. Roger shut the garage door and fired up the heater. Turning to Chase he said, "There is a small cabin attached to this garage. There's a kitchen, bath, and bed. There's also a TV with some movies if you need a break."

"Perfect," responded Chase. "Let's get to work."

The warehouse was about the size of a two-car garage, and the house, which was hard to see from the street, was attached behind the garage. The motorcycle took up very little room in the garage, allowing most of the warehouse/garage to be available for Chase's experiments.

"I'll need to get a few chemicals that I wasn't able to take with me," suggested Chase. "How should we get them?"

"There's a car rental place about a block away from here on the main road," informed Roger. "I'll get a car and we'll make a run to Kalispell in the morning. We need to get food and a few other household supplies as well. I'm guessing we can hold up here for a couple weeks anyway, so we should get all that we need for that period of time."

"Agreed," responded Chase. "But how are you going to rent the car without giving away your ID and location?"

"Good question. I think I'll go over there and see what I can work out while you get yourself setup and comfortable here."

Roger started walking to the main road, which was one block west of the warehouse. On the way he saw a man pull into a driveway with a Toyota Tundra pickup. He approached the man and started a friendly conversation. "I'm just getting setup over here and I need to run to Kalispell to pick up some bags of cement and some tools. Would you be interested in renting me your truck for the day, tomorrow? I'll gladly pay you a couple hundred dollars under the table, just to save me the hassle."

After some additional conversation, the owner of the truck agreed to loan Roger the truck for the day, and no ID checks would be involved. Just an exchange of $250. Roger would pick up the truck in the morning and he and Chase would drive to Kalispell, collect all the supplies they needed, and return in the afternoon.

June 2020, Helena, Montana
Roger's Burnt Out Warehouse

The entire police detective team had arrived at the burnt-out warehouse that Roger had been using for his research on Aztec cement. The fire was completely drowned out and they were stumbling around in the ruins, not really sure what they were looking for. After getting wet, dirty from charcoal, and smelly, Ranel waved to Matthew and Lemery to come over to where he was, and he asked, "Should we let the arson experts do their thing? We're not coming up with anything here."

Matthew asked, "Why did Roger burn this place down? He must have been hiding something, but what was it?"

Lemery chimed in, "We don't know for sure that Roger did burn it down. If he did, I'm guessing he's just hiding his research. My guess is that he ran off to protect what he's been working on. Apparently, someone wants to get at what he's got."

"That's probably all that's behind this mess," commented Matthew, "but I wish we could figure out who is after him. Roger has to be pretty desperate if he's going to go to this extreme effort to hide what he's doing."

Just then one of the detectives waved his arm up in the air, giving the signal that he found something. "What have you got," yelled Lemery.

"I found their burnt-up cell phones," replied the detective.

"Bring them back to the office so our CSI guys can work on them," yelled Lemery. Then turning to Matthew and Ranel he said,

"I'm sure there's nothing there for us to work with, but we might as well let them try."

"I agree," added Matthew.

Lemery yelled out for the entire team to hear, "We're going to head back. We'll see all of you back at the office in the morn-ing."

Matthew asked, "Where did Jill go?"

"No idea," responded Lemery. "She really didn't say much about where she was going or why."

Matthew continued, "She sure took off in a hurry. It was right after she spoke with Eric and Judy. It seemed a little suspicious. Did she leave with them? I wonder where she went?"

Lemery responded with, "I'll give her a call and see what she's up to." He called her number but didn't receive an answer. "That's strange," he commented. "She's usually very responsive."

"Maybe she's in the middle of a stake out of some kind and can't answer the phone right now," suggested Ranel.

Just then a text message came in on Lemery's phone from Jill which said, "*Can't talk right now. I'll contact you later.*"

"Wonder what that means?" asked Lemery, as he read the message.

Matthew also received a text message informing him that the CSI team had found some interesting pieces of evidence, and that he needed to come to the lab to take a look. He informed Lem-ery and Ranel that they needed to head to the lab so the three of them hopped into their police vehicle and left the scene of the burnt-out building, hoping that they might finally have a piece of evidence that had some value.

They drove to the police lab and headed directly to the Lead of the CSI team. Lemery spoke up first, "What have you found?"

The lab technician explained, "I think we have irrefutable evidence of who was behind the attacks at the Falcon gravel pits, and who is responsible for this latest set of murders."

"What's this evidence?" asked Lemery.

The CSI technician sat down at his computer and pulled up a recording. He explained, "We found a small camera-phone in Gerd's office. He was apparently recording the conversation that he was having with a couple of his associates about the burning of the Falcon offices at the gravel pit. But he forgot to turn it off and the next thing we hear is Gerd talking to Pablo, and then there are shots fired.

"So, Pablo was in Gerd's office when he was shot?" asked Lemery.

"Definitely," answered the tech.

"And no one else was there?" asked Ranel.

"Nope."

"But it has to be more than just Pablo that's behind all of this," suggested Ranel. "Who is Pablo working for?"

"There is a larger organization behind it," responded the Tech. He continued playing the recording and they heard Pablo talking to someone on the phone. He asked for Venicia and then talked to her. Unfortunately, they could only hear one side of the very short conversation.

"It sounds like this Venicia is the boss, and Pablo is just carrying out her instructions," suggested Ranel.

"Yep, I think you're absolutely correct," answered the technician. "But there's more. We did a little research on Venicia and traced Pablo's phone communications during this time and we see that the phone number he called was to the International Cement Products Company (ICPC). We did a little more digging on the name and found no one with that name in the company. But one of our contacts suggested that there is a Venicia who is a contractor working for ICPC, so we checked out that possibility, and we did indeed find a Venicia. Unfortunately, she seems to have disappeared. No one has seen her for a couple weeks."

"You're the techie. How do we use technology to find her?" asked Ranel.

The tech continued, "We're already working on the next step. We're tracing the location of Venicia's phone and listening in on her conversations. What's interesting is that over the last day she travelled from the ICPC headquarters in Pennsylvania to Helena, Montana, and she's here in town right now."

"But rather than pick her up, we should keep monitoring her movements and recording her phone calls and text messages. She might be the boss, but we need to capture everyone doing her dirty work as well," explained Matthew.

"I agree," responded Ranel.

Lemery instructed the tech, "Thanks for the excellent work. It looks like you found the evidence we needed to start solving these murders and fires. Let's It seems that the consensus is that we keep monitoring her and send us regular updates of any movement."

"Perfect," responded the tech. "Will do." And he turned back to his computer and continued working.

Lemery turned to Ranel and Matthew and gave them a big smile and said, "We finally have something to work with."

CHAPTER THIRTY-THREE

Rescue

June 2020, South of Missoula Montana

"We need to wait for Bridger to join us before we do anything," insisted Jill after Eric parked the car.

"That may work for you," responded Judy as she opened the passenger door, "But that doesn't work for a mother. I'm going to sneak up to the house and see what's going on."

"You're not going alone," added Eric as he also exited the vehicle.

"I guess I'm going too," added a reluctant Jill. "But this isn't very smart." As they walked, she texted Bridger informing him that they were heading to the farmhouse. He responded asking her to wait and she texted that it was out of her hands.

The three worked their way down a line of trees that followed each side of the driveway, doing their best to stay out of sight from the farmhouse. Judy remained in the lead followed by Eric and Jill.

It was a long driveway, and it took several minutes before they came close enough to the house to see any activity. The front curtain was opened and the three could see in. They were able to see two men standing guard and several people sitting. It was impossible to see the faces of the ones sitting. Six of them could be identified by the tops of their heads and a couple of them appeared to be small children. Judy was convinced that one of them was Lizzy by the color of her hair, but she was not one hundred percent positive.

Lizzy made her way to a large oak tree in the front yard and the other two caught up to her. "What should we do?" Judy asked Jill.

"We wait for backup," Jill responded, referring to Bridger.

"No thanks," answered Judy. "We need to act quickly while they are still getting settled in."

There was no restraining Judy. She crouched down close to the ground as she made her way over to the front of the house. Then she started to work her way around to the side of the house and toward the back, hoping to find a back entrance that the kidnappers weren't guarding.

Jill, in frustration, and knowing that she needed to protect Judy, followed behind her. She knew Judy didn't have a weapon and that Jill's weapon might become important in this attempted rescue. She wasn't going to give Judy her weapon, so she knew she would have to follow close behind. Eric was behind her.

Judy found the back door, went up the porch stairs, and quietly tried to open it. It wasn't locked. Luckily, the kidnappers hadn't gotten around to checking all the exits, as Judy had hoped. She started to open the back door, but to her disappointment, it didn't open quietly. The door squeaked causing Judy to jump back to the ground on the side of the porch and listened. One of the kidnappers, Pablo, came to the door, pushed it open, stepped out onto the porch, and yelled back to his partners, Ricardo and Karl, "There's no one out here. The door was left open and the wind must have moved the door." He didn't see Judy because it was dark, and she had pressed herself against the side of the stairs to where he would have had to look straight down to see her. He never even bothered to look that closely. He slammed the door shut and locked it, disappointing Judy's attempt to get inside the house.

Judy continued working her way around the side of the house, hoping to find another entrance. At the side of the house she found a basement access door. She tried opening that door and again found it unlocked, which didn't surprise her because in Montana people rarely locked their doors.

She opened the access door slowly. There was a small squeak, but since her movements were really slow, the squeak was never very loud. Since the access was in the basement, the kidnappers never heard a sound. With the door opened, she crawled inside the basement. By now Jill and Eric had caught up with her and entered the basement behind her. The three of them listened for the voices of the kidnappers and heard one of them say, "We're not here to hurt anyone. We won't be here long. We need to wait for a call from our boss telling us that it is safe to let everyone go, and then we're out of here. Stay calm and don't cause any trouble and this will all be over soon enough."

Jill whispered, "That's probably not true. All the hostages have seen the faces of the kidnappers, and they won't be safe. The 'boss', whoever that is, will probably instruct them to kill everyone. I wonder if they already did that at the previous farm-house. It doesn't look good for the kidnap victims."

Judy searched around the basement and found a crowbar. Brandishing the bar, she started to slowly make her way up the stairs. Jill again suggested they wait, but Judy wasn't going to let anyone hold her back. No, she knew that her daughter's life was at stake, and she was going to free her or die trying.

Eric was about to follow Judy, but Jill held him back, waving her gun to indicate that she had a better chance with her weapon. Jill followed Judy up the stairs, followed by Eric, who had picked up a baseball bat along the way.

They had mistakenly assumed that there were only two kidnappers, because that is all they had seen in the living room window. But there was also a third, and this put them at risk.

The door at the top of the basement stairs wasn't shut tight, making it easier to remain quiet. Judy pushed it slightly, both to see if it would squeak, and also to have a peek to see what she could see. Luckily, there was no noise. The door opened quietly.

She stepped out into the dark, unlit hallway. Jill followed close behind, pistol at ready. Eric spotted a smoke detector and pointed to Judy and Jill, directing them toward the kitchen. "I'll set off the smoke detector as a diversion," he whispered.

When the two ladies were safely in the kitchen, Eric pushed the button used to test the smoke detector, and the alarm went off immediately. Eric quickly slipped into the bathroom, and waited, baseball bat in hand, for the kidnappers to come running down the hall.

One of the kidnappers, Ricardo, appeared in the hallway and Eric made quick work of him, hitting him hard over the head with the bat. Judy and Jill, thinking there was only one additional kidnapper, charged into the living room, coming from two different directions. The second kidnapper, Karl, who was standing in the center of the room, pulled out his gun and was starting to bring it up when Jill fired a shot, hitting him in the chest. He fell backwards, still trying to take a shot at Jill, but the shot went wild and missed her completely.

Suddenly a third kidnapper jumped up from the couch, pistol at ready and fired a shot at Jill, hitting her in the shoulder. Jill spun around, being knocked by the shot, and her pistol flew from her hand. The bullet had hit her underarm and she started bleed-ing profusely.

Judy immediately jumped in and charged the gunman. The gunman, Pablo, wasn't expecting the attack and was surprised when she grabbed the hand holding the pistol with both of her hands. The kidnapper was strong and was able to swing her around. He punched her hard with his remaining hand causing her to stagger to the side. He started taking aim at her head, just as Eric came running in the room, bat held over his head, ready to hit Pablo, but the hit never happened. Pablo crashed to the floor, blood oozing from his forehead.

It all happened so fast that Eric was stunned. It took him a few seconds to realize what had happened. Pablo had been shot, but who shot him? Then he noticed the shattered front window and realized that someone on the outside had fired the shot. Seconds later Bridger entered the house through the front door asking, "Is everybody safe?"

No one answered.

Judy and Lizzy were already in a big hug which Eric also joined for a few seconds until he realized that Jill was in serious danger. He rushed over to help her. He pulled off his shirt and tied it tightly around her upper arm, hoping to stop, or at least slow, the bleeding.

Bridger was already on the phone ordering an ambulance for Jill. Then he went and checked the three kidnappers. Ricardo had a broken nose and cheekbone and was still unconscious but alive. Pablo was dead from Bridger's bullet to the head. Karl was alive, but seriously injured, blood pumping from his chest. He was conscious but not for long. The bullet to his chest had punc-tured a lung and he was having trouble speaking and breathing.

There wasn't much that could be done for Karl or Jill until the ambulances arrived. It would be about a 30-minute wait, because of their remote location. In the meantime, Bridger and Jill phoned in reports to the remaining team, letting them know what had happened. As they were on the phone Ricardo started to recover, yelling for help. Bridger and Jill were still on the phone, but Judy didn't hesitate. She went over to Ricardo and challenged him, "Who do you work for?"

Ricardo responded, "I owe you nothing. I was just hired to do a job. Your fight is with someone else, not me."

Judy wasn't sympathetic. She slapped him across the face, making sure to hit his nose as hard as possible, causing Ricardo to yell out, "Stop her. She's torturing me. This is police brutality."

"I'm not with the police, so their rules don't apply," she responded as she slapped him a second time. "Start talking you piece of crap before I really hurt you. Who are you working for?" Jill and Bridger turned their backs to Judy, indicating that they didn't see or hear anything. Judy knew she was free to pursue her questioning.

Ricardo yelled again, "You can't do this. I have my rights, and this qualifies as cruel and unusual punishment."

Judy slapped him again and stomped hard on his groin causing Ricardo to scream, "Okay! I'll tell you! What do you want to know?"

"I want names and numbers," replied Judy. "Who's involved in this? And what are their objectives?" She started to raise her hand in order to hit him again.

"I don't know everything, but I'll tell you what I know," responded Ricardo. "Please don't kick me again," he pleaded.

"Start talking," answered Judy.

He handed her his phone and said, "If you look at my contacts, you'll see everything. The most recent phone numbers were conversations with the lady that hired me. Her name is Venicia and she is an agent for Intercontinental Cement."

Bridger heard the comment and came over, "Did you say Venicia?"

"Yes," responded Ricardo.

"Our team back in Helena is trying to catch up with her now. What can you tell me about where she's staying?"

"I can't tell you anything," Ricardo responded.

Judy started to pull her hand back in order to give Ricardo another slap and Ricardo yelled out, "I don't know anything. She just tells me what to do and I do it. She doesn't tell me anything about her movements. I didn't know she was coming to Helena. Don't hit me. I don't know anything more. Pablo might know more. Ask him."

"Pablo's gone," responded Bridger. "He's not going to be telling us anything."

Ricardo shook his head.

Bridger returned to his phone call and repeated everything that Ricardo had said.

Ambulance sirens could be heard off in the distance.

CHAPTER THIRTY-FOUR

Venicia

June 2020, Helena, Montana
Police Headquarters

Matthew finished his phone call with Bridger and called Lemery and Ranel to join him in Duke's office. He tells them everything that Bridger had explained about Venicia.

"We'll keep tracking her and hope she never finds out we have a trace on her," said Lemery.

"Which brings us back to our real question; 'Do we bring in the rest of the team and share this information with them or do we keep this between the three of us?'" asked Matthew.

"This police team leaks like a sieve," complained Ranel. "We can't bring anyone else in or she'll suddenly become invisible. We're going to have to keep it between the three of us."

"I hate this because it basically means we have a worthless team running around doing nothing of value and wasting time," interjected Lemery. "But I agree that we don't have a choice. We're on our own."

"So how do we delegate our activities?" asked Matthew.

Lemery was the first to respond, "I'm going to camp with the CSI techs and watch her activities and listen in on her calls. I'll alert you guys the minute something meaningful happens."

"We should do it in shifts," suggested Matthew.

"I agree," responded Ranel. "How about 6-hour shifts, and I'll take the second shift 6 hours from now."

"Okay," responded Matthew, "And I'll come in 12 hours from now. We're going to be working our back sides off over the next few days, but we finally have something to work with and I don't think any of us wants to waste this opportunity."

"You're right about that," responded Lemery as he headed for the door. "I'm off to take the first turn at it."

June 2020, Helena, Montana
CSI Lab, Police Headquarters

Lemery came to the CSI technician and asked, "Is there a computer terminal I can sit at where I can retrace all of Venicia's activities since she arrived here in Helena?"

"Definitely," was the tech's response as he set Lemery up with one of the empty computer terminals and demonstrated how to follow her activities. "I don't see she's done a lot yet. She came from the airport and went directly to the Holiday Inn. She's gone out to a restaurant, and then returned back to her hotel room. She's sent a few text messages, asking for 'the team' to meet her at the hotel, but there haven't been any responses so I'm not sure if the meeting is going to happen or not."

"What time was this meeting supposed to occur?" asked Lemery.

"Nine PM," responded the tech.

Lemery sent a message to Matthew and Ranel letting them know about the meeting stressing that it might not happen. It's possible that "the team" was destroyed when Lizzy was rescued.

Ranel responded, "I'll be there at eight. I'll set up a GoPro Hero5 video camera somewhere and take pictures of everyone who comes and goes I just have to be careful not to spook anyone off."

"Great idea," responded Lemery. Ranel went up to the hotel early and asked the front desk, "Is there a meeting here later today, say around eight? I just wanted to make sure I was in the right place."

"Yes," responded the desk clerk, not realizing that it was the police that was inquiring. "The meeting will be in Conference Room B down the hall."

"Excellent," answered Ranel and he walked through the front door and out into the parking lot. Then he worked his way around to the side of the building, using the side entrance to re-enter the hotel. He went to Conference Room B, entered the room, and placed a camera on a bookcase at one end of the room, using a fake book with a hole in the binding to disguise it's presence. He also went back down the hall and watched the front desk of the lobby, waiting for the desk clerk to leave. Then he snuck into the lobby and placed another, similar, hidden camera there. Both cameras had plenty of battery charge to give them four hours. Ranel knew that any evidence captured in this man-ner wasn't admissible in court, but he also knew that if he involve-ed anyone else by trying to get a search warrant, he would proba-bly ruin his chances of learning anything about Venicia's activities.

He left the hotel grounds so that neither he nor his car would be spotted, thereby ruining his chance of gaining any evidence. He would return later that evening to pick up the cameras. Then he could watch the videos during his shift in the CSI labs.

**June 2020, Helena, Montana
CSI Lab, Police Headquarters
(The Following Morning)**

Ranel had reviewed the two videos and then texted both Lemery and Matthew to meet him at his office in the Montana State Police offices in central Helena rather than at the Helena Police station where they usually met. After the three of them were together and had undergone the usual greetings, Lemery asked, "What is so important that I would be pulled away from the CSI lab where we are tracking Venicia?"

Ranel pulled up a video clip on the computer and said, "Watch this!"

The first clip showed several people entering the lobby of the Holiday Inn Express. Most of them were people checking in, but several of them either asked for directions or just walked by the front desk. The surprise was that Duke, the Helena police detective who was the original lead on the case and who had been shot, was one of individuals entering the hotel. He was supposedly still in the hospital recovering from his injuries. But apparently his stay at the hospital was now being faked.

The second clip was from inside the meeting room where five individuals sat around a table together. Two were women and the other three were men. The person leading the meeting was a woman of Philippines descent which all Ranel, Lemery, and Matthew immediately assumed was Venicia. One of the men was Duke. Another of the men was Brendt George from the Mon-tana State Police, who had been identified earlier by his accent when a phone call was made.

"Interesting," responded Matthew. "We know who three of the individuals are. And who are the other two?"

"No idea," answered Lemery, and Ranel also shook his head.

"But that's not all," said Ranel. He turned up the volume so they could hear the conversation. It was scratchy but understandable. "Listen to this."

On the recording they heard the following:

Venicia, "At this point what do we know for sure?"

Duke, "We know that the kidnapping of Lizzy Falcon was another disaster like so many of our current operations have been."

Venicia, "What happened?"

Duke, "We sent three boys out there to kidnap her and hold her for ransom hoping to get information about the whereabouts of Roger and his research. We were trying to draw Roger out from wherever he is hiding. Apparently, the threesome was fol-lowed or something like that because as soon as they settled into their hideout they were raided. One guy is dead and the other two are in the hospital under police guard, and the hostages are free. We gained nothing but another black eye."

Venicia, "Scratch the idea of kidnapping. We tried it thrice, once with Roger and then with each of his kids, and it blew up in our faces every time. Why am I paying all you cops so much to make this happen and all I'm seeing is a bunch of screw-ups? You are all totally incompetent."

Brendt jumped into the conversation, "The lead detectives on this case don't trust anyone anymore, least of all us cops. They're off doing their own thing. They know there are moles in the police force and so they don't trust anyone, and they don't share information with anyone."

Venicia, "We tried kidnappings, random assassinations, burning down homes and office buildings, and we still don't have anything."

Duke, "Yea. Who was the idiot that burned down my house?"

Venicia, "That was another screwup. But at least it threw suspicion off of you. Jill's house was part of the plan, and the Falcon offices as well. We wanted to scare off the police and the Falcons. But your house was a mistake. It was supposed to be Bridger's house."

Duke, "So what's the plan now?"

Venicia turned to the second female in the group and instructed, "Maria, tell them the plan."

Maria explained, "Roger has escaped our grasp. We know he headed north somewhere, maybe even into Canada, but he's gone along with his lab tech, Chase. They left all their communi-cation equipment behind in the fire that burned down the warehouse where they were working previously here in Helena. As Venicia explained, kidnapping has been a disaster. Originally there were a couple of attempted kidnappings of Roger, one of which was orchestrated by Roger in an attempt to help him hide out, and a couple were ours which were also failures. The kidnap-pings of Lizzy and Eric were also failures. We're done with kid-nappings.

We have surveillance wiretaps on all the phones of friends and relatives for both Roger and Chase. We're hoping to get a break that way and then we'll go after him."

Duke asked, "Does the lab tech have a family?"

Maria continued, "Not directly. No wife or kids. He has a mom in a retirement home and that's it. He is basically a recluse who lives by himself and plays video games every waking moment that he's not working in the lab. The guy is almost scary in what little life he has."

Brendt asked, "What else can we do?"

Venicia answered, "Not much. We just have to wait until the two of them come out of their shell."

Just then a phone beep could be herd and Maria picked up her phone to look at a message. She spoke up, "We have a sight-ing of Roger and Chase on a motorcycle on the Blackfoot Indian Reservation in northern Montana."

Brendt asked, "How were you able to get that?"

Maria answered, "Satellites. I think we found him. Let's go get him."

Venicia interjected, "I'll rent a small six-seater aircraft and a pilot. Let's all meet at the airport in one hour and head north."

Duke responded, "Sounds like a plan. Let's go."

The meeting broke up with each of the attendees heading out of the hotel to their vehicles.

The video stopped and Ranel shook his head. "I just can't believe Duke would do this."

Lemery agreed, "We learned a lot. But with Duke – I could kill him myself! Unfortunately, we're going to have to explain how we got that information if this ever goes to court."

"Well I'm just thankful that we've made some progress," responded Matthew. "The only question I have is What's the quickest route to Browning?"

"Unfortunately, I can't join you," said Lemery. "I'm tied to Helena. But at least the two of you can go."

Ranel turned to Matthew and said, "We can't afford a private airplane, so I guess we're driving."

Lemery inserted, "The trick is going to be avoiding anyone that would recognize you, like Duke or Brendt."

"We'll have to be careful. But we have to take the risk. I guess we're off. I'll drive," said Matthew, and the three left the building, Matthew and Ranel heading for Matthew's car, and Lemery heading for his own vehicle.

"I'll keep tracking movements on any of the phones and let you know if I see anything useful," suggested Lemery, "especially Venicia's,"

"Excellent," said Ranel as they separated toward their cars.

CHAPTER THIRTY-FIVE

Browning, Montana

June 2020, Browning, Montana
Blackfoot Indian Reservation

The plane trip to Cut Bank, Montana, the closest airport to Browning, was smooth and comfortable. Venicia had ordered a rental van and it was waiting for them when they arrived. They quickly transferred to the van and started the one-hour drive to Browning with Brendt driving.

They arrived in Browning, which has one main street through town and several smaller side streets. There were a couple of grocery stores, and a couple gas stations, but other than that, it was all small shops. The plan was to split up and question the owners of these stores to see if they recognized the picture of Roger.

Brendt, who was white and had a strong Australian accent, was completely out of place as he entered one of the grocery stores. He went up to the service counter where he was ignored for several minutes. He became angry and barked at the clerk, "I'm here trying to get help! I'm looking for an individual who has had a death in the family and I'm hoping you might recognize his picture."

Brendt tried to show the picture to the clerk, but the clerk didn't bother to look up at the picture and just barked, "You're not from around here are you. I don't know who you are. Don't bother me."

Brendt was irritated, flashed his police badge, and barked, "Who's the manager. I want to speak to him."

"I'm the manager. I don't have time for this nonsense," responded the clerk. The badge had the opposite effect that Brendt was hoping for. Rather than causing the clerk to jump to attention, the clerk seemed even more irritated and defiant. He barked, "I have work to do. I'm not your social secretary. Go away."

Brendt slapped his hand on the counter. He was full blown mad. He yelled, "I demand you answer my question!"

Again, the reaction Brendt received was not what he had hoped for. He was immediately surrounded by five large Black-foot Indians. One of them asked, "What's going on here? Is there a problem?"

"Yes," responded the clerk. "Throw this guy out. He's caus-ing trouble."

Brendt attempted to protest, but before he could say anything one of the Indians grabbed him by the back of the collar and yanked him away from the counter and toward the exit. The other Indians followed him in support. Brendt knew he had no choice but to leave. His status as a state police officer had no in-fluence on an Indian reservation.

The other team members split off and went to the gas stations and the other grocery story. Most of them were able to get better cooperation. They found someone willing to look at the picture of Roger, and some had even seen him, but no one had any idea where he was or if he was even still in the area. At the end of the day, all the team learned was that Roger had been in the area about one or two days ago, but none of them seemed to know any more about his whereabouts or his movements.

They started working their way down the streets, going from one shop to the next, hoping someone had seen something, but they didn't learn anything more. At the end of the day they decided to look for a hotel, but no one liked the small hotels that were available in Browning, so they decided to shop for hotels in neighboring cities. They could either drive the one hour back to Cut Bank, which had some chain hotels, or they could travel the half hour to East Glacier, which had some resort hotels. They decided they only trusted the brand name hotels and headed back to Cut Bank, where they settled in for the night.

June 2020, Browning, Montana
Blackfoot Indian Reservation

The four-hour drive to Browning goes through some of the prettiest wheat fields. But you feel isolated and alone, rarely seeing a farmhouse or another vehicle. Matthew and Ranel opted for the back roads because it was a shorter route than going up the freeway which then required a long drive off the freeway to Browning. They didn't mind the drive. It gave them time to think and to discuss strategy.

"What are we going to do once we get there?" asked Ranel.

"No idea," said Matthew. "The Indians aren't going to be a lot of help. They don't like us and will give us any answer that will get rid of us the quickest."

"Are we looking for Venicia and her team, or are we looking for Roger?"

"Good question," answered Matthew. "It would be good if we got to Roger before Venicia does, but we can assume they've already done a lot of questioning and maybe already know where he's located. I think we would raise a lot of suspicion if we asked the same people the same questions. I think we should find out what type of vehicle they rented and get the plate number and keep watch for that."

"Good idea," responded Ranel. "I'll make some calls, as soon as I get enough signal strength to make the calls."

Ranel called the Cut Bank airport and learned that Venicia and her team had arrived earlier in the day and had rented a van. He learned the details of the van and informed Matthew, "They rented a van and headed west, to Browning, but I'm not sure what happened after that. We have a lucky break. They have GPS on the van, and we can find out where they went using that. Additionally, we still have tracking on Venicia's phone. I don't think she realizes how close we are to her."

Ranel turned on the tracking software on his smart phone and entered the van's tracking information. Once he located the van he said, "It looks like they're in Cut Bank. Either they found Roger there, or else they gave up for the day."

"Gave up is more likely," suggested Matthew. "The Blackfeet aren't all that cooperative with strangers. I doubt they learned much from them. Check the tracking on her phone as well and see if she's in Cut Bank too."

Ranel checked Venicia's phone and reported, "Yep. She's in Cut Bank. I think your scenario is the correct one, that they gave up for the day. So, what do we do?"

"We're about thirty minutes from Browning," reported Matthew. "Do we head over to Cut Bank, or do we stay in Browning and wait for them to come to us?"

Ranel suggested, "I'm thinking we'd be better off staying in Browning, and we may even get the local police involved. They're probably willing to help us take down a bunch of strangers. At the very least, we can use them as our eyes, watching for the van."

"Browning it is then," responded Matthew. "Hope you can find a decent hotel."

"There's a decent hotel at the other end of town by the casino and museum. Let's go straight there. And I'll call the local police chief and see if he'll meet us there. I seriously doubt that any of the Browning cops are on Venicia's payroll."

"I'll take your word for it," responded Matthew. "Why didn't Venicia stay at this hotel you're talking about?"

"They probably didn't see it. It's out of town at the other end of town. You wouldn't know it was there if you hadn't seen it before."

Ranel made the call and arranged for the local police chief to meet him in the lobby of the hotel. Thirty minutes later, they arrived at the hotel and the chief was already there waiting for them. "How can we help?" asked the chief as he put out his hand.

"We are tracking a group of individuals who are suspects in several murders in the Helena area and we believe they are somewhere in the Browning area." Ranel held out a picture and the chief seemed to have immediate recognition.

"I've seen them in town earlier today," said the chief. "They left town heading east toward Cut Bank. They were waving pictures around asking if we had seen someone in town, but no one seemed to recognize the pictures."

"Are these the pictures?" asked Matthew as he handed the chief a picture of Roger and his technician Chase.

"Yes, exactly," replied the chief.

"Have you seen these guys?" continued Matthew.

"Yes. They bought some groceries and headed out of town toward East Glacier."

"Then why did the other guy's head toward Cut Bank?" asked Ranel.

"I don't think anyone told them anything, so they headed back to where they came from," responded the chief. "What's with these two guys that they are chasing. What's the story?"

"They have some valuable information, and these other guys are trying to steal from them," answered Matthew. "They've tried kidnappings and extortion. But so far, they haven't been successful. We're here because we're trying to protect those two guys, but they've been doing pretty good on their own. We're just trying to avoid any more murders."

"I've told you all I know," said the chief, "but I'll keep my eyes open and let you know if I see any more of either of these two groups."

"Perfect," replied Ranel. "We desperately need your help." With that, Ranel handed the Police Chief a card with his personal telephone number and walked away.

It was now late and Ranel and Matthew checked into the Glacier Peaks Hotel, next to the casino, found their rooms, and called it a night. Tomorrow they would continue their search.

CHAPTER THIRTY-SIX

East Glacier

June 2020, East Glacier, Montana
The Next Morning

Ranel was slowly getting ready. He wasn't anxious to spend the day in another stake-out, which might very well prove to be a complete waste of the day. But he didn't know what else to do. They had to find Venicia and her team. Other-wise the entire trip to Browning would turn out to be a waste.

The day started with a three-way phone call which included Lemery and Matthew. Lemery explained, "Bridger and Jill were able to get a little more information from the kidnappers. Appar-ently, the reward for getting Roger's research is quite high. We're talking about billions of dollars in revenue to whoever gets the patent on the process he's working on. This cement is flexible enough to withstand earthquakes, and yet durable enough to not erode or decay after thousands of years. If our roads and build-ings were made from this stuff, they'd last forever, or that's what everyone believes. It sounds a little like a fantasy to me, but these guys really believe it and they've put together a team which consists of spies in all three of our police departments, the Helena local police department, the Montana state police, and the FBI. I guess the payouts are hard to resist. They're talking as much as five to ten years wages for some of these guys."

"If that much money is involved," added Matthew, "Then I can see why even murder isn't out of the question. On the sur-face, killing people over cement seemed a little stupid. But when you put a high dollar value on something, then I guess anything is fair game."

"Well I guess we better get out there and find these guys," added Ranel. "I wasn't looking forward to a stake-out, but now I can see this is a big deal."

"It sure is," emphasized Lemery. "Bridger is on his way up there to join you. I tried to discourage him, because he is on sus-pension, but apparently Roger's wife was hell-bent on joining you and Bridger felt he should tag along just to keep her under control. But that's not all. Eric is with them too."

"This is turning into a parade," responded Ranel. "You're sending us a suspended FBI agent, the emotional wife of the victim, and a boy. You've basically given us more to do, and we're already seriously outnumbered. What is Jill's status?"

"She's in the hospital for another day or so. She's not badly injured."

"At least that's good news. But no thanks for sending Bridger and the family up here," added Ranel.

"It's not like I had any say in it. Those guys are coming direct-ly from Missoula to Browning via Flathead Lake." added Lemery. "Good luck to you."

"Thanks," expressed a sarcastic Ranel, and the call was dis-connected.

A few minutes later there was a knock on the door. It was Matthew. "You ready?" he asked.

"Yep," replied Ranel.

"Let's go grab some breakfast and then head on out of here."

Just then Ranel's phone rang. He answered it with, "Hello."

"This is the chief of police in Browning. The van you're looking for just stopped for gas at the gas station on the east end of town. It's a dark blue Toyota van. I thought you'd like to know."

"You bet, thanks chief," answered Ranel and the call was disconnected. Then he turned to Matthew and said, "I guess breakfast is going to have to wait. They spotted our van at a gas station and we better head over there so we can start tracking them."

"You bet," answered Matthew. "I'm packed and ready to go."

With that the two grabbed their luggage, made their way to the car, and sped off toward the east end of town.

As they drove through the center of town, they spotted the van coming in their direction and Ranel reacted quickly, turning right down a small alley, hoping that no one in the van was able to identify them. After the van had passed, he pulled back out on the road, following behind the van, but at a distance far enough so that they could not be identified.

As they reached the west end of the ten-block town, the van slowed to a stop and Ranel had to pull off again, this time into a gas station. The van would either head west toward Glacier Park, or it would head south toward the town of East Glacier. The occupants of the van seemed confused about what direction they should go. Eventually they turned south.

Ranel wasn't in a hurry. He knew that this road didn't have any turn-offs until it reached East Glacier and so there was little chance of losing them. When they were far enough ahead, Ranel pulled out of the gas station and followed their route.

They were about fifteen minutes into their drive when they received a phone call from Bridger. Matthew took the call and said, "What's going on?"

Bridger responded with, "Judy's driving. This is Bridger. We've been driving for a good part of the night and we're almost to Browning. We're just getting into East Glacier so we should be there in about thirty minutes."

"Excellent," answered Matthew. "Stay in East Glacier. Stay off the main road but where you have a good view of the road. We are following a dark blue Toyota van with five people who are the individuals that have been causing all this trouble. The van inclu-des the ringleader, Venicia, Duke, Brendt George, and a couple other new individuals. So, you should be able to spot them when they come through. We are following about ½ mile behind them. You should stay hidden as well. They should arrive there in the next ten minutes."

"Duke is in on this?" expressed an exasperated Bridger.

"Yep. So much for his being in the hospital. From what we can tell, he's been a kingpin behind a lot of this."

"But he was shot, and his house was burnt down. How does that make sense?"

"Apparently that was a mistake," answered Matthew. "I think they were after your house."

"But I don't have a house here."

"Maybe that's what caused the confusion."

"We'll find a place to stake out at the north end of town by the gas station and the post office," responded Bridger. "I'll keep you posted on their movements."

"Thanks," responded Matthew as he disconnected the call.

It wasn't long before Matthew received a text message, "They're here. They stopped in at the gas station. It looks like they're questioning people about Roger. They've spread out and they are hitting every shop, hotel, and bar."

"We'll wait outside of town," answered Matthew. "We'll wait on just the other side of the bridge. We don't want to be too ob-vious."

"No problem. We'll keep you posted."

Matthew turned to Ranel and said, "I guess this little group of vigilantes led by Bridger has turned out to be useful after all."

"Right on," answered Ranel.

It was about fifteen minutes later when another text message came in, "Looks like they found something. They all packed back into their van and now they're heading toward the north end of town."

It was followed immediately by a second text message which said, "Now they turned right and they're going under the railroad tracks. They haven't spotted us, so I think we're still okay to follow behind. I'll keep you posted."

"Be careful. If you're identified by the guys that you know, like Duke and Brendt, we're blown."

"Got it."

After reading the text Ranel turned to Matthew and said, "Let's go!" As they slowly cruised into town, they could see Brid-ger up ahead turning right and driving down into the short tunnel that allowed passage under the railroad tracks to the west side of the city.

CHAPTER THIRTY-SEVEN

Finding Roger

June 2020, East Glacier, Montana
The Same Morning

Venicia challenged Brendt, "What exactly did you learn?"

"The small store in the center of town recognized the pictures and said that they've come into the store the last two days," explained Brendt. "They always head through the tunnel leading to the west side of the city, but they don't say much about where they're staying or why they're here."

"Are they still on a motorcycle?" asked Venicia.

"Yes," replied Brendt, "and there aren't a lot of motorcycles around here so they should be easy to spot."

The van pulled out and drove under the railroad tracks, slowly moving past the East Glacier Park Lodge, a large log cabin structure surrounded by a golf course. Venicia instructed, "One of you get out here and keep an eye out. Jonard, you do it. Roger doesn't know you, so you don't have to worry about being spotted."

The van pulled over and Jonard jumped out of the van close to the driveway towards the Amtrak terminal. The van drove a little further and there was an intersection where the roads veered off to the left and right. Venicia continued, "Maria, you get ready to get out as well. You can hang out in this part of town and let me know if you spot these guys. Try to blend in for Judas sake! Don't blow this!"

"Will do," responded Maria. She climbed out of the van and started walking up the street, hoping to see someone. She stop-ped into the small store and, showing the picture of Roger, asked the clerk if he had seen him.

"Yes," responded the clerk. "He was in here earlier today."

"Do you know where he's staying?" asked Maria.

"I'm not exactly sure, but it's somewhere along the back road east of here," responded the clerk as he pointed towards the back of the store, indicating the direction of the road.

Maria left the store and phoned Venicia, letting her know that Roger was staying somewhere close by. "He's hold up some-where along the east road," said Maria.

"We'll go house-to-house and see if we can find him," responded Venicia. "There's only about ten houses here so it shouldn't be too hard. You stay where you are and keep a watch in case you see someone taking off on a motorcycle."

"Will do," responded Maria as they disconnected the call.

June 2020, East Glacier, Montana
In Roger's Lab

Roger's technician Chase yelled for Roger and he responded quickly and came out to the garage. "What have you got?" asked Roger.

"Watch this," Chase explained. He had two clumps of ce-ment, both about the size of a brick, laid out on a piece of lab equipment which simulated earthquakes. He cranked the earth-quake simulator up to 9.0 and started it up. It was awfully noisy, and the vibrations were so strong that it could be felt on the floor of the garage. One brick of cement started to crumble immed-iately, but the other clump of cement held firm, showing no signs of strain.

"Wow," expressed Roger. "I think we got it!"

"I think so too," responded Chase. "I think we found our earthquake resistant cement. Look at this other brick." Chase walked Roger over to a different machine which pressure sprayed water against a similar brick of cement at tremendously high pres-sure, and the brick was showing no sign of damage. "The pres-sure that I'm shooting against this brick is stronger than the strongest hurricane ever recorded, and I've had this running for over an hour, and there is no sign of erosion. I think we finally have the formula right."

"Give me the final formula and I'm going to patent it immed-iately, before we get any more attempts to steal it," answered Roger. "My personal Patent Attorney, Steve Smith, knows this is coming and is ready for it. He has all the preliminary work com-pleted and is just waiting for the final formula."

Chase handed the formula to Roger and Roger dialed the phone. "We have the formula," Roger said after Steve answered the call. "I'll take a picture of it and text it to you so you can wrap up the patent. How long will it take before we are the sole owners of this patent?"

"Everything is ready and pre-processed so it should be all yours by tomorrow," Steve responded.

The call was disconnected. Roger took a picture of the form-ula and texted it to Steve. Then he turned to Chase and said, "Ex-cellent work. Thanks for getting this wrapped up. I'm sorry that we had to come up here to East Glacier in order to complete the process, but I'm glad we're finished. Now, let's get rid of all the evidence, including the formula, in case we're identified."

Chase interjected, "Easy enough to do," and he destroyed the formula and any experimental data. It was all in his head anyway, and now it was at the patent office as well. "I think I've earned a diet coke. I'm going down to the small store to pick one up. You want anything?"

"No! but I think I'll join you. Let's go to the restaurant and have some huckleberry pie. I'll buy.'

"You have a deal," replied Chase and the two exited out of the back of the building, walking across the back field toward the Whistle Stop Restaurant.

It was a short walk to the restaurant. They entered the outside patio, and the waitress came to their table and handed them a menu. She asked, "How is your day going?"

"Great, how about you?" replied Chase. He noticed her accent, so he asked, "Where are you from?"

"I'm from Germany. I came here to work for the season."

"Do you like it here?"

"Yes. It's so beautiful, here in the middle of the mountains."

The owner of the restaurant came to the table and said, "There was a lady looking for you. She came here about a half hour ago and showed us your picture."

"Who was that?" asked an anxious Roger. "Did she say why she was looking for us?"

"Something about a dead relative. But I didn't believe it. It sounded like a phony excuse."

"What did you tell her?" Roger asked.

"I told her that you were here in town somewhere. She wanted to know where you were staying but I told her I didn't know. She wasn't very friendly. I'm sorry if I did the wrong thing. She did seem a little nervous and anxious."

"No problem. Thanks for the information," added Roger. "If you see her again, please don't tell her anything. I just want to be left alone and that's why I came here."

"Will do," said the owner and she left the table.

Roger and Chase ordered pie and a drink, but they couldn't avoid looking around, watching to see if there was anyone walking the streets. East Glacier was fairly deserted and anyone walking the street would be quickly identified. There just weren't that many people on the streets.

Just then a van drove by, and a girl came out of the little store next to the restaurant and jumped into the van. The van drove off and turned left down the next available roadway. The owner came up to Roger and said, "That was the lady I was telling you about."

"Thanks," said Roger. "I'll keep a look-out for her."

The pair finished their pie and headed back toward the back of the house, using the same route that they had used to come to the restaurant. They kept a watch to see if they spotted the van, and they could see it at the far end of their road. Several indivi-duals had stepped out of the van and were going from house-to-house. Roger and Chase knew this was trouble. They knew these individuals were looking for them and it wouldn't be long before they received a knock on their door.

CHAPTER THIRTY-EIGHT

Tracking

June 2020, East Glacier, Montana

As they drove under the railroad overpass, Eric spoke up, "I knew Roger was coming up here. He was here a few months ago. He said it had something to do with a job, but now I know better. He was finding a hide-out for himself in case it got too hot in Helena. And apparently he decided to use it."

Bridger, who had taken over the driving duties because he was trained in high risk driving, asked, "Did he say anything about this hide-out? Anything that would help us locate it before this band of brutes finds them?"

"He mentioned how convenient it was because it had a large garage which was big enough to include his lab, and that there was a house behind it which wasn't much of a home, but it was sufficient."

"Anything about it being on the main road or off the road?" asked Bridger.

"Nothing like that," responded Eric. "Let me think about the conversation. There was a slight pause. No, I can't think of anything else."

"They drove down the main street of the little community had grown up on the west side of the tracks. It was mostly season-al establishments, like hotels and restaurants, which closed up tight during the winter months. They drove all the way to the end of the community and out into an area called Froggy Flats. There were no more structures past this point, so they turned around and headed back into the community. The mysterious van was nowhere to be found.

"Left, or right?" asked Bridger, as they came to the first intersection. Just then they saw Ranel and Matthew turn west behind them. "It looks like they're taking that side of the main road, so we'll take the other.

Bridger turned left and drove the one block to the end of the road, which then curved right. They had already made the turn when they were suddenly face-to-face with the missing van. Brendt was in the driver's seat of the van and he immediately pointed to Bridger and started yelling something inaudible.

Venicia, who was in the passenger seat, pulled out a gun and aimed it at Bridger, and fired a shot without hesitation. Fortunately, Bridger had already thrown the car into reverse and was turning the vehicle around so that it headed back the way they came. He slammed on the gas and was off and running, making a right turn, and flying past Froggy Flats.

"I want out," yelled Judy.

Bridger, thinking that Judy didn't want to get shot, replied, "Good idea. When I round the next sharp turn, I'll pull over quickly, and you jump out. Then hide and I'll continue the chase."

The mountain road was very twisty, and they had enough of a lead so it wasn't a problem slowing down enough so that Judy could make her escape. She was in the back seat behind the pas-senger seat. She opened the back door and quickly rolled out of the car. Much to Bridger's surprise, Eric, who was in the front passenger seat, had the same idea, and rolled out of the car as well.

Bridger stomped on the gas, slamming the two doors shut. He continued running, allowing the chase, convinced that Eric and Judy were now safe.

But Judy had other ideas, and Eric knew it, which was why he decided to join her. After the pursuit van had passed their location, the two of them started working their way back to the direction of the community where they had encountered the van. They were walking up an incline when they rounded a corner, and just in front of them was a big black bear meandering across the highway. The bear turned to look at them but fortunately didn't have any interest in them. Judy and Eric stopped in their tracks and stood perfectly still. The bear continued in his journey through the forest, and Judy and Eric continued on their way.

Judy gave a quick call to Ranel and told him what had happened. "Are you safe?" he asked.

"We're fine," replied Judy. "But I'm not sure everyone on the team was accounted for. You said there were five that went on this trip, and I only saw three in the van. There must be a couple of them on foot canvassing the area where Roger might be. We need to get over there and protect him."

"Right!" yelled Ranel and he could be heard instructing Matthew where to drive.

The jog back to town took about ten minutes. When they arrived, they turned toward the area where they had encountered the van. They were cautious, just in case they accidentally en-countered someone, but at the same time they aggressively push-ed forward, looking for two individuals who might be canvassing the area.

Without saying a word, Eric pointed down the road, about two-thirds of the way to the end of the short road. Judy saw what he was pointing at. Two individuals, a man, and a woman, were walking around the side of an oversized garage, moving towards the front door of a house that sat behind it.

"We'll just act like a couple of hikers who just happened to be in the area," suggested Judy. "I don't recognize either of them, so I don't expect them to recognize us either. Let's see what those two are up to."

Judy and Eric walked down the road. There were houses on the west side of the road, but the east side was all trees and woodland. They pretended to be discussing their hiking experience, and the bear they encountered. They acted completely disinter-ested in the two individuals, a man, and a woman, that they were stalking.

They passed a house that seemed to fit the description. It had a large garage, so large that it hid the small house that was behind it. Judy and Eric casually passed by the front of the garage and, when they were past the front, they checked to see if the man and woman were looking in their direction. Seeing that they were not being watched, they quickly snuck around the side of the house away from the two visitors. As they rounded the corner of the garage, they heard a loud vibrating noise in the garage, so loud that it would have kept sounds from being heard.

Judy and Eric worked their way around to the back side of the house until they came to the corner where they would be able to watch the two intruders. The two had come to the side of the house where the entrance to the house was located. Judy and Eric could barely hear the knocking of the visitors, the sound in the garage was so loud. One of them, the woman, said, "Let's go around the house and look in the windows to see if we can spot anything. Maybe the garage has windows on the other side, and we can see what's causing all the noise."

They proceeded around the front of the house and the garage and eventually they could be spotted on the far side of the house, working their way toward the back, following the route previously taken by Judy and Eric. They stopped at a window and looking in the window the man said, "I think that's them."

The woman answered, "How can you be sure? The window is so foggy it's hard to see through it."

"I'm not one hundred percent sure. But it's a strong possibility. It's the best possibility we've found so far. There're only ten houses on this road, and this is the eighth. And, so far, there's either no one home or the residents don't fit the description. But here we have two guys running some kind of machinery in their garage. I think it's the best possibility we've had. Let's go in and check it out."

"Let's call Venicia and get her approval."

"That's ridiculous," barked the man. "Do we really need to check with her every time we want to blow our nose? I say we go in."

"Okay," responded the lady.

The man and the woman started working their way toward the back of the house, but just as they were turning the corner around to the back of the house the man found himself rolling on the ground in pain, rubbing his nuts, and the woman found her-self flying through the air, landing flat on her back, with a knee pressed against her larynx.

"Wow," responded Eric to Judy. "That Mixed Martial Arts training you've been doing has really paid off." Judy had given the man a well-placed kick in the groin, followed by a judo flip on the lady. Neither knew what hit them. It all happened too quickly.

Eric, using his shoelaces, tied up the hands and feet of the man. He tied the hands together behind the man's back and then tied one of his feet up to the hands. It was nearly impossible for the man to move. Then, using the man's shoelaces, he did the same to the lady, who tried to put up a fight, but Judy quickly put an end to her attempts by giving her a hard punch in the upper stomach, under the ribs near the lungs, knocking the wind out of her. Once the two were successfully tied up, and Judy and Eric were again able to stand up, Judy asked, "Who are you and what are you doing here?"

The man answered first, "We're just a couple of hikers who got lost. You have no right to brutalize us like this. I'm going to press charges."

Judy started laughing, walked over to the man, and slapped his face as hard as possible. "If you're going to threaten me, I'm going to make it worth the trouble. Now, answer my question."

"Like is said, we're hikers here on vacation," the man repeated.

Judy slapped him again, set her foot on his balls, pressing down hard on what was already a painful area, and repeated, "Who are you and what are you doing here?"

By now the woman had regained her breath and responded to Judy, "What's it to you? Who are you and why do you care?"

Judy said, "I'm Roger's wife and you're here stalking him and trying to kidnap him or worse. And I'm here to stop you. Now quit with all the false pretenses and answer my question. Who are you? And who are the three people in the van?"

Both the man and the woman were surprised by Judy's frankness and they said nothing. Judy pressed down harder on the man's nuts and Eric proceeded to stomp his foot on the woman's crotch. Eric spoke up with, "What's going on here. If you plan on getting out of this alive, you better start talking."

"I'm going to press charges for police brutality," barked the man.

Eric answered the threat with a threat, "At the rate we're going here, you're not going to be alive to press those charges. And since we're not police, I'm not sure who you'd press police bru-tality charges against. You're really talking stupid talk."

Again, the two fell silent. Fear started to show in their faces. They could see that Judy and Eric were as desperate to find out who they were.

"Okay," said the lady. "I'm Marie and this is Jonard. We both work for Venicia, who is a contractor working for Intercon-tinental Cement. But you probably already know all that anyway. We're here to find Roger. That's all we know. If there's more to the story, we don't know it."

"And who are the people in the van?" asked Eric.

"Venicia, Duke, and Brendt," replied the man. Judy and Eric each took their foot off their victim's crotch. There was a noticeable sigh of relief from the two.

"Duke and Brendt are cops, correct?" asked Judy.

"Yes," replied Marie. "They were paid a lot of money to be inside moles so we could keep track of what the police were doing."

"You guys are responsible for all the killings and burning down buildings, right?" asked Eric.

Marie had a confused look on her face and became defen-sive, "We're not responsible for those things. Venicia had multi-ple teams working and we don't know anything about the other teams. We weren't clued into their activities. But we didn't burn down any buildings."

"Come on man. Untie us. This is hurting! We have told you everything we know." cried the man.

"Fat chance of that happening," answered Eric. "We're not about to give you the chance to turn against us."

Just then they all heard the rusty hinges of a door opening.

CHAPTER THIRTY-NINE

The Chase

**June 2020, East Glacier, Montana
(Back to Bridger a Half Hour Earlier)**

Bridger rounded a corner and in front of him was a slight turn-out, beside which was a lot of brush. He slowed to a crawl to drop off Judy. He didn't expect Eric to jump out, but he understood why he did. If an encounter occurred, Eric wasn't going to leave his mother to fend off the bad guys by herself. Bridger was now on his own.

Slowing down had given the van that was chasing him a chance to close a lot of the distance between them and now he was once again within range, allowing the riders in the van to take shots at him. He could hear them shooting at him but most of the shots went wild. The movement of the vehicles, and the distance, made pistols almost useless. They weren't much use except at close range, but they were trying to shoot at him, hoping for a lucky hit.

Bridger decided to take advantage of the fact that he had a car with a lower center of gravity than the van that was chasing him. That meant that he would be able to round corners faster. His vehicle would be more stable. With each corner he was able to put more and more distance between himself and his pursuers. He was driving all over the little town - taking turns at every op-portunity. Soon he was out of range and they quit wasting their bullets trying to shoot at him.

Bridger rounded another corner followed by a long straight-away. The van was gone. It was no longer behind him. He was surprised. He assumed that something had gone wrong and the van was no longer able to continue the chase. Either they crashed the van, or it must have broken down. Bridger slowed to a stop but left the engine running. He kept a close watch in his rear-view mirror, but the van did not reappear. He swung around to retrace his route.

He had to return using the same road that he had just travel-led. He was risking encountering the van, but he didn't care. He had to bring this whole, stupid escapade to an end. He had to find Roger and make sure he was alright. And what about Judy and Eric. He hoped to God they had gotten away safely.

June 2020, East Glacier, Montana

"Hurry up," Venicia yelled. "He's getting away."

"This van is top heavy," was Brendt's barked response. Mix-ed with his strong Australian accent, the comment sounded al-most comical.

Nevertheless, he pushed the van around the next corner, and it came up on two wheels.

"Hold it," yelled Venicia in fear. "You almost flipped us you idiot."

"I told you. This van is top heavy," barked Brendt.

"Okay. I see what you mean," responded Venicia. "Don't kill us!"

Duke was taking the occasional shot at Bridger's vehicle, with no luck. "This is a waste of time. We might as well be shooting up in the air."

Just then two beat up old pickups came racing up behind the van. They were honking their horn and waving for the van to pull over.

"Ignore them," barked Venicia.

The pickups kept honking and when there was a bit of a straight-away the lead pickup swung out into the other lane, raced to the front of the van, pushing the back of the pickup against the front of the van, and forced the front of the van to the side of the road. The pickup had the front of the van blocked and they could go no further.

Three Indians jumped out of the cab of the pickup and a couple more jumped out of the back of the pickup. Another three came from the second pickup which had parked tight against the back of the van.

Venicia was in shock, "What in Judas is this about?"

The lead Indian came up to the driver's window of the van and Brendt rolled down the window. "Are you guys crazy or something? You nearly killed us," barked Brendt.

"You're the one that's crazy," barked the Indian. "You don't come on our reservation and go around shooting. What were you shooting at anyway?"

"We're police officers in pursuit of a criminal. And you're interfering with a police operation," yelled Venicia.

"Tell your squaw to shut up," barked the Indian at Brendt. "You're on the res. You have no damn jurisdiction here; I don't care who you think you are. You don't go around shooting here without a permit. You don't have permission to even have a gun, let alone go driving down the street shooting it off."

"Like I said, we were in pursuit of another vehicle. And now you've let him get away."

"I didn't see any other vehicle. I only saw YOU shooting. You almost tipped the van over back at the last turn. You must be drunk or on drugs or something. I'm not going to let you drive any further. You need to step out of the vehicle."

"This is crazy," barked Brendt. "We need to continue our chase."

"Not today mister," commented another Indian who had come up to the van's window. "You're done with your little ad-venture for today." Then, in a very harsh and stern tone he said, "Now get your ass out of that van before I have to drag you out."

Brendt could see that there was no hope for a quick solution. He would have to comply. He opened the door of the van and stepped out onto the pavement.

The second Indian did a quick body check to make sure Brendt didn't have any concealed weapons and he found a gun strapped to his lower leg. The Indian took the gun and gave Brendt a shove.

Next out of the van was Venicia, and she was searched as well. Her search looked more like molestation, but the Indian was able to locate a small pistol on the inner thigh of her right leg.

As she was being searched a car drove by in the opposite direction. The Indians paid no attention to it, but Brendt noticed that Bridger was the driver. He was about to draw attention to the car, but Venicia gave him a look and shook her head side to side indicating that she didn't want any attention given to Bridger. Bridger would just complicate this entire process and get the local Indian police force involved, and that could take hours. No one spoke up or reacted in any way allowing Bridger to drive back towards East Glacier.

Next came Duke. They took his handgun and then found a second gun strapped to his back next to his belt.

Satisfied that they had discovered all the weapons the three were carrying, the second Indian climbed into the van and searched it as well. He found a couple more weapons. Once he had climbed out of the van, he instructed the first Indian, "I think we found everything." Then turning to the three-some, he said, "Thanks for the weapons. We'll keep these because you brought them on the reservation illegally. I strongly recommend you leave Indian territory now."

Venicia demanded, "You can't just take our guns. We have a permit for them. You have no right to take them!"

"You have them illegally and you were using them illegally. That's enough reason. We can go down to the police station and discuss this further if you like."

She knew she wasn't going to win, so she said, "Fine. Maybe we can work a deal. We have some bad guys we need to capture and maybe you can help us. How much would it cost to get your help and support?" Even if she found Roger now, she didn't have anything to threaten him with. So, she had an idea. If you couldn't beat them, pay them to join you!

CHAPTER FORTY

The Chase Continues

June 2020, East Glacier, Montana

Ranel and Matthew arrived at the little off-shoot part of East Glacier that was located on the west side of the tracks. They recognized no one as they slowly cruised past the small hotels on the left and the restaurants and stores on the right. They arrived at the north end of the community and found themselves in the open area of Froggy Flats. They drove to the end of the flats, looking for a place to turn around. They found a small logging road that they used for their turn and they were just finishing the turn as Bridger came up behind them. Both cars pulled over to the side of the road and Bridger went to Ranel and Matthew's car.

"What the hell is going on?" questioned Ranel.

"Judy and Eric texted me they are walking around the back side of the town, looking for the two guys that were not in the van any longer. The other three, Venicia, Brendt and Duke, are held up down the road behind me. It looks like they riled up some Indians, I think because they were shooting at me. But our focus right now needs to be on the other two that are looking for Roger. We're pretty sure he's in that community somewhere, but we don't know where."

"Did you try calling Judy? Keep trying her phone and let's get back into town." said Matthew.

"When you get to town, take the first left and follow it around," suggested Bridger. "That's where we encountered the van that chased me and started shooting at me. I'm sure Judy and Eric must have gone that way as well."

"Will do," commented Ranel as he started to drive off.

Bridger returned to his car and drove off in the same direction. When they arrived at the community, Ranel and Matthew took the first left as instructed, and followed the roadway all the way to the end. Bridger stayed on the main road, acting as look-out in case he saw anyone running away.

Ranel and Matthew saw nothing, so as they reached the end of the road they turned around and headed back the way they came. As they drove up the road they were surprised. They encountered Venicia's van, trailed by two older pickups, streaking straight at them at high speed. They texted a warning to Bridger, "I think we're in trouble."

June 2020, East Glacier, Montana

Judy and Eric reacted quickly to the noise by moving to the corner of the house that was hidden from the door. Judy was closest to the corner and she peaked around the corner to see who was coming out. She heard Chase's voice and he said, "I don't see anyone out here. I'm not sure what you heard. It was probably an animal."

Then she heard Roger answer back, "Don't worry about it. Come back into the house and lock the door."

Unfortunately, Maria and Jonard also heard the voices and Maria was the first to quickly yell out, "Help. We're being attacked by some crazy people here."

Chase said, "Roger, there is someone out in back. We better check it out."

Roger responded with, "I bet it's a trap to get us out of the house."

Judy yelled out, "It's Judy and Eric. Come out here Roger. We want to show you something."

Seconds later Roger and Chase were at the back of the house. Roger asked Judy, "What the heck are you doing here? And how did you find me?"

Judy answered, "You guys are missing out on all the fun. We had to rescue Lizzy earlier and now we're here to rescue you. You may not know it, but there's a group of five guys trying to hunt you down. And they got this close to you," she said as she pointed at Maria and Jonard.

"We better get our butts inside quickly before any more of these guys show up," commented Chase.

But Roger had other thoughts. He grabbed Judy and gave her a big kiss, and said, "I missed you. I'm glad you're safe. I love that my wife has to rescue me!"

"Well I guess you missed me," responded Judy.

"Hurry. let's move it," commanded Chase.

"I can't believe these guys found me," continued Roger as they quickly moved toward the door and went back inside. "I thought East Glacier would be remote enough that no one would find me here. I guess I'm not safe anywhere."

Chase and Eric pulled Maria and Jonard inside as well. Once inside Roger turned to Maria and angrily demanded, "What the hell do you guys have planned? How many of you are there? Who's in charge?"

Marie looked away and did not answer.

Roger stomped on her knee. She screamed out in pain. Then Roger repeated the questions.

Maria barked out, "Leave me alone. I don't know anything. You're as good as dead anyway. The rest of my team is going to catch up with you and that will be the end of it for you."

"What do you want," this time it was Jen challenging Maria.

"I don't know, and I don't care," lied Maria. "I wasn't hired to get Roger and that's all I know."

This time it was Jen who was irritated, and she slapped Maria across the face.

"You stupid coward," screamed Maria.

But Jen aimed her weapon at Maria's stomach and said, "Then I'll have to get rid of you so you can't press charges."

Maria screamed, "You jerks! I don't know anything."

Jonard jumped in, "You idiots are doomed. We have a whole team here. I can't wait to see what they do to you and if they don't beat the crud out of you, I'll make sure I get the pleasure."

Chase ran off to the garage and returned with a couple two by fours, a hammer, and some nails. Then Roger and Judy shut and barred the door by nailing the two-by-fours across it.

Roger instructed Eric, "Get these two idiots down into the basement. Tie them up good and tape their mouths shut."

"Good thinking," responded Chase and he and Eric followed Roger's instructions. The two captives were soon secured and out of the way.

When Roger, Judy, Chase, and Eric were all together again Roger instructed, "Let's make sure everything is secured. We may be in for a fight and we need to be ready."

"Agreed," replied Judy. "We have several police officers out there trying to help us. Bridger, Matthew, and Ranel are all out there trying to find us. I'm going to call them and tell them our location and our situation."

While Judy was on the phone, Roger commanded, "Spread out! We need someone at each side of the house, keeping an eye out for any activity." Roger provided each of them with a weapon and plenty of ammunition. He had originally stocked up the East Glacier location for hunting, but now, in desperation, he hoped he could use it as a hideout.

"Will do," replied Chase. "I'll take the front by the garage and watch through the garage door windows." Judy went to the north side of the building, watching through the glass door. Eric went upstairs and positioned himself on the south side of the building, where he had the best view. And Roger, re-boarded up the main entrance. They waited.

Judy, in a display of frustration, challenged Roger, "What is this all about? Why is there an army after you?"

"It's about cement," was his response.

"Cement?" doubted Judy. "Who kills for cement?"

"Someone who's greedy," was the only response she received, and then the room fell to silence, everyone listening for activity outside. "They're after my formula."

June 2020, East Glacier, Montana

"I got them," Duke yelled out, scaring everyone half to death.

"You've got what?" barked Venicia.

"I've got Maria and Jonard," he replied. "They're about halfway between here and the end of the street."

"Signal them to come out," commanded Venicia.

"I already did. And there's no response. It's as if they have lost access to their cell phones."

"Let's assume they shut their phones down so as not to make noise. And they're not hearing us," responded Venicia.

"What's going on," asked Ranel. "I thought the Indians had arrested these criminals. Now it looks like they've become part of the team."

"It doesn't look good," responded Matthew, as they sat in their car at the end of the road waiting for the on-coming vehicles to arrive.

Suddenly and unexpectedly Venicia's van and the two pick-ups stopped about halfway down the road, and Venicia could be seen climbing out of the passenger side of the van. Duke and Brendt climbed out as well and the three started walking towards the side of a garage and towards the house behind it. Two of their new Indian companions also followed, but four others remained in their pickups. Matthew stated, "I guess they're not after us. Looks like they think they know where Roger is."

They watched carefully to see how Venicia and her team would react. At first it seemed like they were being ignored. Unfortunately, it wasn't long before shots rang out and the front windshield of the car exploded into a million small chips of glass. Both Ranel and Matthew were quick to duck down behind the dashboard of the car.

"That was a shotgun," commented Ranel. "That had to come from one of the Indians. Venicia and team didn't have shot guns on them."

Before he could say any more, a second round of shots rang out, this time blowing out the back window of the vehicle. Ranel and Matthew opened their door and jumped out of the car, using the door as a shield. "The shots are coming from the second pick up," yelled Matthew. There was a guy standing in the back of the second pickup, using the roof of the pickup to prop up his rifle.

"Got it," said Ranel who was in a better position to take the shot. Without first extending a warning, two quick shots rang out from Ranel's pistol, and a large crash could be heard, which was the Indian falling over onto the bed of the pickup. "This is going to turn out to be a jurisdictional nightmare," mumbled Ranel. Non-resident cops shooting an Indians on an Indian reservation would become a paperwork nightmare and a court battle all on its own. Ranel had just put himself into the middle of it.

Rather than put an end to the shooting, Matthew and Ranel were now barraged with shots coming from several different directions. All three of the remaining Indians were now taking random shots in their direction. Matthew waved Ranel back into the car. They threw the car into reverse and started backing away from the gunfight. They weren't giving up. They were simply trying to reposition themselves. Once out of shot gun range, they stopped the car and climbed out.

CHAPTER FORTY-ONE

Showdown

June 2020, East Glacier, Montana

Chase was the first to send out a call to the others. He yelled back to Eric, Roger, and Judy and said, "They're here! I see eight in total but three or four of them are staying behind in their pick-up."

"There were only three in the van," asked Judy. "Where did the rest come from?"

"It looks like they picked up a bunch of Indians to help them out."

"They just want Roger's formula," replied Judy. "Which means Roger and Chase are probably safe, but the rest of us are expendable."

There was a knock at the door. Everyone inside remained quiet. Then Venicia yelled out, "We know that Jonard and Maria are in there. We have tracking devices on them, which tells us that Roger is in there too. So Jonard and Maria must be hostages. Roger, do you really think that you can hold out against us? We have a small army out here. I'll give you one more chance to open this door, and then we're coming in. We're not here to hurt you, but if you won't work with us then who knows what can hap-pen."

Eric was upstairs and could see someone trying to climb up to the upstairs window, hoping to sneak in that way and come up behind Roger. The intended intruder, one of the Indians, arrived at the window and tried to open it. He found a pistol aimed at his face through the window. He let out a yelp and fell down on the roof and pressed himself against the wall, too quick for Eric to react. Eric was now unable to see him.

Venicia tried the door handle, but the door would not open. She waved to Duke to bust down the door. Duke came in and slammed his shoulder against the door. It creaked but didn't budge. "They have some kind of barricade against the door. We're probably not going to be able to get in that way."

Duke was furious, pulled out his pistol, and started shooting at the door's lock. "Stop that you idiot," barked Venicia. "The door is barricaded and shooting out the lock won't get the door opened."

Brendt spoke up and pointed to a window that was next to the door, "Let's just go through the window." He took a rock and threw it at the window, causing the window to shatter. Then he took a small piece of firewood from the firewood pile next to the door and broke the window out completely so that anyone climb-ing through the window wouldn't get cut up.

The base of the window was about five feet off the ground. For someone to climb through they would have to be boosted up. "Who's going to go through?" asked Brendt.

"I'll do it," said Venicia. "Stoop over so I can climb up on your back."

Brendt leaned over, still standing up, so he would be high enough. Venicia unsuccessfully tried to climb on his back but fell off and landed on the ground on her butt. Duke came over and offered her a hand. She tried again to climb up on Brendt, this time holding onto Duke's hand with one hand and placing her other hand on Duke's head to give her balance. She was almost standing up. She let go of Duke, thinking she had her balance when she suddenly fell backwards right on top of Duke who ended up grabbing her butt and pushing her back up. She reach-ed inside the window and held onto the inside windowsill. Then she swung her right leg up and into the window. She started to slip again and once again Duke's hand was on her butt, helping her to maintain her balance. This time he gave her an extra push which gave her the momentum to go flying through the window, landing on the floor inside the apartment. She was lying face down on the ground and before she knew what was happening, she felt a knee pushing down on the center of her back, holding her to the ground.

"What are doing here? What do you want with Roger?" Judy said.

Venicia was surprised by the unexpected female voice. "I want his formula. I want his research." Demanded Venicia. "And if you don't give it to me, we'll shoot this place to pieces and then burn it to the ground."

"Who are you working for?" asked Judy.

"I don't know. I'm given instructions from higher up and I just obey," she lied.

"Put your hands behind your back," demanded Judy.

Venicia's reaction was unexpected. She started squirming and fighting. First she swung her feet up and kicked Judy hard enough to knock Judy off. Then Venicia started to get up and Judy grabbed her by the hair, pulling it hard enough to knock Venicia off her feet and forcing her to stumble. But Venicia caught herself on a table and started to stand up.

Judy reacted quickly, grabbing Venicia again by the hair and pulling her hard. This time she pulled her over toward the window. Stumbling and falling, Venicia ended up flying out the window, crashing into Duke during her flight, knocking him over and landing on top of him.

"You're supposed to be searching the house. Not flying back out the window," complained Duke. "What was that all about?"

"That bitch in there threw me out the window," complained Venicia.

"There's a female in there?" asked Brendt. "Who is she and where'd she come from?"

"How should I know," barked a frustrated Venicia as she tried to climb off Duke and stand up.

Brendt swore, "OK, going through that window didn't work out."

"Why don't we just burn the place down?" asked Duke as he sat up.

"I'm tempted to do that, but then we may destroy the very thing we've come here for," responded Venicia. "It's tempting, but too risky."

"Then what do we do?" asked Brendt.

"I think we're stuck with just holding out," she responded. "Let's cut their power and shut off their water. And let's just keep a guard on the place. They'll have to come out eventually."

"I hate waiting," complained Brendt. "Besides, we have Indians attacking the place and you're suggesting we sit around shutting off their water and power and wait for them to come out? That's nuts. The attack is on! Let's go get them."

"Of course! That was a stupid idea," she responded. "But let's send the Indians in first."

Just then a couple shots were fired on the opposite side of the building. "Go find out what that's all about," Venicia commanded.

Brendt cautiously ran toward the back of the building and around the corner to the south side.

"This is ridiculous," complained Duke. "We're professionals and we're being held off by a couple amateur geeks. I wish we had some smoke grenades, so we could put an end to this circus."

Venicia nodded her head in agreement, but she had no suggestions to offer.

Then he whispered, "I'm going to go around this building a see if there's any other access point that we may have missed. Maybe there's something that's not guarded."

This time Venicia nodded and by the look in her eyes Duke could see that she strongly agreed. "While you're at it, shut off the electricity and the water."

"Will do," he agreed. He started off, working his way slowly around the building.

In the meantime, Brendt had made his way around to the south side of the building just in time to see one of the Indians running off toward the front past the garage. "What's going on?" yelled Brendt.

"That crazy guy up there is shooting at me," replied the exasperated Indian. "I didn't sign up to get shot." He turned and ran around the corner and across the front of the garage.

Brendt looked up at the upstairs window but saw nothing. But he was convinced that the Indian was telling the truth. He had heard the shots. He wasn't convinced that the shots were aimed to kill. They were probably only intended to scare, and that worked perfectly.

Brendt decided he would climb up on the roof of the first story and work his way to the second story window in the hopes whoever did the shooting had convinced himself the threat was gone.

Brendt's climb was noisy. If he was trying to sneak up on the window, he wasn't doing a very good job. He made it to the window and as he tried to sneak a peek through the window, he heard a shot. At the same time, he felt a pinch on his leg. Looking down he saw blood and realized that he had been shot in the leg. Whoever was in the house had shot him through the interior sheetrock and exterior wood plank wall. Neither was strong enough to hold off the bullet.

Brendt quickly climbed back down off the roof, but it was painful. Once down he tied off the area where he was shot using his shirt. Luckily, a bone was not hit. The bleeding had to be stopped.

Duke came around the corner and saw what had happened. "Get whoever is shooting at us!" yelled Brendt.

CHAPTER FORTY-TWO

Shootout

June 2020, East Glacier, Montana

Venicia was furious. How could the simple snatch and grab assignment of a couple of geeks become so difficult? Nothing seemed to be working out. From the very beginning, members of her team were getting killed for the stupidest reasons. And now they're sitting in northern Montana close to the Canadian border, doing an old-fashioned siege on an old shack. In the end they might come up with nothing. What a mess. Plus, it was only a matter of time before local law enforcement would arrive.

She had heard the additional shot on the opposite side of the building but didn't know the cause. She assumed it was a warning shot, trying to scare off her team. Just as she was pondering her failures, four of the Indians came up to her, shotguns at ready, and looking very threatening.

"We've had enough of this nonsense," complained one of the Indians. "Whoever's in that building is shooting at us. We're going to have to shoot up the place, whether you like it or not."

Venicia spoke up, "But you can't do that. You may destroy the very thing that we're here to recover."

"Don't care," responded the Indian. "Nobody shoots at us!"

The Indians lined up facing the door and aimed their shotguns. They fired off several rounds at the door, blowing it to pieces. Then they reloaded and fired off another round, blowing away any obstructions that were blocking the doorway.

One of the Indians walked up to the door and kicked away the bullet-ridden door and frame opening the access to the building. He was about to step through the door when a shot rang out and he fell backwards unto the ground. His companions ran up to him to see what had happened. He had been shot in the leg and his leg was broken, causing him to lose his balance and collapse. They picked him up and helped him to one of the pickups, put him in the passenger seat, and drove off with him, taking him to the nearest medical facility which would require a 30-minute drive to Browning.

The Indians put out the word and ten minutes later an additional force of Indians arrived, shotguns in hand. "This is becoming an all-out war," exclaimed an exasperated Venicia. "I've completely lost control of this situation. What was earlier just a stand-off has now become a gun battle."

A group of five Indians, shot guns at ready, charged into the building. The first persons they saw was Maria and Jonard com-ing up from the basement, and without asking any questions and thinking they were part of the team shooting at them, they pro-ceed to blast the two of them with several shotgun rounds. Then they yelled out, "We've got them. We shot the two who were shooting at us."

Venicia yelled back, "Is there a woman amongst them?"

"Yes," responded an Indian. "A man and a woman."

"Let me come and see," said Venicia. She entered the building and went to where the shooting had occurred. She was horrified to see her two companions lying dead on the floor in a heap of blood. "That's not them," she yelled out in fury. "They're still in here somewhere. Find them!"

Two of the Indians went down the stairs to the basement and found no one there. The other three Indians went upstairs to see what they could find. In the meantime, three other Indians had entered the house and they proceeded to search the main part of the house to see if they could find Roger and his companions. But none of them had any luck. There was no one to be found.

They went out into the garage and found all of Roger's experimental equipment, but still nobody. Venicia was beside herself in frustration. She searched for papers, hoping to find the formula. She found nothing.

How could Roger have escaped? Then she heard a pair of shots around the back side of the house and she ran off to see who was shooting.

June 2020, East Glacier, Montana
A Few Minutes Earlier

Ranel and Matthew had worked their way around the neighborhood and had arrived at the back of Roger's house just in time to meet up with Bridger. The three of them watched the drama that was unfolding at the house. They saw that someone upstairs and inside the house had shot at the Indian and scared him off, and then had shot Brendt, causing him to come off the roof. They also saw Duke helping Brendt. They came up behind Duke and Brendt and aimed pistols at their heads, threatening them to keep quiet but Brendt decided to yell out anyway, causing Ranel to shoot him in the head.

Duke kept quiet and so Matthew and Bridger tied him up and tied his mouth shut while Ranel climbed up on the roof and went over to the upstairs window where he found Eric. "We need to get you out of here. There is an entire army of Indians stand-ing at the door and they're going to come charging in any minute. Can you round up your guys and have them come out this win-dow?"

"Yes," replied Eric. "I'll get them up here quickly."

Eric went off and Ranel waited for him to come back. Then, one at a time, the four that were in the house, Roger, Judy, Eric, and Chase, snuck out of the window, across the roof, and climb-ed down to where Bridger and Matthew were waiting for them. Eric, the last to come out, could hear someone coming up the stairs behind him. He quickly and quietly made his escape.

Once on the ground, Matthew pointed everyone toward the back of the house, hoping to take them to his car, but as Chase and Judy rounded the southwest corner of the house, a pair of Indians were standing there waiting for them, shotguns at ready. They put up their arms, indicating surrender, and the rest of the team that was behind them came to a quick halt, realizing that Chase and Judy had been spotted. Bridger came to the edge of the house and took a quick peek around the corner. He saw the two Indians. He knew if he didn't act fast, the remainder of the war party would be on top of them soon. One of the Indians let out a yelp, letting everyone else know that he had found some-thing. The yelp triggered Bridger's reaction. He stepped around the corner and fired off two shots in quick succession, putting a bullet hole into the forehead of each of the two Indians.

Everyone started running off in the direction that Matthew had indicated earlier, but it was too late. Shots were being fired in the direction of the escapees. Chase took a shot to the back of his legs, causing him to fall to the ground, and Roger received a single bullet hit to the back of his left arm, breaking the bone. He also fell to the ground. Ranel was less fortunate. He received a shotgun hit to the back of the head. He was dead before he hit the ground.

The rest of the team, which now included Eric, Judy, Bridger, and Matthew, also fell to the ground hoping to avoid being shot. Matthew and Bridger had guns and they took aim at their attack-ers, firing several shots in rapid succession. Within seconds two more of the Indians had hit the ground with shots to the body. The battle was now reduced to Matthew and Bridger, the only individuals carrying weapons on the one side against Venicia and a group of four Indians on the other. Of Venicia's team of five, three were now dead and one was incapacitated. She was all that was left.

A fierce battle ensued. Venicia hid behind the northwest cor-ner of the house, while the Indians took a variety of positions; one lying on the ground, one in a prone position, one hiding be-hind a section of broken fence, and the last remained standing, acting as if he were invincible.

Venicia took careful aim. She was a marksman in her own right, and she knew how to handle a gun. The Indians took random, wild shots in the direction of their targets, hoping to get lucky and hit something.

Venicia's skill paid off and she hit Matthew in the left shoulder. This made it harder for him to control the targeting of his pistol. The four Indians were also lucky. One of their wild shot-gun shots struck Judy, peppering her back, the back of her legs and buttocks, causing her to yell out in pain.

The Indian that was in the standing position was soon shot and fell to the ground. A second Indian, the one hiding behind the fence, was also shot in the stomach and fell to the ground.

The gun battle continued, with no one seeming to gain any advantage. Then suddenly, and unexpectedly, Venicia fell for-ward and face first hit the ground. The Indian that was in the prone position looked around to see why Venicia had fallen, and he was also shot suddenly and unexpectedly, but not from the front. He was shot in the head from behind. The remaining Indian, seeing that the rest of his team was now dead or injured, threw up his arms and surrendered. Then Chase stepped out from the corner of the building. He had successfully snuck around the building, picking up someone's gun on the way, and made the final two kills. He yelled out, "I knew everyone was wrong. I knew that some good would come from me playing all those video games."

CHAPTER FORTY-THREE

Wrap-up

June 2020, East Glacier, Montana

Duke was the only one left of the hired assassins that had been sent out to capture Roger. The Indians that were left collected their dead. Local police were on the scene even before the shooting had ended, and they were quick to round up all the remaining participants in order to find out what had happened. Considering the large number of Indians that had died, this investigation wasn't going to be pretty. The FBI and state police badges didn't impress anyone on the reservation, least of all the local police.

While sitting at the Browning police station, waiting for his turn in the interview room, Roger received a text message from Steve Smith his patent attorney which read, "Your patent is secured. You are now the proud owner of all the rights associated with your new cement formula. I already received several inquiries and two of them even came with offers to purchase the rights to your patent. You just became a multi-millionaire. Con-gratulations."

Roger forwarded the message to Judy, who was in the hospital recovering from her wounds. Then he added, "Guess you mar-ried the right guy after all."

Judy responded with, "I'm just glad we made it out of all of this alive. We paid a big price and took a huge risk to get that patent. I wasn't sure we were going to make it there for a while there."

The police were in the process of interviewing Duke who pro-ceeded to spill the beans on the entire operation, as far as he knew it. He was recruited by Venicia and her team late in the game, so he wasn't privy to all the details, but he knew that the objective was to get Roger's formula, either by coercion or by force; whatever it took. When asked why his house was burnt down, he responded, "Gerd was instructed to scare off the police. Jill and I were the primary targets behind the investigation. Gerd didn't know that I had joined the team earlier that same day, and he proceeded to shoot up and later burn down our houses, thinking that was what he was supposed to do. Idiot!"

"And what about the shooting up and burning down of the Falcon property?" questioned the police officer.

"That was all about intimidation. Unfortunately, we weren't the only team in play. There was someone else who did the shooting, and we assume they were after the same thing that we were after. I'm pretty sure it was a second team that was under the direction of Venicia. But somehow, after their attack on the Falcon offices, they disappeared. For some reason they dropped out. We were never sure who they were and why they disap-peared so suddenly. Venicia never shared that part of the plan with me."

"What about the attack on your car; the one that sent you to the hospital?" asked the officer.

"That was before I became involved," he replied.

"Tell me what you know about the organization behind all of this."

"I can't tell you anything," replied Duke. "My contact was Venicia. She's the one who paid me and she's the one who gave me instructions. She never informed any of us who she was working for. She always said that was on a 'need to know' basis and we didn't need to know."

"I guess we'll find out for ourselves and make sure this becomes public information," Roger stressed angrily.

The officer turned to Roger and asked, "I'm just not understanding what the big deal is here? We're talking about cement, for Pete's sake. Why would you kill people over cement?"

Roger, attempting to calm down, knew he had to offer some kind of explanation, so he said, "To understand why this is so important we need to go back about 2000 years and look at two isolated and separate parts of the world. Both the Pre-Aztecs and the Romans, independently, had developed the ability to build roadways and buildings with a cement that has remained weather resistant and durable through all sorts of environments, including earthquakes. Their cement roadways are still in existence today. But our cements that we use throughout the world only last a few years, at best, and in snow country like here in Montana, we're lucky if they last five years. So, the ability to come up with a cement that would last for thousands of years would be consid-ered invaluable. I have come up with the formula for this cement and we have encountered two groups that have been attacking us. There are the groups that see this as an incredible financial opportunity and want my patent for the money. And there are groups that don't want this information to get out because it will damage their current businesses."

"Do you have this magic formula for cement that will last thousands of years?" asked the officer.

"Yes," was Roger's simple response, still hesitant and a little angry. "What I don't understand is how two, so-called primitive societies, completely independent and isolated from each other, could each develop something so advanced that our scientists, including extremely intelligent chemists, today have spent decades trying to duplicate, and have still come up with nothing."

"Maybe they weren't so primitive after all," commented Duke.

"I would have to agree," responded the officer. "Now let's get back to this little war that you guys have been waging." The offi-cer attempted to return to the events of the day but seemed to get nowhere.

The further investigation of Duke, Roger, and the remainder of the team didn't shed any new light on the disaster that had cost so many lives. In the end, Duke admitted that he was related to Joe, the bumbling idiot who died at the Holter Lake cabin. He and Joe were collaborating with Gerd to kidnap Roger, but the entire effort went horribly wrong and steadily became increasingly more complicated by the minute. Then Gerd was killed by higher powers that he supposedly represented, and they took over. Venicia led that effort and represented this higher power, and it became impossible for Duke to back out, even though his house and his family were mistakenly attacked. In the end, Duke went to prison for his involvement. Even though he wasn't directly involved in any of the murders, he still received a long prison sentence since he was a collaborator.

Roger was fined for the fire he started at the warehouse in Helena but didn't end up serving any jail time. He had to rebuild the warehouse at his own expense. And the rest of the team was penalized by the injuries they had to suffer.

In the end, Roger became a household name in the cement industry, having produced a cement product that was stronger than traditional cements, yet flexible and pliable enough to with-stand most earthquakes. His formula made him an international hero amongst developing countries that were often ravaged by earthquakes.

And of course, the Falcon family lived happily ever after. Or at least as far as this story goes.

June 2020, Helena, Montana
(One Week Later)

Eric arrived at Lucca's restaurant slightly before Jill. Jill was still sore, but the stiches had been removed and she was healing quickly. "How wonderful to see you up and about," commented Eric, who greeted Jill by putting out his hand.

Jill would have none of it. She grabbed his face, putting one hand on each cheek. She pulled his face toward hers and gave Eric the kiss he had been dreaming about for the last week. Then she took his hand and said, "Are you as hungry as I am?"

"Yes, but I have a more important question."

"What's that?" asked Jill.

"Are you ready to move back in with me now that the case is solved? Are you ready for us to seriously get to know each other?"

Jill just smiled.

ABOUT THE AUTHOR

Gerhard Plenert

Gerhard, obsessed with the world of fantasy is an internationally recog-nized author having written and published books for organizations like the United Nations, and for various universities in the United States, Japan, and Europe. This will be his sixteenth book.

He also has 150+ articles published in journals and magazines around the world. His publications have been endorsed by companies like Black and Decker, AT&T, and FedEx and by internationally recognized bestselling authors like Stephen R. Covey. He travels internationally and works as a business consultant.

VISIT THE AUTHOR

SOCIAL MEDIA

Facebook
https://www.facebook.com/authorgerhardplenert

LinkedIn
www.linkedin.com/pub/gerhard-plenert/1/b0/75b

Twitter
https://twitter.com/GPlenert

WordPress Blog
http://gerhard338.wordpress.com

Websites
www.donnaink.shop
www.gerhardplenert.com

GIFTS AND EXPRESSIONS

PLENERT CREATIONS

Gerhard Plenert

Dr. Gerhard Plenert
WWW.DONNAINK.COM

Montana Rising and Small World Series Titles

Montana Bleeds
The Siege of the Small World
The Uniting of the Small World
Saving the Small World

Nocturnum's Muse Imprint
DonnaInk Publications. L.L.C.
17611 Aquasco Road
Brandywine, MD 20613
www.donnaink.shop
(910) 528-4347

dpInk

Donnaink Publications, L.L.C.